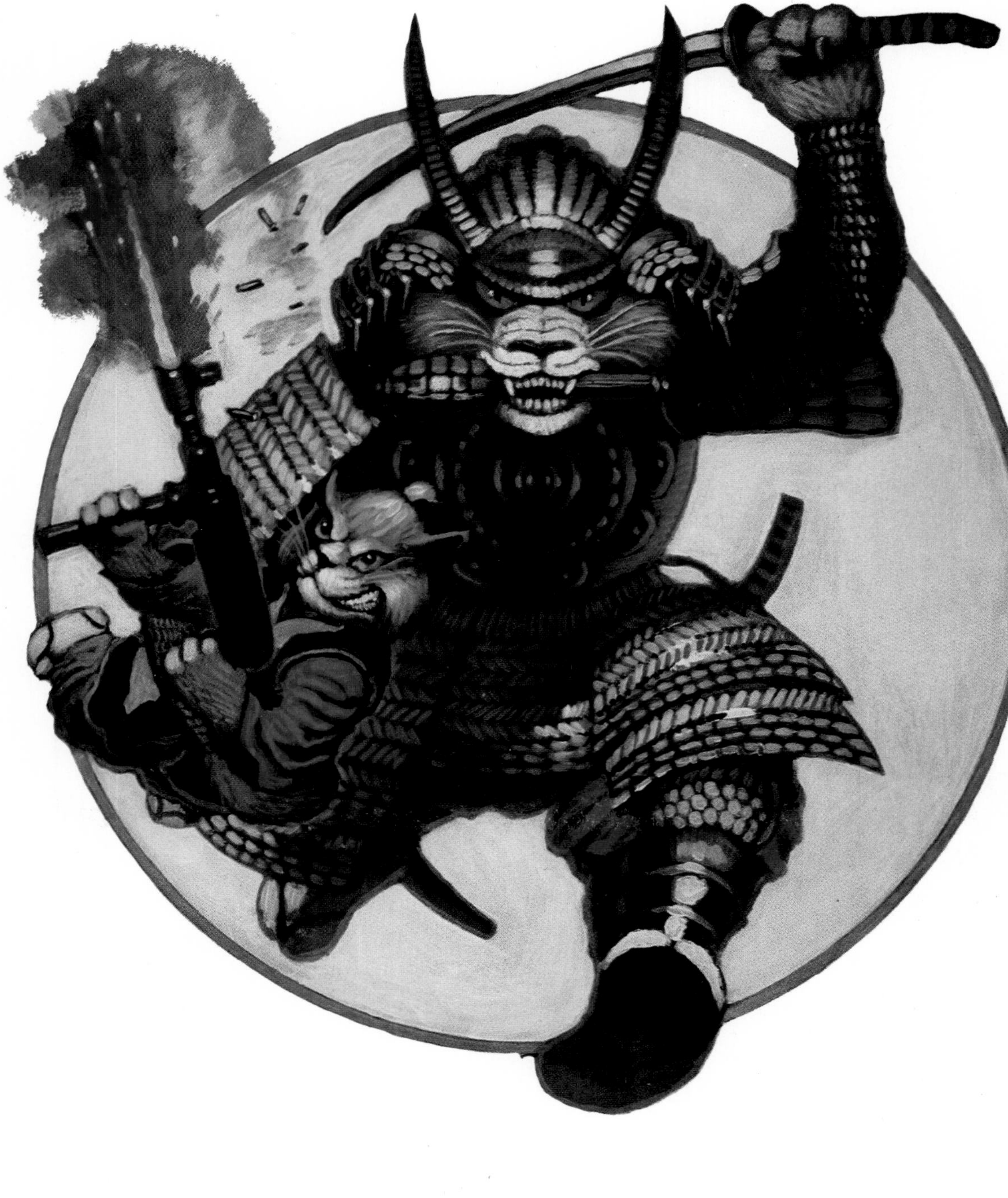

THE ADVENTURES
OF
SAMURAI CAT

THE ADVENTURES OF
SAMURAI CAT

MARK E. ROGERS

TOR

A Tom Doherty Associates Book

This is a work of fiction. All the characters and events portrayed in this book are fictional, and any resemblance to real people or incidents is purely coincidental.

THE ADVENTURES OF SAMURAI CAT

Copyright © 1984 by Mark E. Rogers

All rights reserved, including the right to reproduce this book or portions thereof in any form.

Reprinted by arrangement with Donald M. Grant, Publisher, Inc.

Cover art by Mark E. Rogers

First printing: October 1984

A TOR Book

Published by Tom Doherty Associates, Inc.
49 West 24 Street • New York, N.Y. 10010
ISBN: 0-812-55246-6   CAN. ED.: 0-812-55247-4

Printed in the United States of America

0 9 8 7 6 5 4 3

DEDICATION

This book is dedicated to my parents; and also to Bill Heath, because he thought the cat was a dumb idea.

ACKNOWLEDGEMENTS

I would like to thank Barb Lantry, for selling the project in the first place; I would also like to acknowledge contributions by my wife Kate, Sam Tomaino, Nancy Lebovitz, Greg Palmer and Judy Gerjuoy, Charles E. Shedd III, Twyla Kitts, Erboyb, Darp, Chris Wilson (ye!), Mary Weigmann, Tom Miller, Jeeve and Stackie, Jay and Jan, Cathy and Michael, Frank Clough (good enough), Karen Angulo, Liz Cole, the members of Galadrim and of Clam Chowder, and all my other friends except Joe Serrada.

Actually, now that I think of it, leave Tom Miller out of there too, because he moved to Ohio.

THE ADVENTURES
OF
SAMURAI CAT

*Sixteenth-Century Japan — a land suffer-
ing through the long night of* Sengoku Jidai,
*the Age of Battles, a period of constant civil war,
of anarchy and terror, of savagery and bloodshed
and lots of other good stuff. The social order was
shaken to its core; class distinctions blurred as
military prowess became all-important. With
luck, even a peasant could slash a place for himself among the mighty.*

   Even a cat . . .

Armor of Miaowara Tomokato
Momoyama Period
Armouries
Tower of London

KATEMUSHA

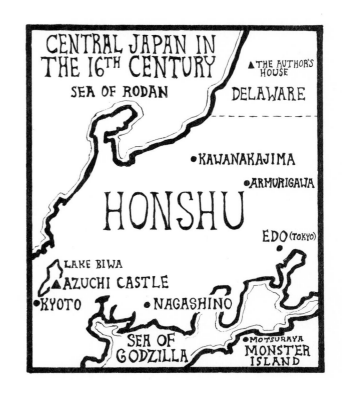

CENTRAL JAPAN IN THE 16TH CENTURY

▲ THE AUTHOR'S HOUSE

SEA OF RODAN

DELAWARE

• KAWANAKAJIMA

• ARMURIGAWA

HONSHU

EDO (TOKYO)

• LAKE BIWA

▲ AZUCHI CASTLE

• KYOTO   • NAGASHINO

SEA OF GODZILLA

• MOTSURAYA

MONSTER ISLAND

The word spread swiftly. *He* was dead. Miao-wara Tomokato, the deadliest of Tokugawa Nobunaga's warriors, the most terrifying fighter in all Japan had died in a minor skirmish.

Many were the sighs of relief breathed by Nobunaga's enemies. With Tomokato at his side, Nobunaga was invincible, his overlordship of Southern Honshu utterly assured.

But without Tomokato . . .

The wolves gathered quickly, but none so quickly as the army of the formidable Takeda clan, which had always formed the backbone of resistance to Nobunaga. Thirty thousand mounted warriors, eager to fight and die, entered his territory, led by the impetuous Takeda Katsuyori. Quickly they threw an iron ring around Nagashino Castle, held by one of Nobunaga's vassals. The defenders sent out a series of sorties which were easily routed. Katsuyori and his men were jubilant.

But on the third day of the siege, the Tokugawa host arrived, led by Nobunaga himself, and as night fell, they dug in on a ridge below Mount Gambo, to the west of the castle. Working in shifts, the troops erected bamboo screens to serve as firing-platforms for their matchlocks, while Nobunaga rode up and down the lines giving commands, torchlight gleaming redly from his black-lacquered Italian morion and breastplate.

The work was finished near dawn. Tension rose among the troops, now that they no longer had tasks to distract them. Mutters passed from man to man, though complete silence fell whenever Nobunaga rode by. Everything about his voice and appearance bespoke complete confidence, but his men were not reassured. Looking across at the Takeda campfires, they knew that they were badly outnumbered, and also that Nobunaga planned to let Katsuyori's cavalry come agonizingly close to his own lines. If the onslaught went unchecked, the bamboo screens would go down in splinters, the arquebusiers would be trampled in the dirt, and all hope of victory would vanish.

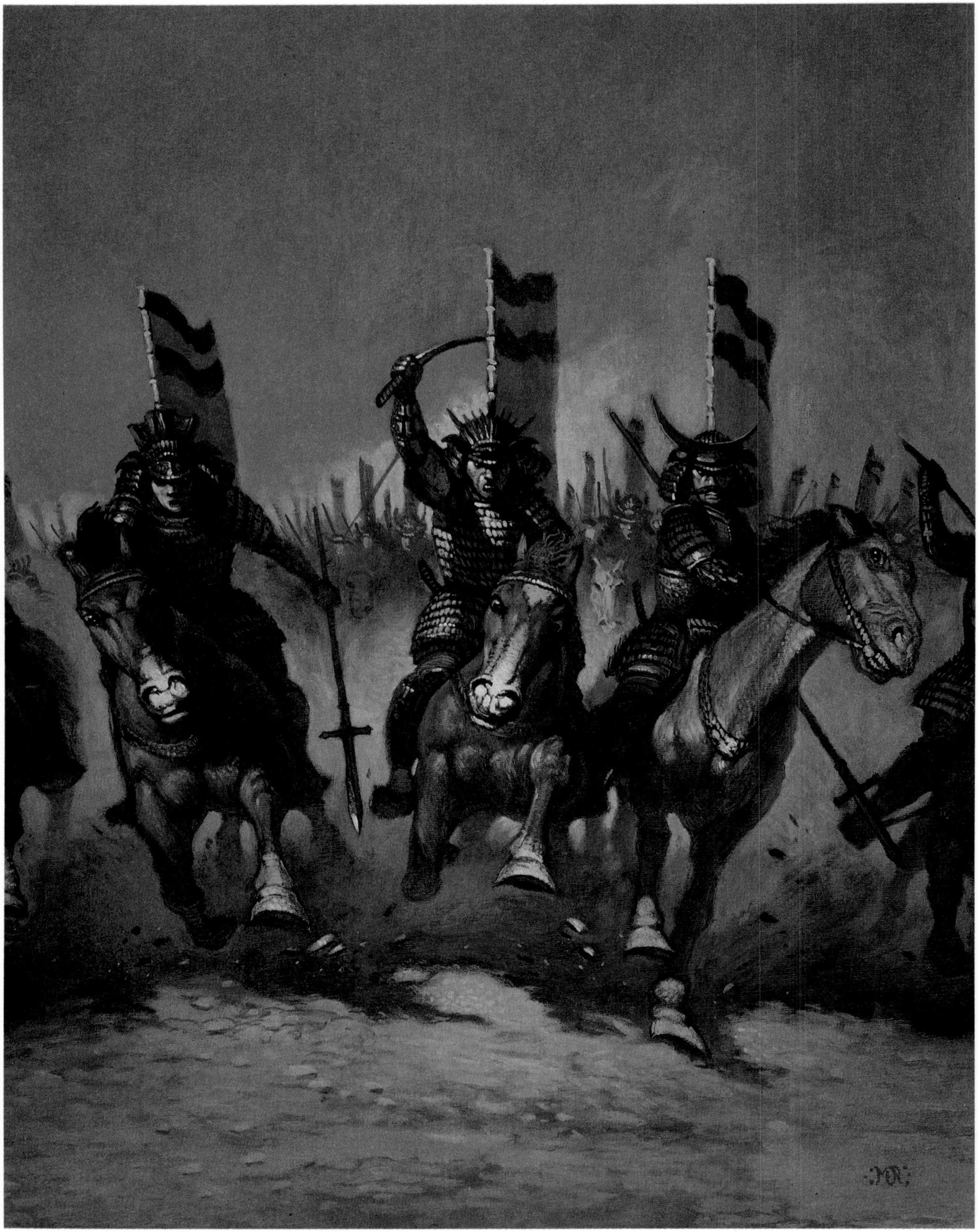

Still, Nobunaga laughed and jested as he rode up and back; and he was as sure of himself as he seemed.

The sky lightened, purple to blue to pink. Cloud-linings kindled, blazing with bright color. Flaming orange, the sun rose, its fiery glow flooding across the land.

The Takeda clan came on.

They advanced like a slow dust-storm, dark mounted shapes with banners at their backs. They halted just outside matchlock range.

Nobunaga watched them, pleased. Everything was going as expected.

On the plain beneath, Takeda Katsuyori stared up at the ridge, squinting in the raking sunlight. He was unimpressed by Nobunaga's deployment. The Tokugawa guns would take many of his men. But Nobunaga did not have enough to break the charge. And if the charge were not broken, Nobunaga would lose. It was as simple as that.

Clad all in black lamellar armor, astride a great black charger, he oversaw the ordering of his host. Dusty as they were, his warriors were a splendid sight, sumptuously accoutered, helms flanked or surmounted by tall horns, or crescent moons, or spiky sunbursts. A few were armored European-style, with breastplates and morions. Each had a rectangular banner, or *sashimoto*, attached to his back; the flags snapped and fluttered in the breeze. Spears rested on shoulders, or were couched under mailed arms. The horsemen were stern, iron-faced men; here and there a gargoylish *mempo*, or armored mask, grimaced up toward the enemy on the ridge.

Katsuyori's foremost general, Babu Nobuharu, rode up beside him.

"All's ready, My Lord," Nobuharu said.

Katsuyori grunted, and led him and his other generals up onto a hillock beside the host. All eyes were on him as he produced a golden signal-fan and raised it high above his head. Then, with a ferocious bird-of-prey shriek, he brought it down.

The Takeda host started forward, swiftly picking up speed. Hooves pounded into the earth, flinging great ragged clods skyward. Dust billowed. Tackle clattered. Laced neckguards flapped behind gold-decked helms. Spear-shadows raced along the ground. Dusty spearheads shone dully above, thirsty for blood. The army rumbled across the flats like the shockwave of an earthquake, a *tsunami* of armored galloping fury.

The front ranks splashed across the narrow stream running along the foot of the ridge, and started up the slope towards Nobunaga's lines. There was no gunfire from the heights yet, even though they were now well within range. But the riders gave little thought to this, intent as they were on reaching the crest. Even more fiercely they spurred their mounts, and the great-hearted beasts responded magnificently. The headlong speed of the charge actually *increased* as the samurai pressed up the incline.

"Superb," said Tokugawa Nobunaga admiringly, smiling as he watched them come. They were now two hundred yards from the top. He took out his signal-fan, drew himself erect on his horse, standing in his stirrups.

On the slope beneath, the Takeda samurai drew even closer to the bamboo screens. They had begun to wonder about the lack of fire from the defenders. More than one now suspected a trap. But they would not retreat. They were so near, only a hundred yards away. And how could any trap withstand the awesome force of their onset?

Nobunaga's smile widened to a grin. His fan flashed silver as it swept down. Off to the right, in the center of his lines, several footsoldiers pushed over a bamboo screen, knocking it forward.

The entire Takeda front rank watched the screen fall and knew the trap was being sprung. They steeled themselves to meet the unknown challenge. They were brave men, courageous men — heroes all. They feared nothing.

Well, almost nothing.

Out over the toppled screen, gleaming resplendent in his white-laced lamellar armor, longsword bare and shining bitterly, strode Miaowara Tomokato.

Samurai Cat!

Terror seized the vanguard of the Takeda host, horse and man alike, as they recognized him, appalled to see he was still alive. Eyes bugging, horses stopped dead in their tracks as though they had slammed into an invisible wall. Riders hurtled forward from their saddles, breaking their necks in the dirt. Rumbling out of the dust behind, the Takeda second rank smashed into the fear-paralyzed horses. Beasts and men thudded to earth in a vast tangle of dead and dying bodies. The third rank piled up, and the fourth and the fifth and the sixth, and by then, the mound of fallen was so huge that it proceeded to roll back down the slope, into the remaining horsemen. When the dust settled fifteen minutes later, it was clear that the entire Takeda army was wiped out.

From his vantage-point Takeda Katsuyori

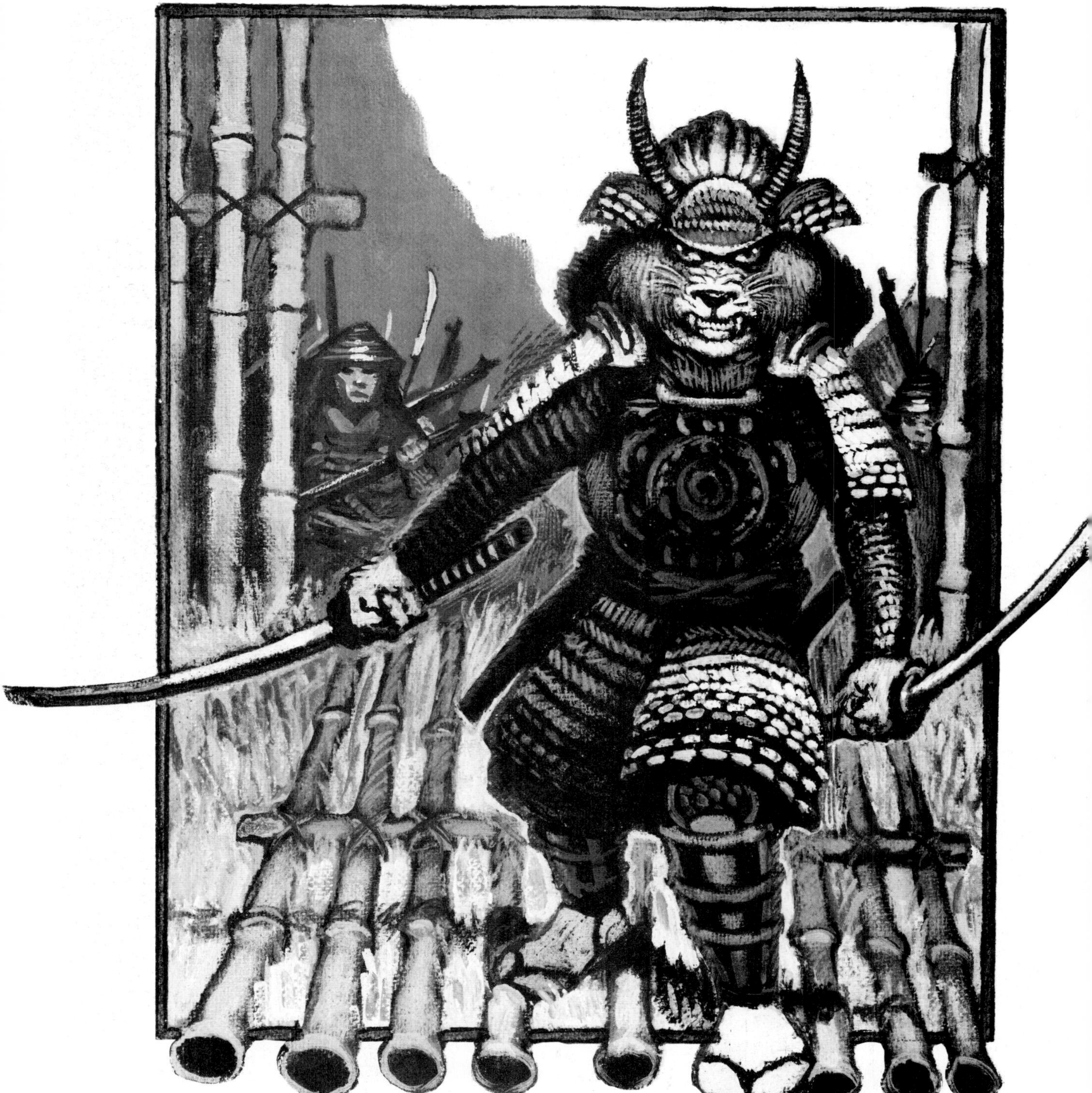

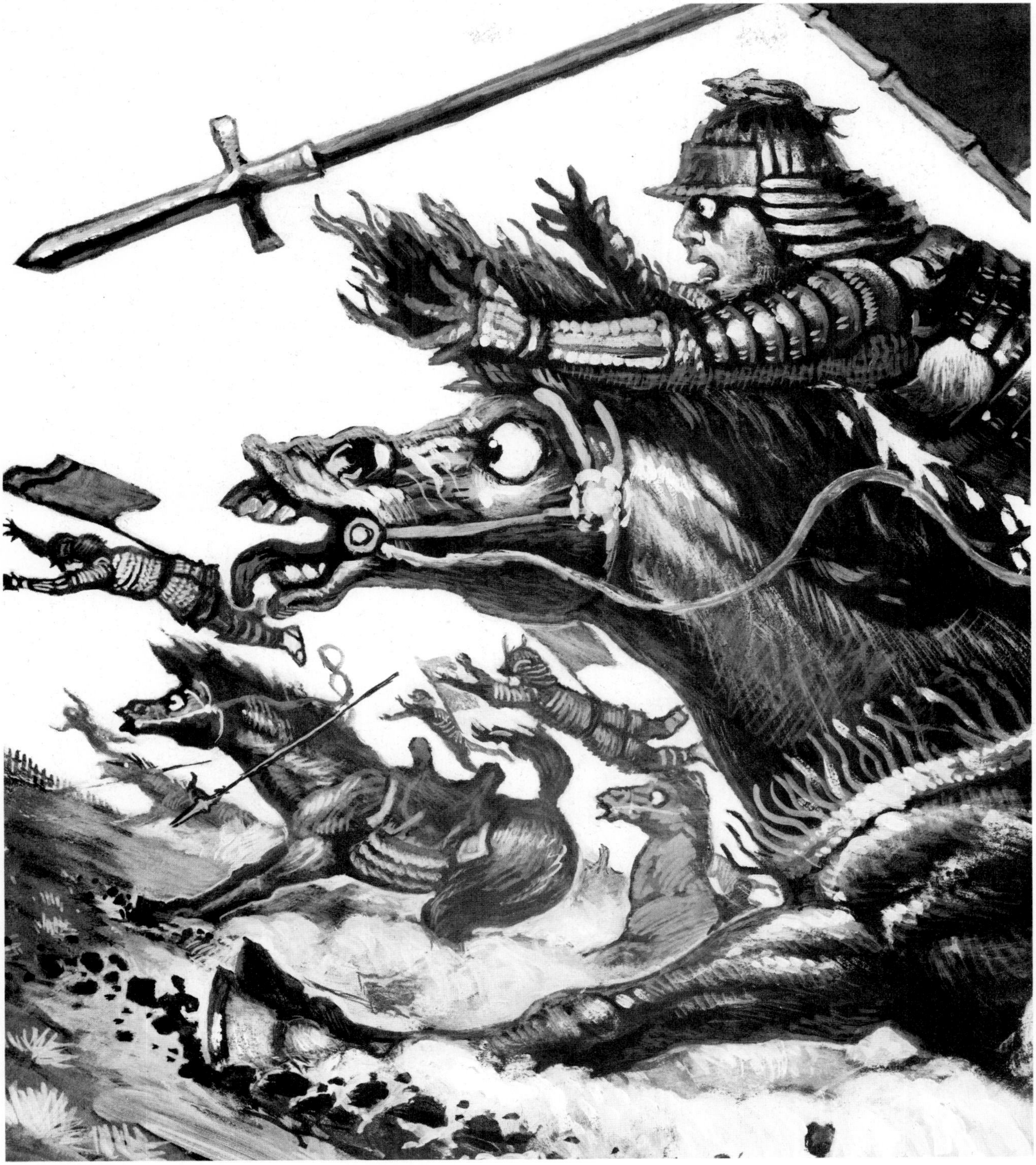

surveyed the grim scene. "Fudge," he gritted.

Dismounting, he took off his armor, and committed *seppuku*.

"Well," said Babu Nobuharu to another of the Takeda generals, "there goes Katsuyori."

His colleague nodded solemnly.

Behind the Tokugawa lines, however, all was jubilation. Carrying Tomokato on their shoulders, cheering footsoldiers bore him over to Nobunaga, setting him down beside the lord's horse. Tomokato bowed, slicking back his whiskers with one orange paw as he lifted his head, face impassive. The soldiers hushed.

"Your plan worked well, My Lord," the feline said.

"Did you have any doubt it would?" Nobunaga asked.

Tomokato shook his head resolutely. "A samurai does not doubt his lord."

"A perfect samurai does not," Nobunaga answered.

Tomokato bowed again, blushing beneath his fur at the compliment.

Nobunaga summoned his generals. "We must be off as soon as possible. Also, messengers must be sent to the clans still advancing on my territory.

I want them to hear what happened today."

As they strode off, Nobunaga smiled inwardly at the thought of his victory. The Takeda forces were utterly destroyed. In all Japanese history, no clan had ever suffered such a defeat. His fame as a general would live forever. And more importantly, the Takeda clan would be no threat to his heirs when he and the cat were gone.

The army was on the march within the hour, pushing to meet a possible thrust against his Northwestern holdings.

But in the following days, as his messengers returned, it became obvious that he had nothing to fear, for the time at least. Without the Takeda clan to engage him on his Northeast frontier, the other clans were unwilling to attack, and would probably remain so for years.

The army disbanded. Nobunaga and his closest retainers withdrew to Azuchi Castle, his great stronghold outside Kyoto, built on a promontory rising six hundred feet from the waters of Lake Biwa. They spent the rest of the summer in peace, pursuing refined and civilized pleasures.

As Autumn drew near, Tomokato sought out Nobunaga, kneeling before him on the *tatami* in the castle's great audience hall. The cat looked out of place among the richly garbed courtiers; he was plainly dressed, wearing a simple blue kimono marked only with the scarlet paw-print device of the Miaowara clan.

"I would like to ask a favor of you, My Lord," he said.

"Name it," Nobunaga replied.

"I thought that since the land is at peace, I might go and visit my brother Shimura for a day or two. I haven't seen him in over a year, even though he lives so close by, and . . . "

"Permission granted," said Tokugawa Nobunaga, with a gracious smile.

"Thank you, My Lord," Tomokato said, bowing. Rising, he backed out of the hall. Before long he was on the road from the castle, riding his small white pony. After a time he spotted a patch of yellow flowers. Dismounting, he picked one, and continued on his way, sniffing the blossoms contently while humming a gruff military tune. Warm breezes swept the fur on his paws and tail, rustled in the trees nearby. All was right with the world.

Miaowara Shimura was Tomokato's elder by several years, and had once been as formidable a warrior; but a bullet-wound in the leg had put a halt to his career as a samurai, and he had taken to living the quiet country life with his wife and children, supported by a pension from Nobunaga. He was a great orange tabby like Tomokato, slightly taller, though he had grown into cheerful chubbiness through inactivity. But while he had given up the way of the sword, he had become an excellent poet, something he had always wanted to do; and though he rarely ventured far from home, his verses had a splendid reputation throughout central Japan, disseminated by Nobunaga's scribes.

Tomokato arrived at Shimura's house midway through the afternoon. His brother greeted him warmly, surprised and delighted to see him. For politeness' sake, Hanako, Shimura's wife, served *saké;* Tomokato partook, though he normally avoided all strong drink. Shimura's sons, a young and boisterous crew, clustered about, gaping at their famous uncle.

"He doesn't look so tough to me," Shiro announced loudly. He was a grey kitten with yellow-green eyes.

The other kittens and Hanako gasped. Tomokato ignored the comment. Shimura laughed.

"How can you let him insult your brother that way?" Hanako demanded. "He'll never learn

manners if you laugh at him. It'll only encourage him."

Shimura sobered immediately, harrumphed. "You're right, of course." He looked sternly at Shiro. "Apologize to Uncle Tomokato."

"It's not necessary," Tomokato said aloofly.

Shimura relaxed, but catching a sharp glance from Hanako, said: "Really, brother, it will do him good. Shiro, apologize."

Shiro thrust his jaw out defiantly, pointing a small paw at Tomokato. "Just look for yourself," he said. "He's not nearly as tough as you are, father — and you're only a poet!"

"Shiro!" Hanako shouted.

By then, Shimura's wrath was aroused. "Just a poet, eh?" Instantly his paws shot out, and he grabbed his rebellious child. Getting up, he took the struggling kitten into another room and spanked him — quite thoroughly, if Shiro's cries were an indication. Presently Shimura returned, with Shiro dragging along behind. Shimura knelt beside Tomokato.

"Apologize," he grated to Shiro, who rejoined the other kittens.

"I apologize to you, father," Shiro said, fighting back the tears brimming in his eyes.

"Now apologize to your uncle."

Shiro eyed Tomokato, who stared calmly back at him. The kitten opened his mouth to speak, then snapped it shut again.

"Shiro . . . " Shimura said.

"I apologize, uncle," Shiro said quickly, almost as if he were trying to spit some bad taste from his mouth.

"I accept your apology," Tomokato said gravely.

There was a short but uncomfortable silence.

"I understand, Tomokato," Hanako said, "that you played a great part at Nagashino."

"A great part?" Shimura said before Tomokato could answer. "I've heard he won the battle singlehanded."

"Lord Nobunaga's plan won the battle," Tomokato answered, embarrassed. "I was simply a part of it."

"Come now," Shimura reproved. "Let us judge for ourselves. Let's have the tale."

Genuinely uncomfortable at first, Tomokato described Nobunaga's plan, the events leading up to Nagashino, and finally the battle itself. When he was done, Hanako and several of the kittens prodded him into telling more of his adventures.

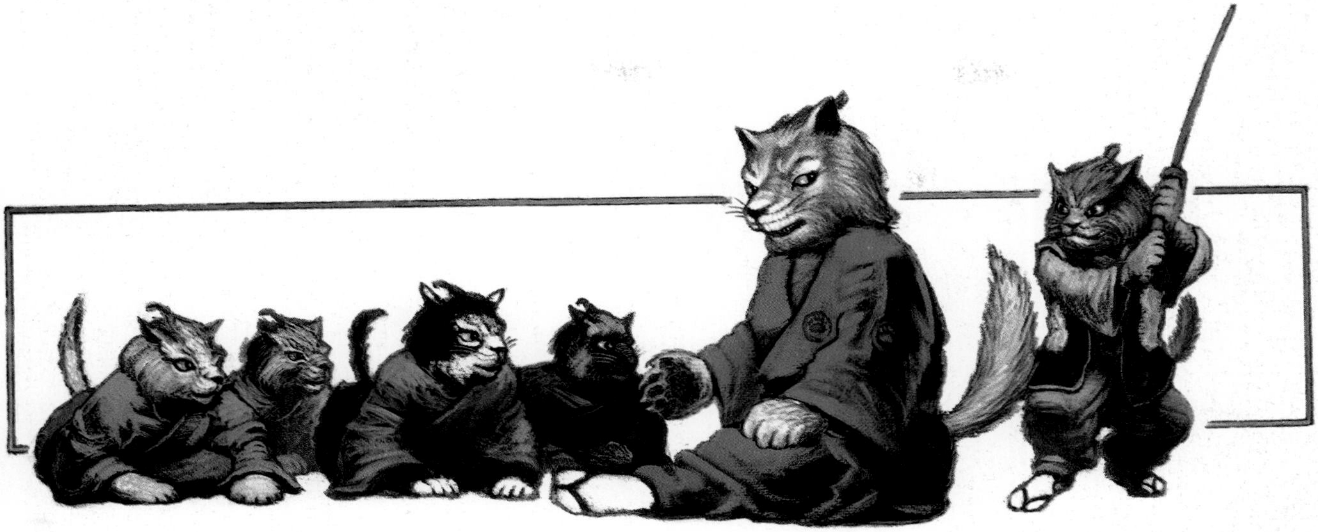

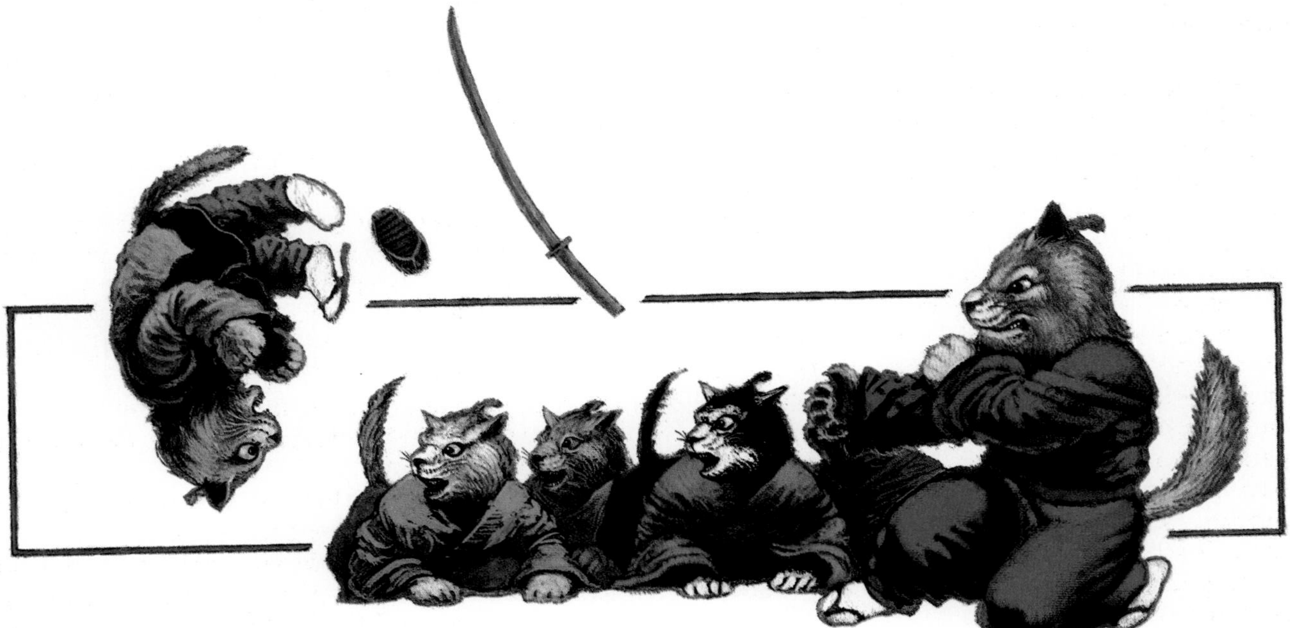

Warming to the task, he reeled off exploit after exploit.

While he was relating his deeds at the battle of the Anegawa, a tax collector arrived, and first Shimura, then Hanako, went out to deal with him. The kittens continued to listen to Tomokato, utterly fascinated.

All save Shiro, that is. He was gone. Slowly he had worked his way behind his brothers, and had slipped out through a side door when he thought there was no one looking.

As Tomokato explained how he had put Asai Nagamata's troops to flight, Shiro, armed with a wooden training sword, or *bokken*, quietly slid back a panel and came out behind him, advancing stealthily. His brothers noticed him at once, but made no sound. Being more than a bit mischievous themselves, they wondered how far he would get, delighted by his audacity.

Tomokato, however, noticed the kittens' sidelong glances and their barely concealed smiles. He had seen Shiro slip from the room and guessed that the little brat was trying to sneak up on him, intent on seeing just how formidable his uncle was. Tomokato smiled to himself. Brat or no, the child had nerve. And he could certainly move quietly. Tomokato's hearing was exceptional, but he had not caught the slightest sound.

He went on with his story as if nothing were happening, watching Shiro's brothers closer than they guessed. All at once he noticed their bodies tensing and knew Shiro was about to strike.

Instantly Tomokato twisted aside. Shiro's *bokken* swept down. Before it could strike the floor, Tomokato plucked the hilt from Shiro's paws and tossed the wooden blade across the room, then sent Shiro spinning after it. The kitten shrieked as he sailed through the air, landing flat on his back, thudding against the thick *tatami* by the wall; his cry was cut off as the wind was knocked from his lungs.

Shimura, having heard the shriek, rushed into the room.

"What's wrong?" he demanded.

"Why, nothing," Tomokato replied serenely.

Shiro gasped and coughed.

"But *what's* the matter with *him?*" Shimura asked.

"He got too excited by my stories," Tomokato answered, never blinking.

Shimura nodded, eyes glinting amusement and suspicion in equal measure. He went back out.

"Now where were we?" Tomokato asked

Shiro's brothers, who were all giggling mightily. "Ah, yes . . . " He resumed his story where he had left off.

Two mornings later, Tomokato prepared to depart.

"Are you sure you cannot stay one more day?" Hanako asked.

"I'd really better get back to the castle," Tomokato replied.

"They just can't do without you, eh?" Shimura asked.

"I'm not so sure about that," Tomokato answered. Suddenly he felt a tug at his sleeve and looked down. It was Shiro.

"Please don't leave, uncle-*san*," Shiro said.

"I must," Tomokato said.

"Well then," Shiro said, "take me with you. I want to be a samurai."

Tomokato let slip a small laugh. "You're too

young. But when you're older you may come to the castle." He looked quickly at Shimura. "If your parents approve, that is."

"But I want to go *now!*" Shiro said, and he stamped his white-socked foot. "I want to be a samurai just like you."

"That's a tall order," Shimura said.

"Well, he comes from the right stock," Tomokato observed. "And he *is* brave enough." He looked back at Shiro, poked him gently in the stomach. Shiro, who hated being patronized, gritted his teeth. "But he's *still* too young."

Tomokato went to the stable and saddled up. He said goodbye in the small courtyard; then, with Shimura and his family calling farewell, he rode off through the gate.

He passed through greenclad valleys, and stopped near noon to eat the lunch Hanako had prepared for him. Before long he was on the road again, following it through the depths of a dark humid forest for many miles. When he came back out into the open, he was very close to home.

But he took no comfort in that. Not when he saw the black smoke billowing above the hill that stood between him and the castle. Clapping heels to his mount, he galloped to the slope and started up. Sick horror welled in his stomach as he reached the crest. The smoke was pouring out of the castle, rolling from the upper storeys. Even at that distance, he could tell that the whitewashed walls were riddled with bullet-holes and yawning shellpits. The main gate had been blasted in.

He spurred down the slope. The dirt road, and the grass on either side of it, were ripped by great caterpillar tread-marks. Several blazing Tiger tanks, corpses sprawling over their hulls and turrets, almost blocked the track up ahead. He began to pass dead samurai, dead Cossacks, dead Romans, dead trolls. An arrow-riddled dragon in a Red Army uniform lay tangled in the sword-hacked wreckage of a recoilless rifle. Apaches and Japanese spearmen, still struggling even in death, clogged the hatches of a fabulous landgoing replica (equipped with balloon tires and Atlas shock absorbers) of the *Merrimac.* An entire platoon of Ostrogoths with Uzi submachine guns, their bodies tattered and bloodied by dozens of sword-strokes, lay in a ring about a single bullet-torn samurai. Al Capone and Bugs Moran, their bitter rivalry behind them, were strewn in pieces by the castle threshold. They had laid the mine that had destroyed the main gate, but had misjudged the length of the fuse. Tomokato, despite his horror

and rage, marvelled at the insane bad taste of their green-and-purple pinstripe suits.

He dismounted and entered the castle. The halls were littered with the dead of all races, some human, some not. The air was thick with smoke and reeked of blood and gunpowder. Picking a path over the corpses, he made his way as quickly as possible to his lord's audience-chamber. The fighting had been fiercest there, he could tell. The walls and ceilings were thoroughly splashed with blood, and huge holes had been chewed in them by bullets and cannonfire and swords and Black Flag. Giant insects were nailed to the ceiling with spears. Gauchos and Zulus were nailed to the insects with arrows and harpoons. On one side of the room the nose of a Heinkel bomber manned by Mongols had smashed through the wall. On the other side the dragon-prow of a viking ship protruded through a mass of splintered timbers. A severed turret from Dover Castle lay atop a mound of butchered conquistadors and pygmies. And everywhere were Nobunaga's dead samurai.

Tomokato wept with rage as he surveyed the scene. He began to rush back and forth, looking for his master, guessing Nobunaga had made his stand here. It was not long before he found his lord's decapitated body and, nearby, Nobunaga's severed head. He clutched the head to his chest and whispered: "If any of the butchers survived, My Lord, I pray, I beg the gods to deliver them to me."

"Let's not drag the gods into this," the head replied. "Put me down, and I'll tell you who you want and where to look."

Tomokato put the head down. He was more overjoyed than surprised that his master still had some life in him. Nobunaga was a tough old bird.

The lord ran through a long list of names and addresses. "And last but not least," he said, "there is Fugu Otoko."

"Otoko," the cat growled. "The Blowfish Who Never Smiles." He had fought Otoko before — at the Battle of the Anegawa.

"Last I heard, he was living in exile," Nobunaga went on. "In Catzad-Dûm. He'll probably go back there."

Tomokato grunted, looking slowly about the room, eyes settling at last on a dead Venusian with a spiked throwing-star stuck in its left head.

"Why are all the rest foreigners?" he puzzled.

"I did a lot of travelling when I was a teenager," Nobunaga explained, with a shrug of his shoulders, which were several feet away. "Got

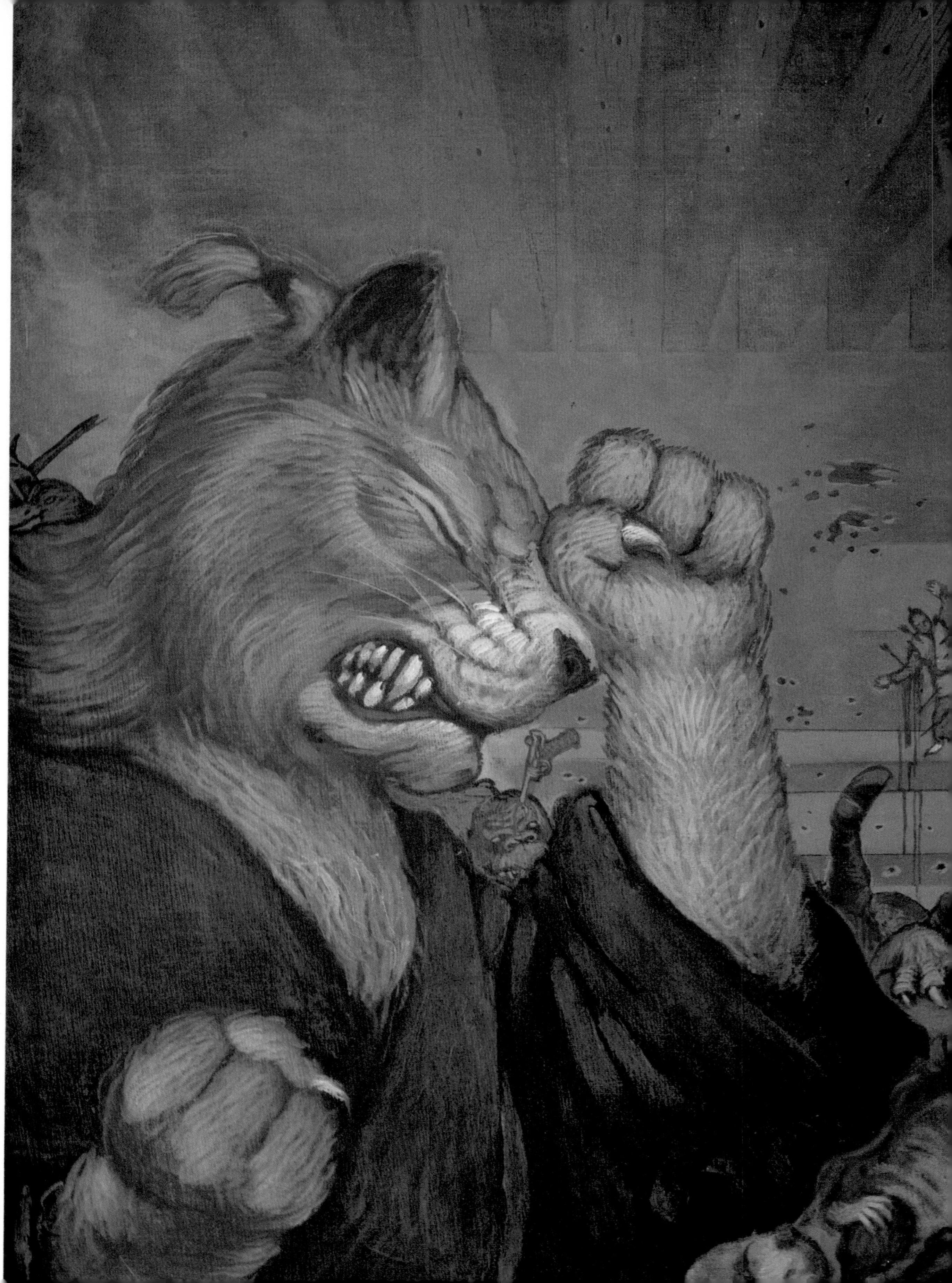

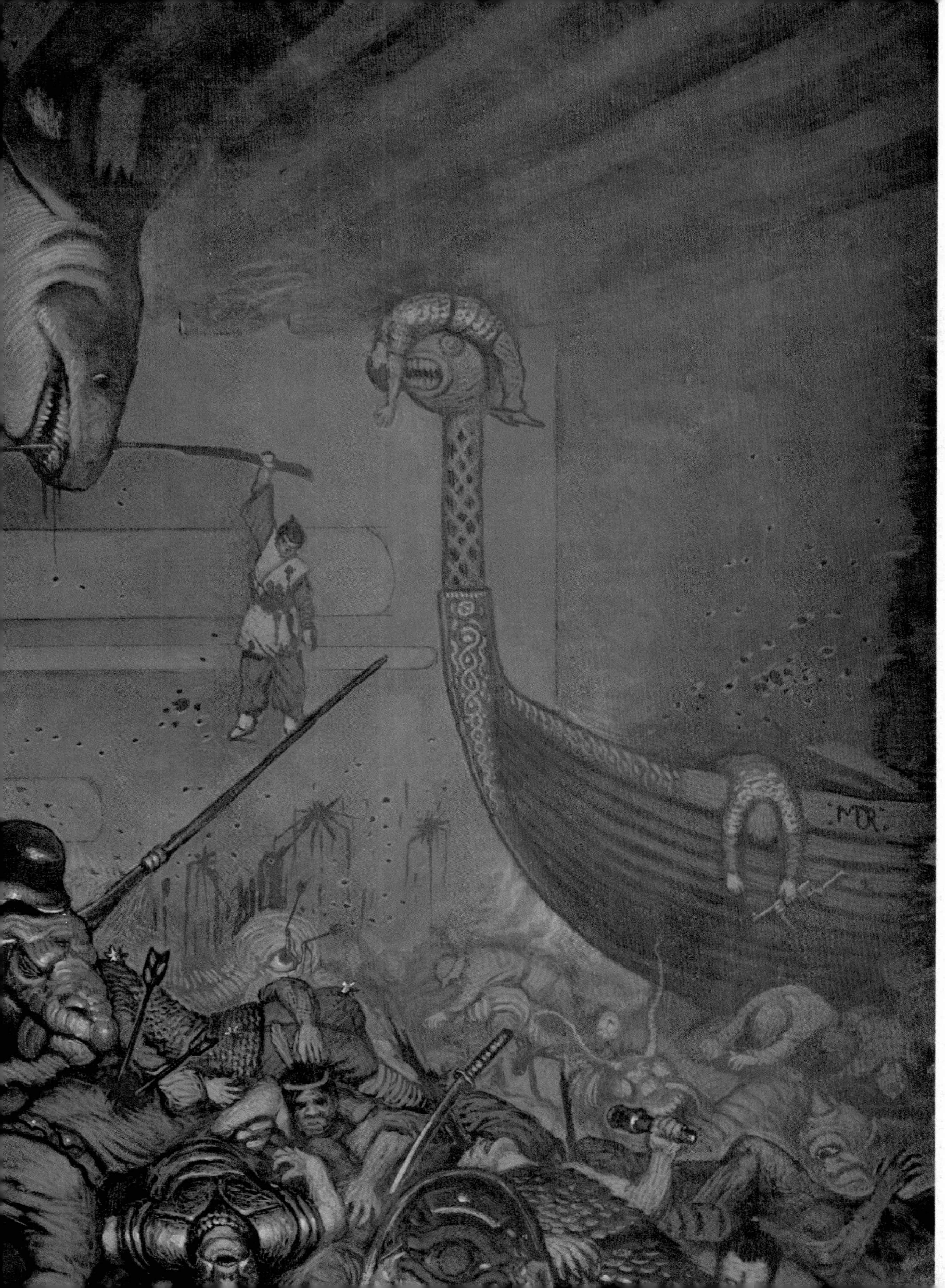

pretty wild sometimes. Made a lot of enemies."

"If only I'd been here!" Tomokato cried, clenching his paws.

"They knew you'd be gone," Nobunaga replied, dribbling a thin, tastefully small trickle of blood from one corner of his mouth. "They had wizards and diviners among them. Otoko told me, when I was captured. How he gloated! He'd seen to it that his allies knew all about you; that's how he got them to hold off the attack — until you were out of the way." He gasped, grimacing with pain. "I'm done for. This is the end."

"My . . . My Lord . . . " Tomokato faltered.

"Avenge me," Nobunaga said. "Happy trails, faithful one." His eyes closed, and his jaw went slack.

Tomokato bowed to him, rose and turned. He was already forcing the grief from his mind, replacing it with steely determination. He would make the bastards pay. . . .

"One more thing," Nobunaga called behind him.

Tomokato looked back.

"Remember what the sage said: 'A giant monster may be cowed by high-tension wires or oxygen destroyers, and be stayed from levelling Tokyo; but the warrior sees only his duty, and does it. . . . ' " A hissing breath passed between Nobunaga's lips, and his eyes closed again.

The cat bowed his head, turned, and strode grimly from the hall. First he would phone Akira Yamazaki, a Kyoto funeral director, and tell him to report to the castle for the challenge of his career. Second, he would go to his own chambers and armor himself. And finally, he would set forth from the castle, a masterless samurai, a *ronin*, a warrior with no responsibilities save vengeance for his lord.

"On the other hand," Nobunaga said, back in the audience-hall, "as the monk Mitsubishi Zero once put it . . . "

But Tomokato was by now too far off to hear that lungless wisdom.

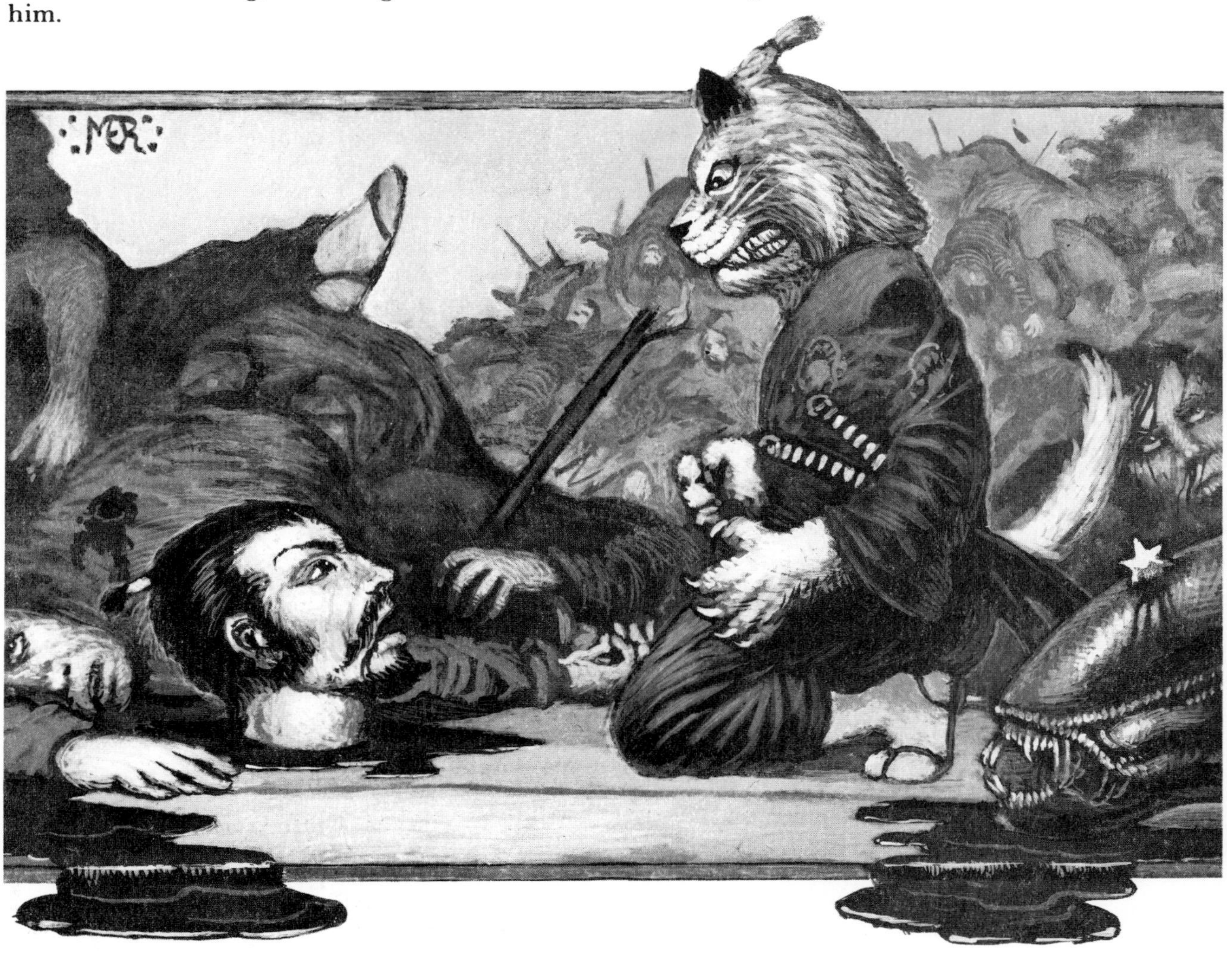
MER

THE BRIDGE OF
CATZAD-DÛM

CURLY RIVER

MT. ALMURIC

PLAY MISTY FOR ME MTS.

• WILMINGTON

BRANDYWINE

RIVER BRANDYWINE

GULF OF LOON

DELAWARE

▲ THE AUTHOR'S HOUSE

RIVER HOWYADUIN

■ BRANDYWINE RACEWAY

CATZAD-DÛM

BAVARIAN ALPS

DOGGON-DOR

MINAS MUFFLER •

CHINCOTEAGUE

MIDDLING EARTH
(TOWARDS THE END
OF THE THIRD AGE)

NEAR HARAD

• HARAD'S DEPT. STORE

FAR HARAD

Upon leaving Azuchi Castle, the attackers had split up. All but a handful reached the coast and took ship. Otoko sailed back to exile: the others returned to their homelands. Able to catch and kill only a dozen or so before they left Japan, Tomokato seethed with frustration, but finally resigned himself to the prospect of having to track them down one at a time. And Fugu Otoko, he decided, would be at the head of his list. . . .

From: *Cat Out of Hell: A Biography of Miaowara Tomokato,* by William Shirer and A. J. P. Godzilla

Tomokato climbed to the crown of the rocky hill, the setting sun at his back. Across from him, summit stained red by the day's dying glare, was the Western cliff-wall of Catzad-Dûm. His shadow was a grim black blot on the crimson-lit rampart.

He stared down into the deepening gloom between the hill and the cliff, picking out the great doors of the ancient cat-mansion beneath their frowning stone lintel. Before the threshold was a large dark pool, its surface motionless. Pale vines from the cliff-wall trailed down into the water. They matted the surface of the precipice — everywhere except for the doors. Tomokato thought it strange that they should be so conspicuously absent from the area; he thought it even stranger when he realized that they had been *pruned* away — a clearly heart-shaped opening surrounded the entrance. What manner of hands had done the work? He felt a certain anxiety, but not enough to challenge his rigid self-control.

Tomokato turned, watching the sun's glaring disc begin to sink beneath a mountain-ridge. A chill breeze sprang up, stirring his whiskers. His paw clenched on the hilt of his *katana,* or longsword. He wondered if he would ever see the light of day again, but he knew it did not matter. His lord had been cruelly, treacherously butchered. Fugu Otoko had had a hand in it, and Otoko had fled into the vast recesses of Catzad-Dûm. Tomokato's soul ached with the lust for revenge. His slitted eyes seemed almost to smoke, like newly-congealed obsidian. He smiled slightly, showing his wickedly pointed teeth. He was the very image of ferocious martial resolution.

Just before the sun dipped from sight, a crow flew by, and was almost too awed by the sight of him to continue flapping.

"What a stud," the bird mumbled to himself, winging erratically southward.

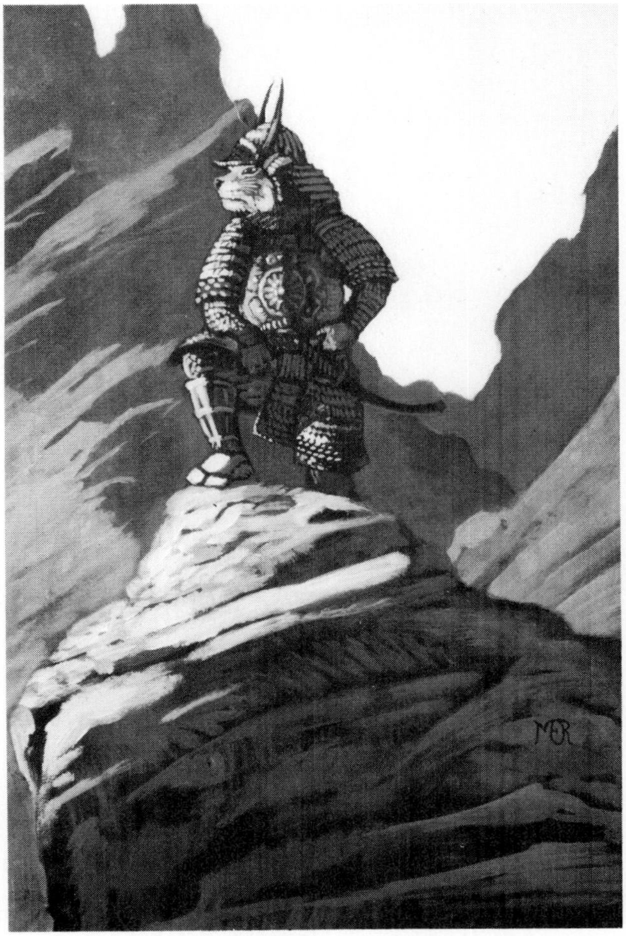
MER

Tomokato turned again, and clambered down the darkened eastern side of the hill, towards the mere. Flanking the cliff-wall for some distance, the water blocked direct access to the doors. But he saw he could skirt it on the left, and climb along the vines until he gained the entrance.

Coming to the mere's edge, he worked his way round, towards the wall. As he walked, he heard a low gurgling sound, and thought he saw bubbles rising in the water. After a time, small sluggish waves began to lap the stony shore. He paused, wondering what all this might portend. However, duty called, and he continued fatalistically on his way.

He reached the creeper-covered rock-face and began to climb sideways to the doors. As far as he could tell, the bubbling had stopped, but still he looked back at the water from time to time, though he could not see much in the thickening darkness.

He hauled himself closer and closer to the entrance. The bubbling began again. Craning his

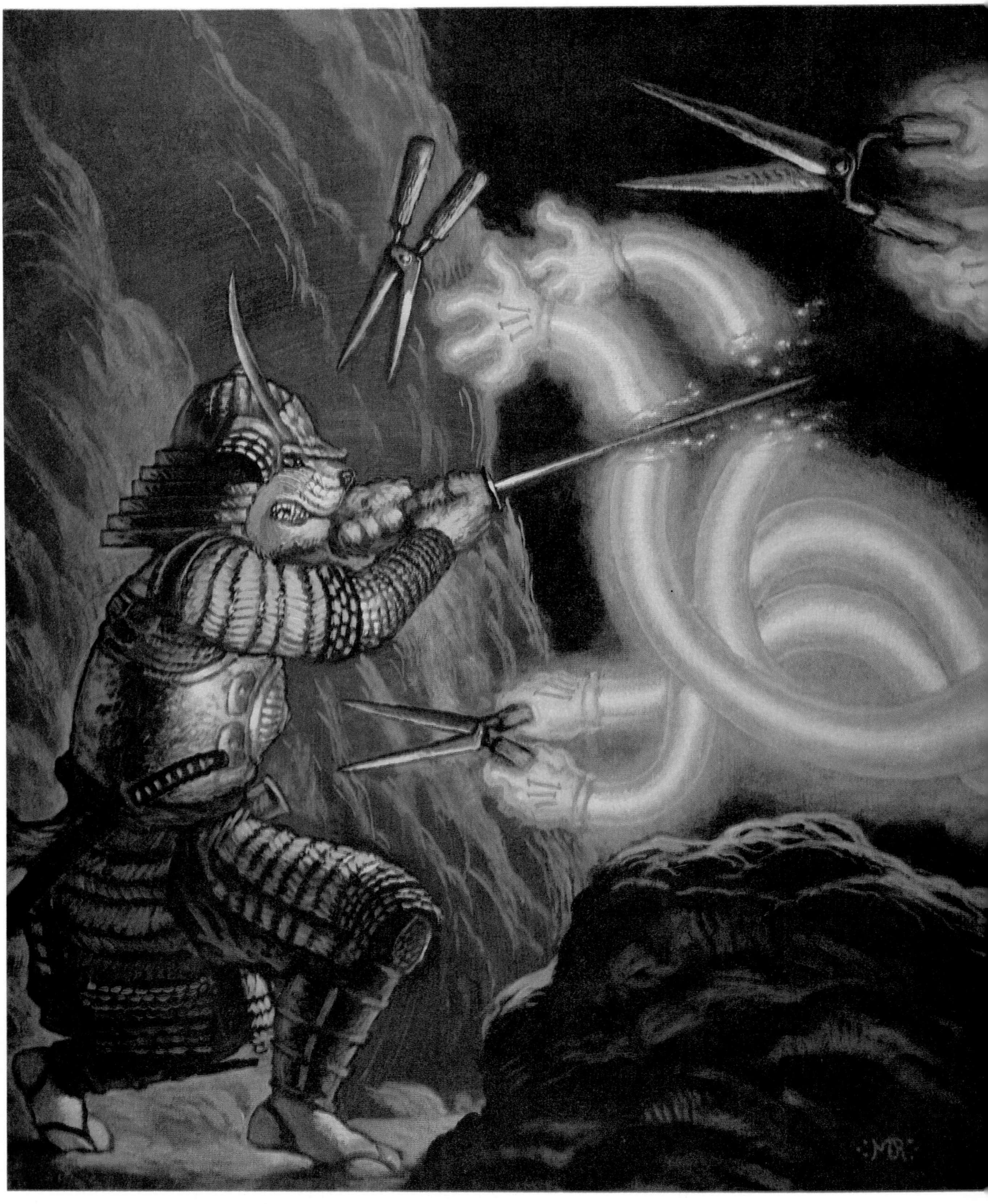

head around, he thought he could see a yellowish glow in the center of the pool, but he was not sure.

Finally he climbed down before the doors. Again he thought about the mysterious pruning around the entrance, wondering what manner of hands had done the work.

He ran his paws over the cool stone faces of the doors, feeling an inscription, and the crack between the valves, but nothing else. There were no handles, nothing for him to open the doors with.

As he stood pondering the problem, the bubbling grew suddenly much louder, and yellow light flooded the doors and the cliff-face. He snarled and spun, whipping out his *katana*.

The mere seethed before him, glowing like golden lava. Effulgent tentacles rose dripping from the boiling depths. Each ended in a four-fingered hand sheathed with a white Mickey Mouse glove; each hand clutched one handle of a pair of garden shears. Dozens of bright clacking blades swept towards the cat.

Tomokato stood in a ready position, holding the longsword in front of him, gripping the hilt with both paws. The Gardener in the Water did not daunt him. He was ready to fight, ready to die.

"Inoshiro Honda!" he screeched. "Sessue — *Hayakawa!*" As the last word rang from between his proud gleaming fangs, he severed the first two hands with a single virile Scarlet Tapeworm stroke. Still clutching their shears, the hands dropped into the mere, trailing a dark ichor that stank like sweat from the very armpit of Satan.

More arms swirled in. The *katana* whirred and flamed, slicing through tentacle after tentacle, whistling in a constantly repeated *Datsun Tempura*, or Divine Whirling Outboard Motor Propellor Blow. Tomokato could hardly breathe without inhaling the rancid ichor splashing through the air. Gurgling shrieks bubbled up from the Gardener as its hands were amputated in twos and fours and sixes. Fallen shears clanged on the stones.

Before long, the creature had had enough, and yanked its darkly-spurting tentacles back beneath the surface. It retreated to its lair, mind roiling with pain and dread. Even so, it had to admit to itself that that cat was sure one Hell of a stud.

Up above, Tomokato wiped his blade on a trouser-leg, then sheathed the sword. As the Gardener fled, the darkness had swarmed in once more; but several severed hands had landed near

the cat, and they were still glowing, though not as brightly as before. He picked one up and used it for a lamp, turning to read the inscription on the doors. The message, carved in cat-runes, said:

Pedo Meow a Minno.

Say *meow* and enter.

Tomokato scowled. The soft utterance did not come easily to his war-hardened windpipe. He thought it vile, effeminate, a sound unbecoming to a cat steeped in *Bushido*, the Way of the Warrior. Still, he forced himself: *"Meow,"* he said, and spat.

Immediately the dark runes began to fill with orange fire. An incandescent purple cat-head, complete with party-hat and noisemaker, appeared above the inscription. The noisemaker uncurled, and there was a sharp razz. Then the device was shifted to one side like a cigar. A word-balloon issued from the cat-head's mouth; in it were flowing letters that read; *You're in!*

The doors creaked inward. Lighting his way with the glowing hand, Samurai Cat strode forward, into the thick musty gloom of Catzad-Dûm. Ancient dust puffed underfoot. Rats and spiders scuttled from his path.

The passage leading from the doors was low-ceilinged and wide. On the walls were cunning bas-reliefs, of stylized cats in armor battling porks and giant fleas, or using vacuum cleaners in what appeared to be extremely dusty chambers, or skiing, or descending in bathyspheres; several of the carvings showed cats doing all these things at once, laughing grimly and stylistically.

Tomokato pressed on, sniffing the air. Faint but pungent, there was an unmistakable odor mingling with the smells of damp stone and decay that hung in the tunnel. There were still porks in Catzad-Dûm. And he knew that his prey would be with them.

Pressing in and out of side tunnels and galleries, he followed the pork-smell, going ever downward into the bowels of the labyrinthine cat-mansion. He passed through abandoned kitty-litter storage-chambers, made his way in and out of treasure-rooms, skirting piled hoards of moldering cat-toys. Sneering slightly, he stalked through the chambers of crumbling cat-houses where the pleasure-seekers of Catzad-Dûm had amused themselves of old. There were pornographic pictures on the walls, but he was unmoved by them, save to contempt. He was a born ascetic; no erotic mosaic could arouse him.

He went down winding stairs and ramps, striding over narrow flywalks that spanned black abysses. The pork-smell grew ever thicker.

Reaching an intersection, he halted as a yellow light turned red. Footsteps echoed from a tunnel off to his left. A bluish glow appeared inside, limning the opening. Casting down the gardener's hand, he reached for the hilt of his *katana*.

Clad all in grey, an old greybearded man entered the intersection, carrying a great gnarled staff; from its tip the blue glow came. He signalled, and eight other people, of various races, came out. There were two other men, a dwarf, an elf, and four small chubby fellows with furry feet.

"Damn it all," said one of the men to the greybeard, "I told you we should have turned right at the Burger Ki—" He broke off suddenly, having noticed the cat. The others turned. Tomokato regarded them inscrutably.

"Don't worry about him," the old man said. "It's just another one of those D and D toesuckers. Come on."

They passed from the intersection. Tomo-

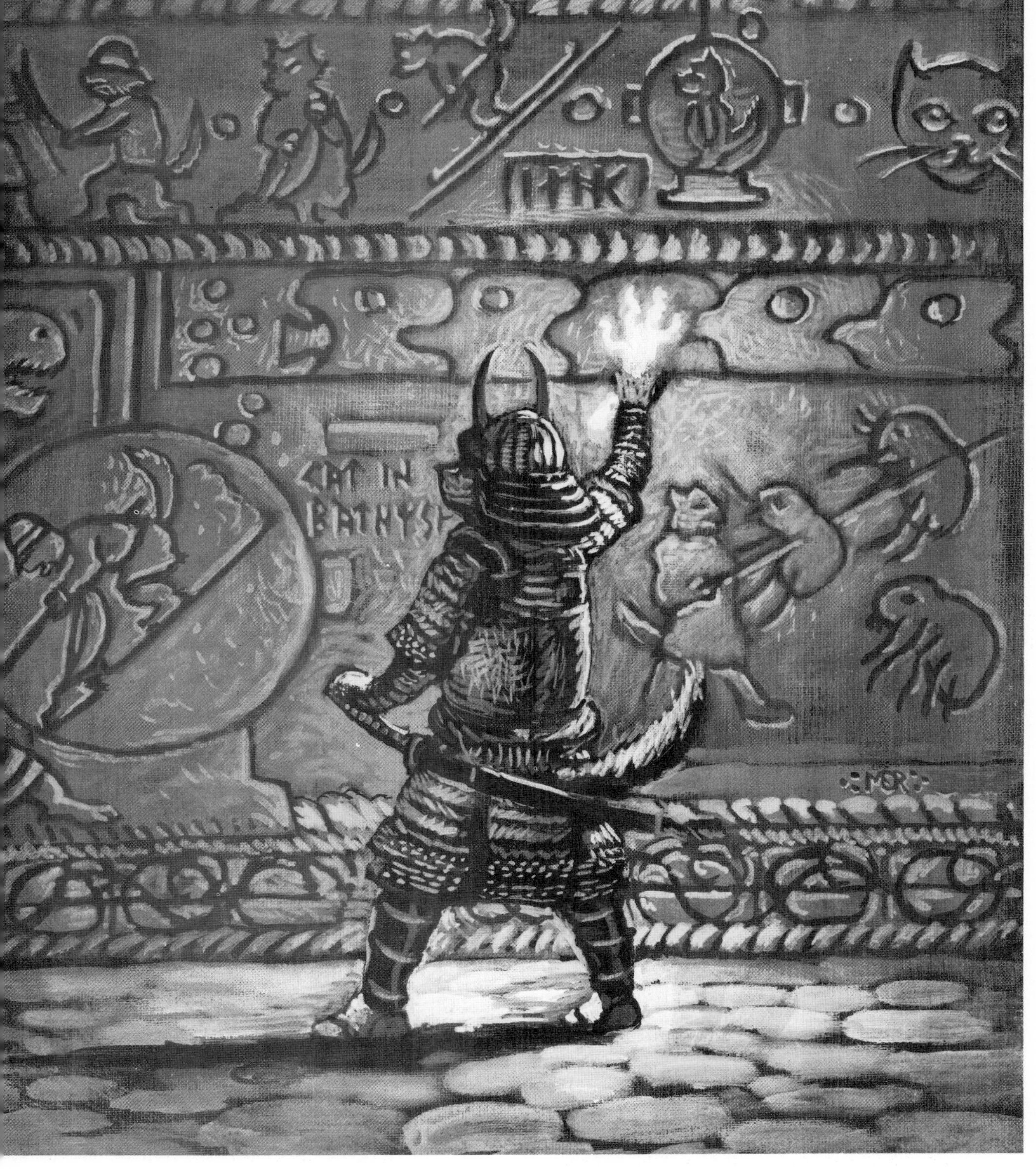
CAT IN
BATHYS

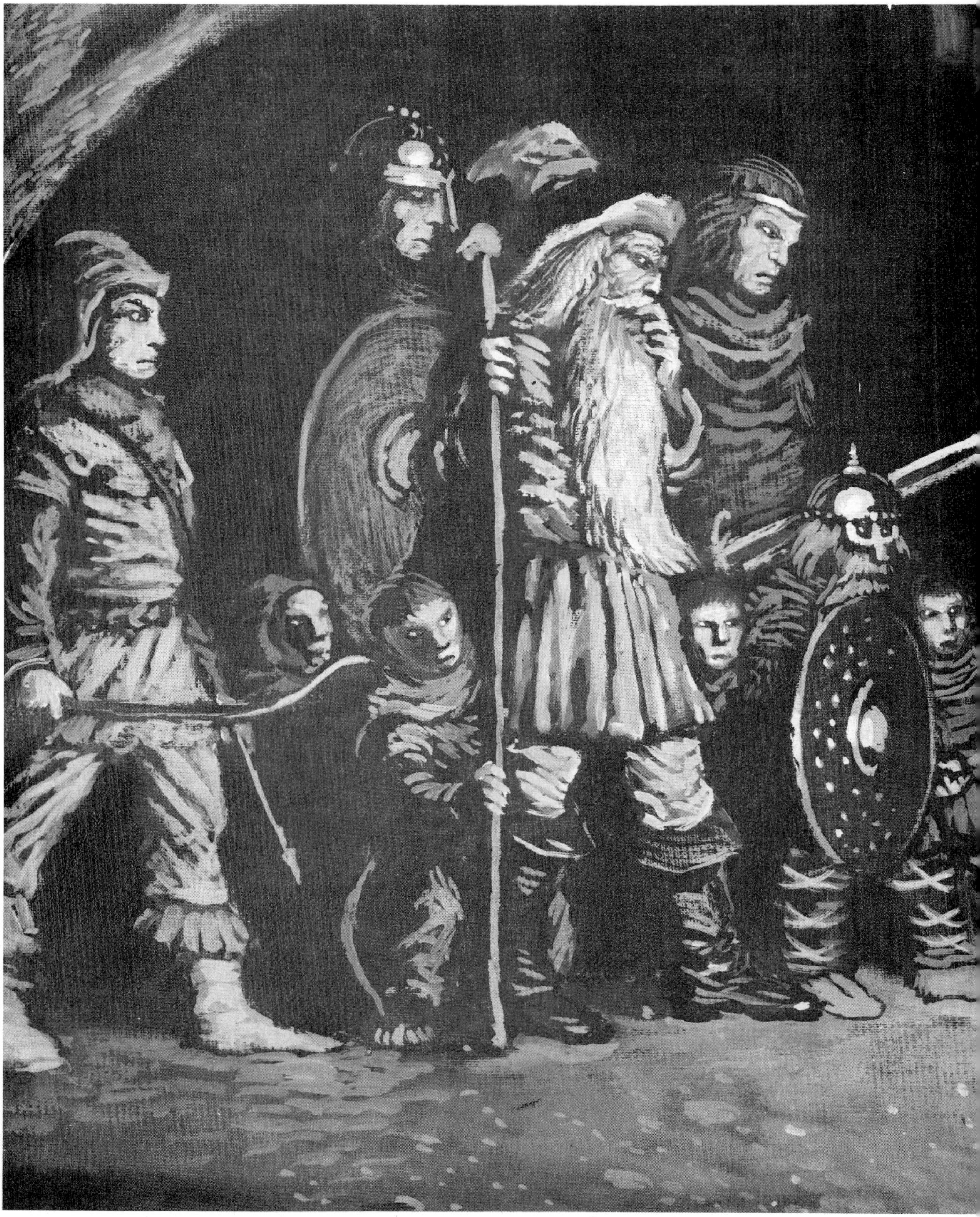

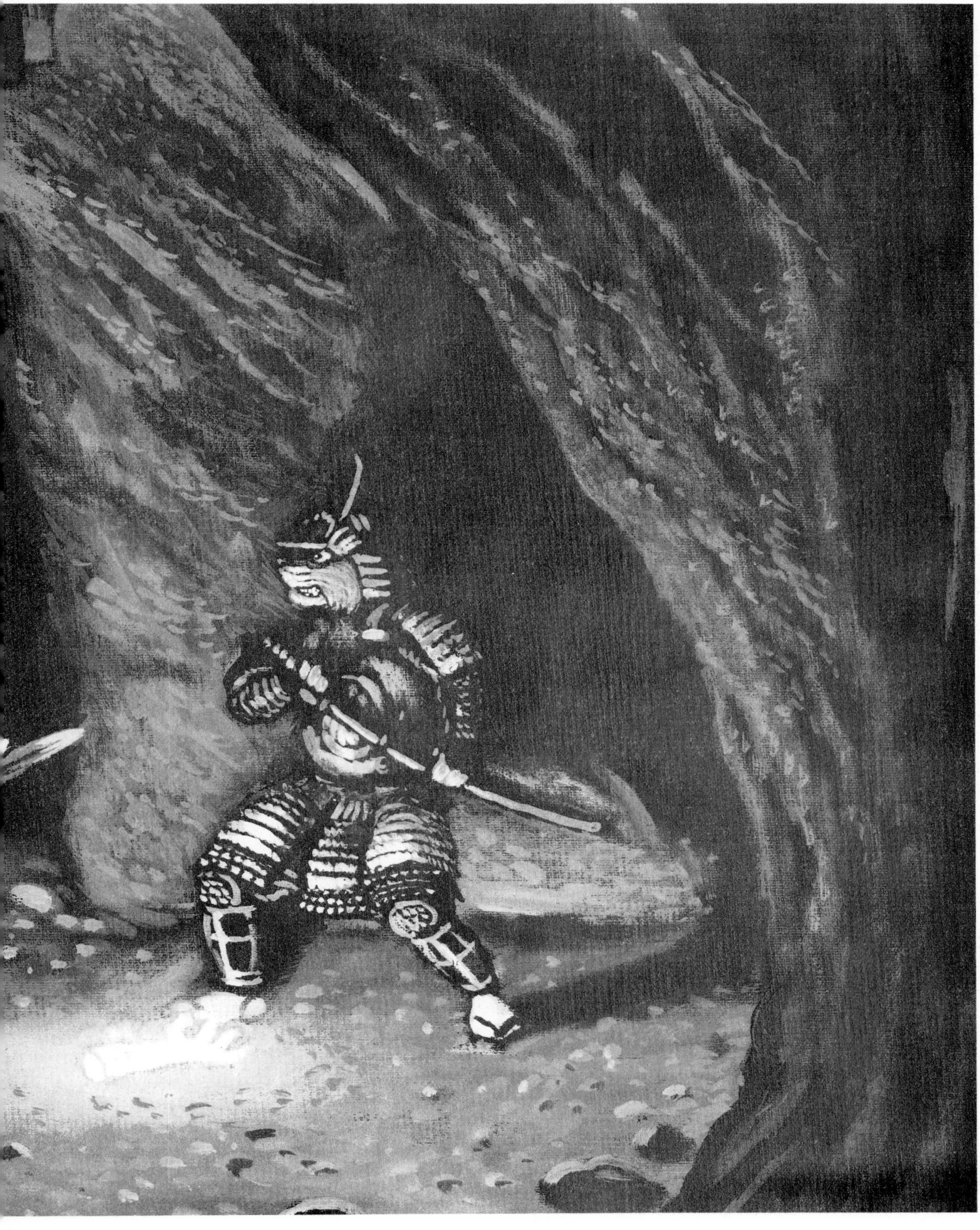

kato picked the hand back up, and continued on his way. The pork-smell led him to a spiral staircase which he descended for several hundred feet. Upon reaching the bottom, he went into a small chamber and squatted down to rest. Gazing upwards, he saw a circular opening in the ceiling. A distant blue glow appeared at the top of the shaft. He heard voices, and presently a small head and shoulders were silhouetted against the glow. There came a hollow whistling, and a rock clanged off his helmet. He snarled and jumped to his feet, still looking up the shaft. He saw the small figure jerk back from the edge of the well.

"You little bastard!" came the far-off, echoing voice of the old man. "That's the last rock you throw in on this trip!"

All at once a falling body was outlined against the blue light. Tomokato stepped aside as one of the small, furry-footed fellows splattered against the floor of the chamber.

The cat shed no tears.

He squatted down again, and after ten minutes felt sufficiently rested to push on. He descended into a section of catacombs that was half-flooded with dark water. Crammed into narrow niches, mummified cats lined the walls, some of them two to a shelf. Feline corpses that had floated up from submerged niches bobbed about him as he waded

along waist-deep. He reached a section where wealthier cats had been laid to rest; their niches were larger, some quite expansive, with room for all manner of grave-goods, which included electrum-headed scratching-posts and platinum milk-bowls; there were stacks of mummified mice and canaries for the felines to torture in the afterlife, and a very few of the richest cats had had their favorite humans put to death with them, to slave for them for all eternity.

The pork-smell grew stronger and stronger. Tomokato drew his *katana*, coming up into a dry corridor.

The clop of hooved feet sounded ahead of him, beyond a bend in the corridor. There was snuffling laughter. He slipped into an alcove and waited. Disturbed, centipedes and tarantulas dropped on him from above. Calmly he brushed them off and quietly stepped on them.

The clopping sounds came closer. A troop of porks, at least thirty of the pig-snouted horrors, pushed past the alcove. They wore byrnies of scale or chain-mail, and plated thigh-guards, and carried Schmeisser submachine guns. Battleaxes and potato-masher grenades were hooked to their belts. On their helmets crouched iron frogs, tipping top-hats; on each link or scale of their mail was written the name of Porky the All-Wise, the Most Compassionate. The foremost pork wore a sashimoto-style banner which read: *Your pearls or your life.* None of them noticed the cat, even though he was well-lit by the gardener's hand; they were too intent on stroking their Schmeissers.

Silently he slipped from the alcove and followed them. Going down a side tunnel, they entered a vast torchlit chamber. Two huge porks stood guard at the threshold; they did not see Tomokato until it was too late. His sword blazed, tracing out the terrible spiralling flips of the maneuver called Popping the Duck. The porks died without a sound, heads cloven, legs chopped through at the knees, intestines knotted like pink bowties around their necks.

Blood dripping from his blade, Tomokato crossed the threshold. The chamber was full of porks, but all of them had their backs to him. Before them, on a tall, dáis-mounted throne, sat Fugu Otoko, The Blowfish Who Never Smiles. But Otoko was no mere blowfish. He was half carp. And his sword was cruel.

Looking at him, Tomokato remembered returning to Azuchi Castle, finding the chambers strewn with dead, finding his lord beheaded. . . .

:YOUR
PEARLS
OR
YOUR
LIFE:

Rage flooded his mind. *"Akira Kurosawa!"* he shrieked, and waded through the porks before him, smiting right and left like a furball from Hell. Arms and heads leaped from shoulders at the sighing kiss of his steel. Porks turned to face him, snouts written with surprise; he sent their souls winging to piggy damnation. Guts slithered to the floor. Blood splashed in gigantic gouts. Snorts of pain filled the air Grinning with maniacal frenzy, the cat mowed down foe after foe, like slaughter-lust incarnate. He disdained the axes that barely missed him, the bullets that grazed his fur, the grenade blasts that utterly dismembered him and spattered the ceiling with his brains. His blade was a whirlwind of sheer shrieking violence. And fi-

nally, the last pork in the chamber was slain.

Stained head to foot with reeking gore, he strode towards the dais. Fugu Otoko had not stirred. He regarded the cat with obvious amusement. But as Tomokato came closer, Otoko signalled; there came a thunderous flapping of leathery wings, and a huge pinioned demon-shape landed between the dais and Tomokato. The cat halted, eyeing his new foe. The monster's mane burned furiously, and its eyes smoldered a baleful crimson. It held a flaming sword and a whip of many thongs; taking both weapons in its swordhand, it extended its free palm toward Tomokato, and growled in a voice thick with contempt:

"Give us a tip, my love."

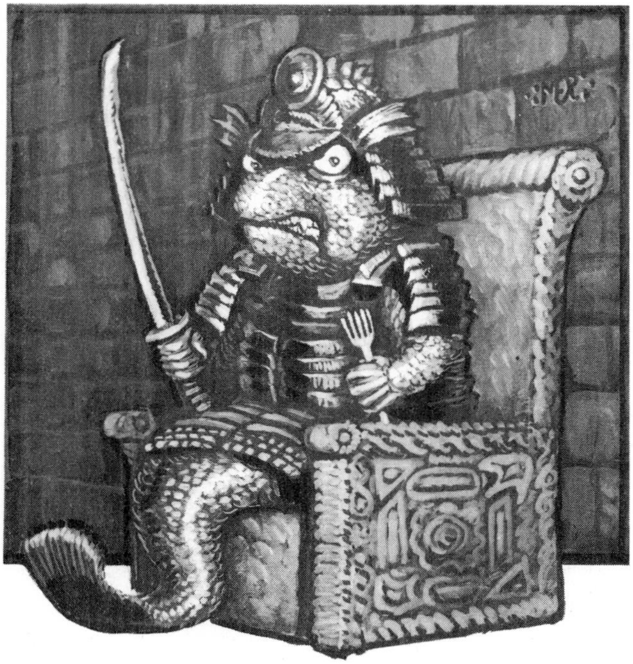

Tomokato was brave indeed; even so, he shivered with realization. The demon wanted a tip. . . . It was a *B'aalhop.*

But despite his terror, the cat steeled himself. He gripped his bloodied sword, prepared to spring. The B'aalhop studied him, saw the courage and determination in the feline's eyes.

If only we didn't have to fight each other, it thought to itself. *I could be friends with a cat like this . . . definitely a stud.* Sighing, it switched the whip back to its free hand, tensing to receive Tomokato's attack.

The cat let out a sudden, terrific battle-shriek: *"Eiji Tsuburaya!"* he cried. The scream bounced ringing from walls and floors and ceiling. Cracked loose by the reverberations, a stalactite plummetted. Before Tomokato could charge, it struck him on the helmet, dashed him senseless to the floor.

Head aching, face caked with dried gore, Tomokato woke. His pulse throbbed heavily, thickly in his temples. He was hanging upside down, paws tied behind his back, ankles bound by the rusty chain that suspended him from the ceiling.

He looked left and right. He was no longer in the throne room, but in another chamber of comparable size. The far side was almost completely dark, but he could make out a shadowy colonnade. On the near side, Tiffany lamps illuminated a mural depicting a New England fishing village in which Dick Van Patten was being devoured by a horde of mutant shrimp.

Good, Tomokato thought. He hated Dick Van Patten.

A moment later, a door banged open in the mural, and scores of porks rushed in, surrounding Tomokato. One wore the cat's *wakazashi* and *tonto.* Another brandished his captured *katana* in his face. Behind the porks loomed the massive form of Fugu Otoko. The Blowfish Who Never Smiles was smiling now, leering triumphantly at Tomokato.

"Soon," Otoko chortled, "you join Nobunaga in Hell!"

His henchmen edged closer to the cat, snuffling. Spears and gun-barrels were pushed up against the feline's face and body. Several grenades were tied to his throat with barbed wire, and two more were stuffed up under the brim of his helmet.

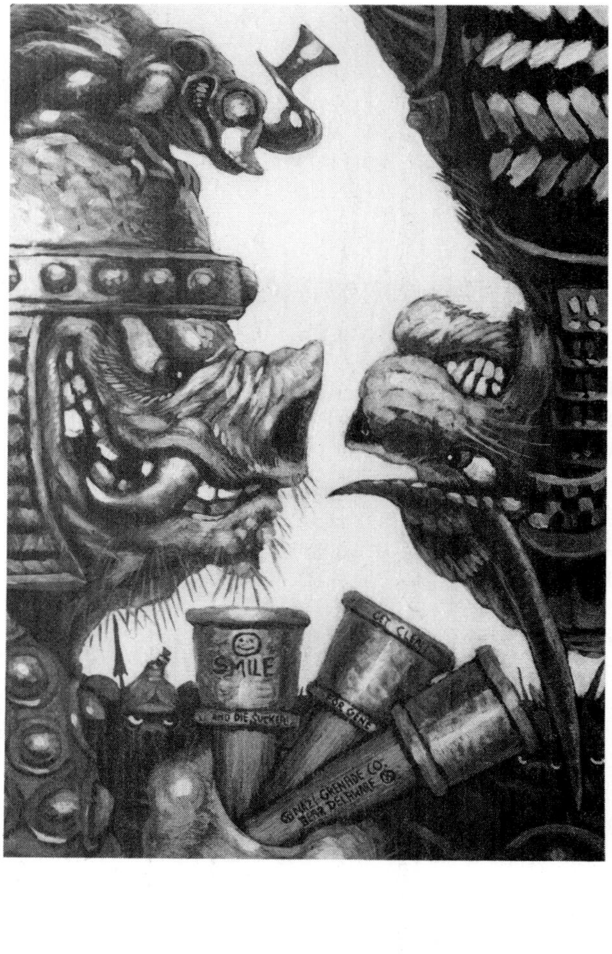
SMILE

"All right, my delightful boot-slaves," Otoko grated, drooling, eyes seething with feral lust, his mind a furnace of hate and sadism; molten earwax dribbled from the sides of his scaly head, and he thumbed the edge of his sword with merciless abandon. He was already bleeding pretty badly. "Let that sucker have it!"

Pork-fingers tightened on schmeisser-triggers; pork-hands began to prime grenades; pork-axes rose, poised to strike; pork-spears drew back, their bearers readying themselves for deep, soul-satisfying, wonderful jabs.

Suddenly there was a loud crash and a series of shrieks. Smiting furiously at the porks, a platoon of semi-human D and D fanatics poured into the chamber. Distracted from Tomokato, the porks turned to slaughter them, but before the fight was done, several wild schmeisser-bursts cut the cat's bonds, and he clattered to the floor. Instantly he was up, snarling. Grabbing a fallen submachine gun, he spun, spraying out a deadly circle of lead. Blood erupting from their bullet-riddled bodies, fifteen porks toppled as if they had been shot. Before the rest could recover, he flung down the empty gun, primed the grenades attached to his throat, tore them free, and hurled them, one after another, among his surviving foes. Explosion after explosion filled the chamber with roaring fury. Pork-corpses flew like ripped ragdolls, but miraculously, Tomokato was unscathed. Gashed by shrapnel, slinging blood out of their eyes, the handful of porks still on their feet tried to charge him. Snatching up a D and D-er's severed head,

he rolled it across the corpse-choked floor, knocking them over like tenpins. As they struggled to rise, he drew out the grenades that hung like deadly ear-rings on either side of his head, primed them, and tossed them. The porks came apart like shotgunned tomatoes.

Tomokato retrieved his blades, looked around for Otoko. Otoko was gone. Yet there was a whiff of blowfish and carp-smell in the smoke-bittered air, and the cat followed it from the chamber. Shortly he came to a narrow bridge. A flaming gulf yawned beneath it. Fugu Otoko stood on the far side, beckoning with his sword.

Growling, Tomokato stepped out onto the bridge of Catzad-Dûm. After a few paces, he heard the beating of vast pinions. The B'aalhop landed between him and Otoko, hefting its terrible weapons.

"You might as well jump over the side now, *cat,*" Otoko yelled. "Save us all some trouble."

But Tomokato continued to advance, *katana* in his right paw, cocked behind his head, *wakazashi* held low on the left.

The B'aalhop laughed in admiration, and its flaming mane blazed brightly. Then, trailing a sheet of fire, it charged, burning sword streaking like the exhaust of a rocket.

Tomokato made no sound. With a swift sidewards Heaven Unicycle blow, he shore through the bridge in front of him. Leaping over the cut, he ducked the lash of the B'aalhop's whip, bounded over a stroke of the flaming sword, and slipped between the demon's legs. Turning, he repeated

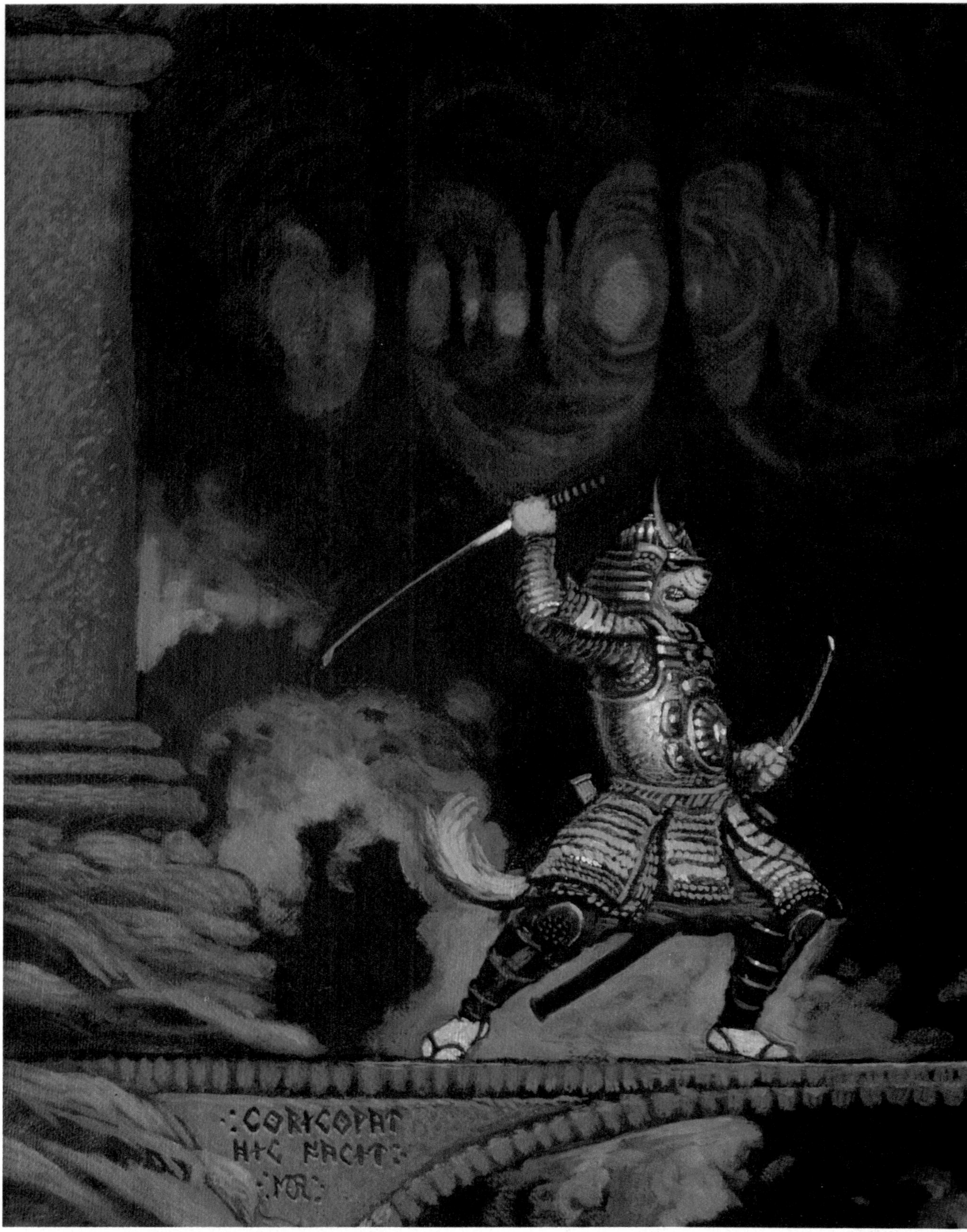
:CORYCOPAT
HIC FACIT:
:MR:

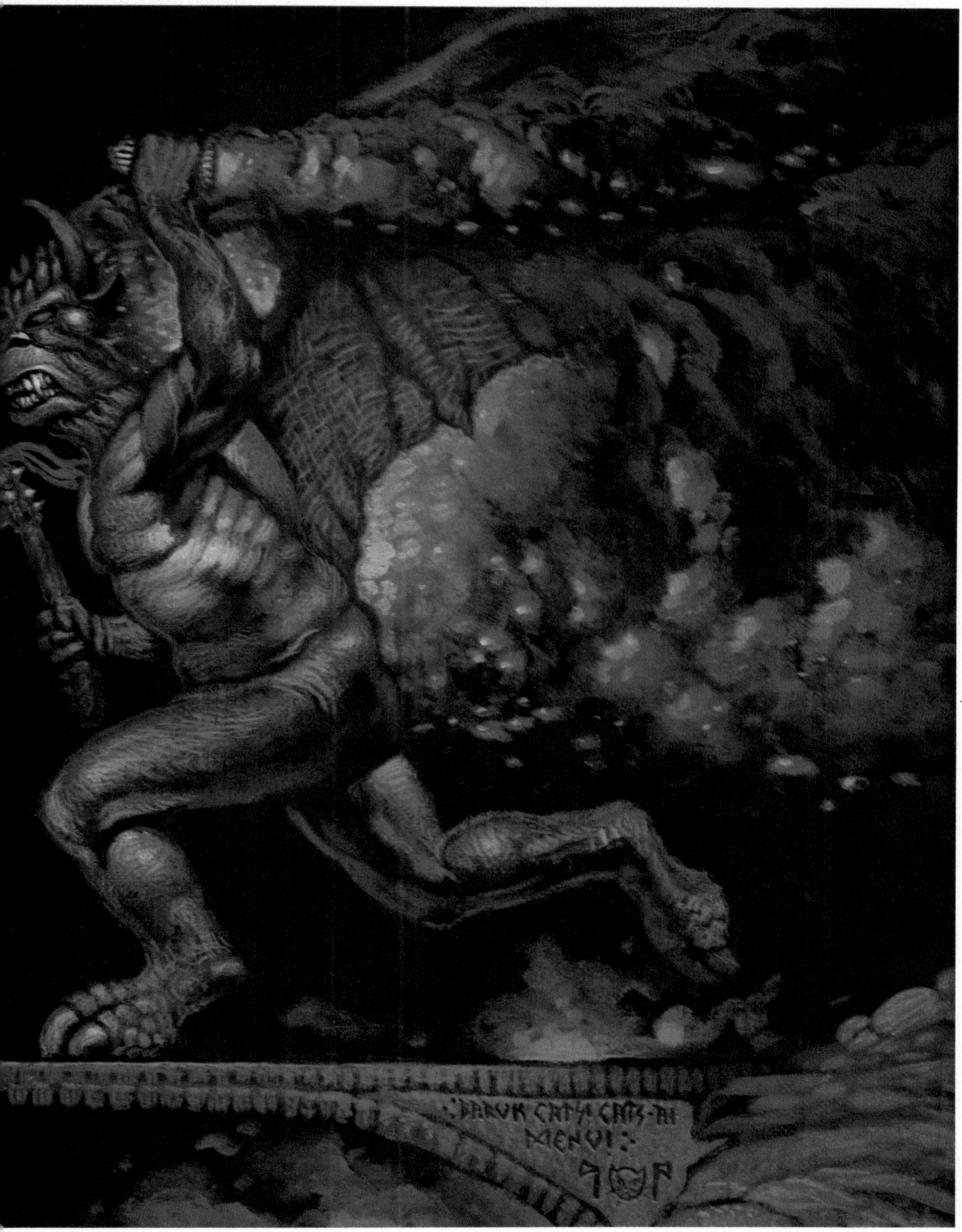

blades met, Otoko whipped out a Luger, fired. Tomokato whirled his *katana.* The bullet spanged off the longsword, rebounded into Otoko's chest. Otoko had never even seen the deflecting stroke; looking very puzzled, he coughed and shrugged, fired again. Again the cat parried. This time the bullet rebounded into Otoko's face. Otoko staggered, looking even more exasperated than before; he examined the pistol as blood rivered out of the hole where his snout had been.

"I don't believe this," he said, and fell over the side of the bridge.

"Toshiro Mifune!" the cat shrieked triumphantly, and sheathed his swords. Then he strode into the torchlit tunnel ahead, secure in the knowledge that he had fulfilled his obligation in the matter of Fugu Otoko, exacted payment in full on The Blowfish Who Never Smiles.

But there were others who still owed their blood, others who had aided in the killing of his lord. . . . Wilbur Wartley, for instance. . . .

Grabbing a torch, he made his way up from the depths of Catzad-Dûm, following the scent of the fresher airs. He emerged at last in a mountain dell on the eastern side of the ancient cat-mansion. For a time he watched the light of day growing in the sky, then looked down the slope. Some distance away, he saw seven bedraggled figures, the remnants of the party that had passed him at the red light. The greybeard was not among them. Tomokato went down to them.

"What happened to the old man?" he asked.

"He fell into shadow," said one of the men. "He did not escape."

"It was his own damn fault," said the other man. "I told him, we should've turned right at the Burger King. . . . "

Tomokato grunted. Then, with a slow swagger, he passed down the hill.

"If only we'd been led by a cat like that," said the elf, nudging the dwarf.

The dwarf nodded in appreciation. "What a stud!"

the Unicycle blow, slicing stone as if it were the merest lichee-nut. Even as the B'aalhop began to spin, the center of the bridge dropped out from under it, and with a terrible cry, the demon plunged into the abyss. Incredibly, it made no use of its wings as it plummetted.

"Fly, you fool!" cried Fugu Otoko. But the B'aalhop vanished in the flames.

The cat turned once more, and grinned terribly, hellishly at Otoko. Otoko read his doom in the feline's smile, but stood his ground, readying his blade.

Tomokato rushed at him. Just before their

THE BOOK OF THE DUNWICH COW

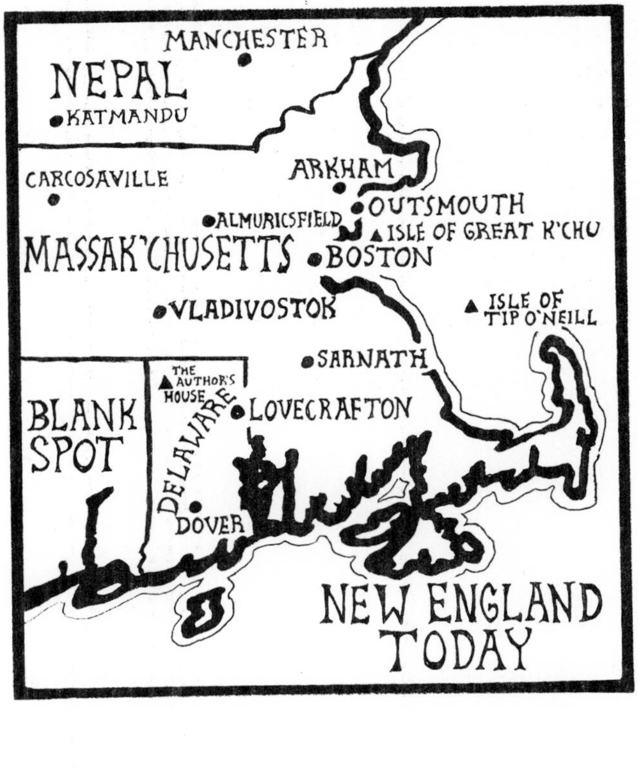
MANCHESTER
NEPAL
KATMANDU
CARCOSAVILLE
ARKHAM
OUTSMOUTH
ALMURICSFIELD
ISLE OF GREAT K'CHU
MASSAK'CHUSETTS
BOSTON
VLADIVOSTOK
ISLE OF TIP O'NEILL
SARNATH
THE AUTHOR'S HOUSE
BLANK SPOT
DELAWARE
LOVECRAFTON
DOVER
NEW ENGLAND TODAY

The cat took ship, sailing for America via the Bay of Belfalas, the Sea of Rhûn, and the Panama Canal, looking for his next target, the New England sorcerer, Wilbur Wartley. But he did not find his prey at the address Nobunaga had given him, which was just behind Arnold's Garage in West Kingston, Rhode Island; nor was the sorcerer at the forwarding address Tomokato extracted from Wartley's housekeeper. But certain clues kept the cat on the trail, and finally, after a long chase that led from Massachusetts to Maine, through Nepal and back to Massachusetts again, Tomokato began to realize he was closing in on his foe. . . .

— *Cat Out of Hell*

As the ancient bus clattered and wheezed its way down from the hill, bumping along the winding, rutted road, Tomokato peered through the cracked window, searching the night outside. The road twisted sharply to the left, and he had his first glimpse of Outsmouth. The town's lights shone dimly, murkily, like luminous fish in the depths of the sea. He could make out nothing else about the town; the moon had not yet risen, and the gloom was thick.

The bus wove southward again. His view was cut off. He sat back, looking up toward the front of the bus. Besides himself, there were only two passengers and the driver; all three were ragged, furtive types clad in ill-fitting baggy black overcoats, and wearing black wide-brimmed hats. Even when Tomokato first entered the bus, and passed by them on the way to the back, he had not seen their faces. But he had noticed they all smelled like fish. The bus reeked with their odor. It made him incredibly hungry. Throughout the trip he had been continuously appalled to find an insidious urge almost overwhelming him again and again, a desire to go up and eat his fellow passengers. He had never wanted to eat human beings before. He told himself it was simply the smell. They were returning to their home, to Outsmouth. It was a fishing-village, or so he had heard. That explained the odor. . . .

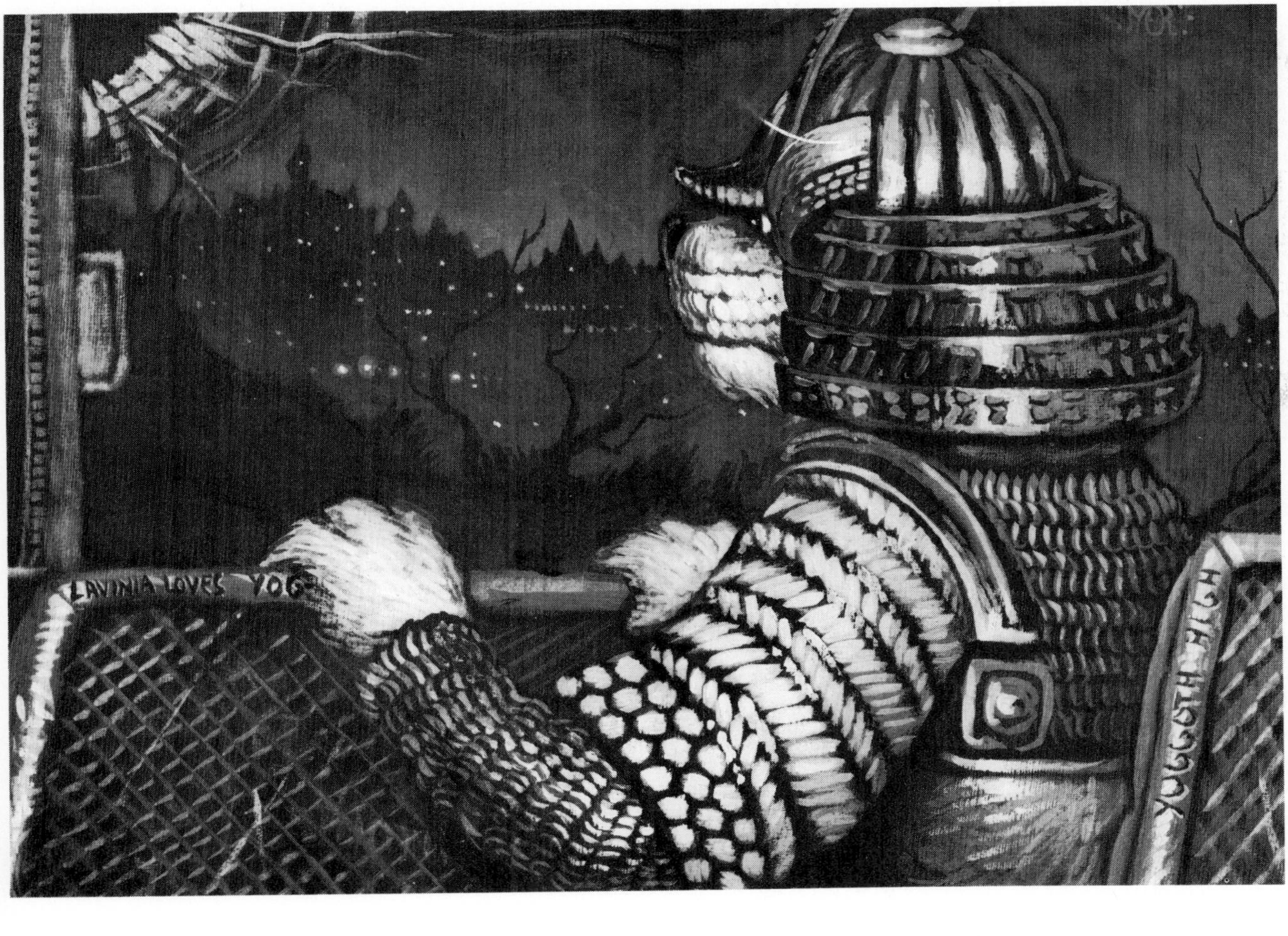

LAVINIA LOVES YOG
YOGGOTH HIGH

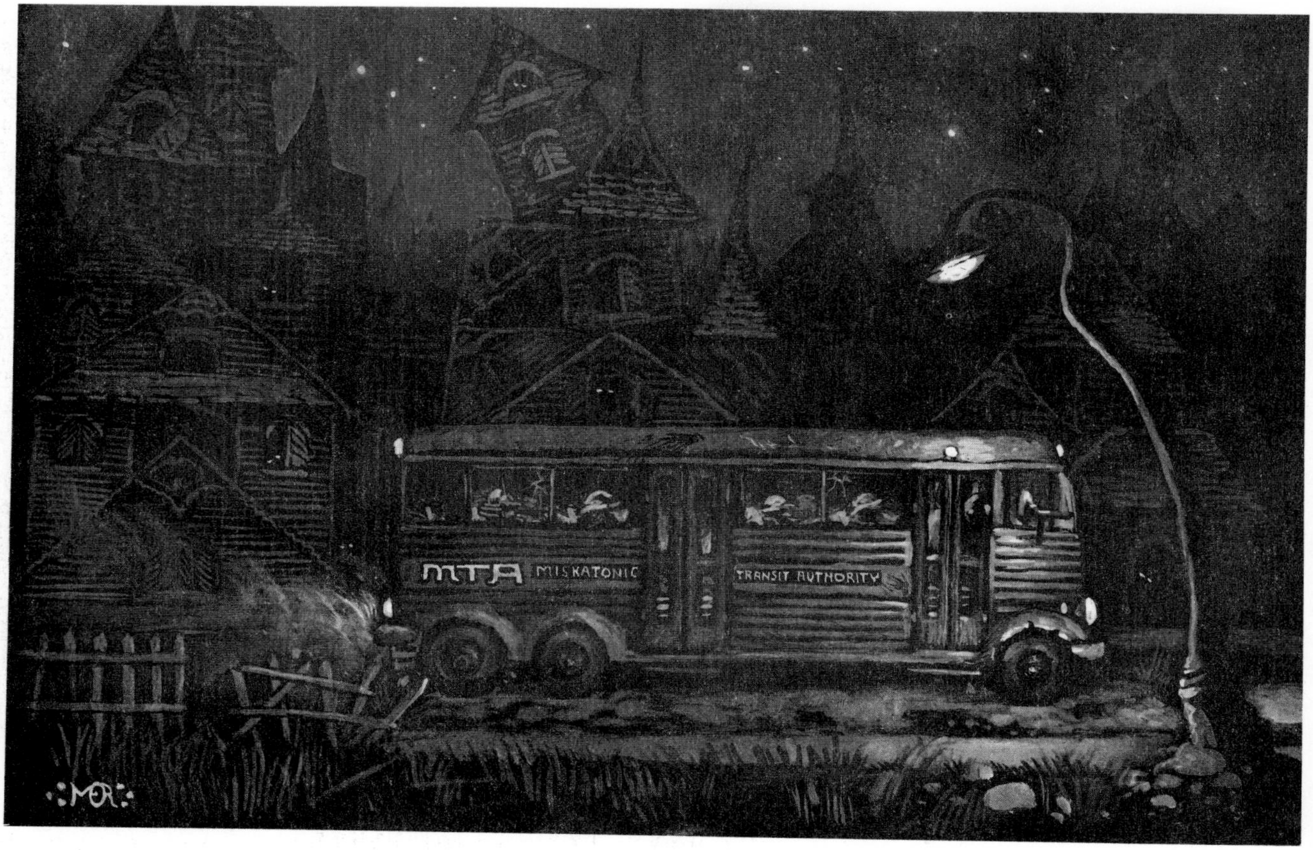
MTA
MISKATONIC
TRANSIT AUTHORITY

The urge came over him once more, and once more he fought it, struggling to keep his mind on something other than that delectable fishy smell. He forced himself to think about his mission. He had to find Wilbur Wartley and kill him. Sorcerer, necromancer, murderer, Wartley was heading for Outsmouth. And Tomokato would be waiting for him, in the town library. The cat would spring when Wartley tried to withdraw that hideous tome of occult lore known as *The Book of the Dunwich Cow*. . . .

The bus reached the fringes of Outsmouth. For some distance the road followed the convolutions of a black river that snaked through the town, emptying into the Atlantic beyond. A few leaning streetlamps shone here and there along the roadside, illuminating leprous, rotting shacks – at least Tomokato thought they were shacks at first. Then he realized they were only the *roofs* of shacks, resting on the ground. Dozens of detached attic dormers, their windows shuttered or boarded over, flanked the road.

The bus gasped its tubercular way toward the center of the town. The buildings Tomokato saw grew more and more elaborate, though they had fallen into peeling, squalid disrepair. Each was a large ramshackle collection of dormers piled one on top of another. From ground to roof, the structures were nothing but shuttered attics. A vague dread gnawed at the cat's mind as the complex shingled façades slipped by; the feeling was heightened every time he saw a hunched, overcoated figure shamble along the cracked and crazily-tilted sidewalks, or vanish furtively inside an alley at the bus's approach. The fishy odor had increased dramatically ever since the bus entered the town, and was thickening almost palpably as the conveyance neared Outsmouth's center; but the cat hardly noticed it now, fascinated and repelled as he was by what he glimpsed through the windows. As strange as he found the United States, he suspected strongly that Outsmouth was even stranger than the average American town. There were few businesses, and those belonged to attic-contractors of one sort or another, or attic-brokers, or attic-cleaners. There had once been several restaurants, fast-seafood joints; they had not caught on. The bus passed their burnt-out shells. Mounted on poles, a ring of cowskulls surrounded one charred Arthur Treacher's. Human skulls circled the Long John Silver's just down the way.

The bus came to a large, relatively well-lit town square, and lurched to a halt, coughing and squeaking and spitting. Before getting up, Tomokato looked at the buildings surrounding the square. All were the now-familiar dormer-piles — all save one, the local Elk's Lodge. Despite the eerie, blue-green floodlight which bathed it, he found it a comforting sight; his lord Nobunaga had been an Elk. But suddenly the cat realized the letters above the door no longer spelled out BPOE, but BPOF — the lowest tyne of the E had been crudely painted out. He wondered what the F stood for — then noticed the statue at the base of the stairs. It was of a fish. He pondered that for a moment. The Benevolent Protective Order of Fish?

The bus's engine sputtered and died. Getting up, Tomokato started for the front. The other two passengers and the driver were gone. He had not heard them leave. Nonetheless, he was alone in the ominous silence.

He paused. His eyes fell on a spiderweb strung between two rows of seats. A fly was wrapped mummylike in the silken net, a spider advancing slowly upon it.

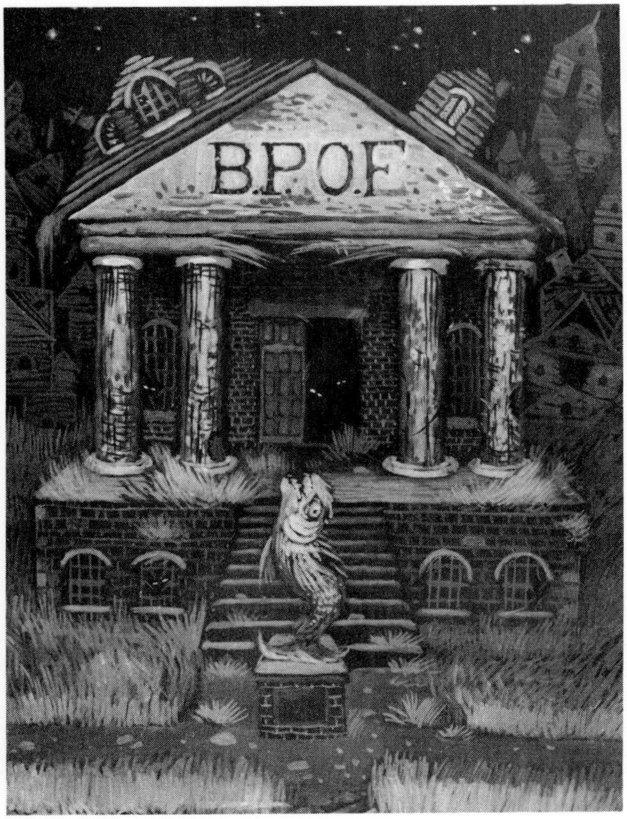
B.P.O.F

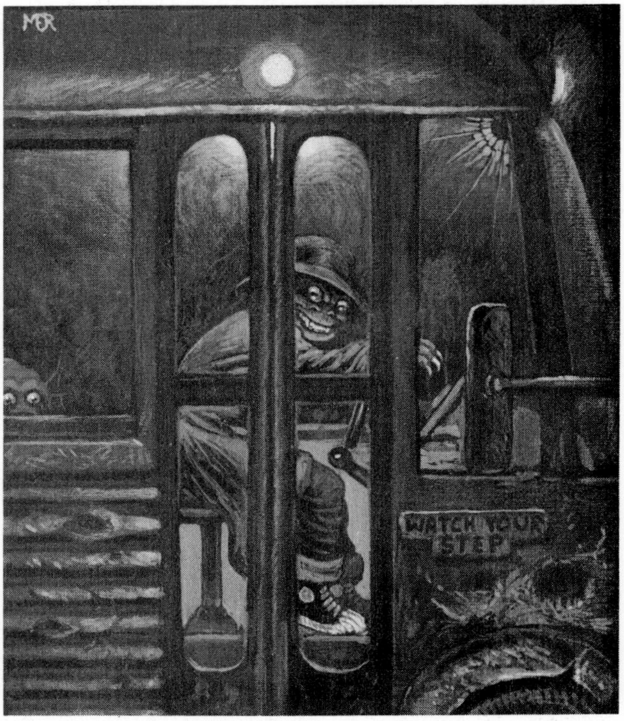
WATCH YOUR STEP

"Help me!" cried a thin, tinny voice.

With a start Tomokato realized it had come from the fly. He bent closer. The fly seemed to have a *tiny human head.*

This is really peculiar, Tomokato thought.

"Help me!" the fly cried again, just before the spider started chowing down on its face.

Without warning, the overhead lights went out. Tomokato clutched at his swordhilt, looked out one side of the bus, then the other, then the back. He could see neither the driver nor the passengers heading away from the bus. He went up to the front, peered out through the windshield. Still, there was no sign of them.

He turned toward the door. It snapped open immediately. He halted, eyeing it. Summoning all his speed, he leaped out. The door sighed shut behind him. He whirled. The bus's interior light came back on, and the engine sputtered. Hunched over the steering wheel, a blot of darkness, was the driver. Tomokato thought he saw round, green eyes glowing in the shadow of the fellow's hat, and thought he read some unfathomable mockery in them. The bus roared as if it had a jet engine under its hood, and shot from the square like a meteor, trailing a cloud of smoke and flame.

The cat looked about. On the far side of the square he saw a tall booth situated in a pool of light

from a streetlamp, a sign over it proclaiming "Information." He padded over.

The booth seemed empty. He knocked on it. A belch sounded hollowly from behind the front panel, and a tall old man, frightfully emaciated and abominably unwashed, rose above the counter, looking for all the world like John Carradine, wobbling slightly, a bottle of Bali H'ai in one hand. Normally the cat would have been repulsed by his appearance, but as the first recognizably terrestrial creature he had seen in Outsmouth, the ancient drunk was a strangely reassuring presence.

"What kin I do fer ye?" the oldster asked.

"Can you direct me to the town library?"

"Fer a bit o' drinkin' money, I might."

Tomokato flipped him some currency. The drunk smiled, pointed to a street joining the north side of the square.

"Jest follow that street thar. Yew can't miss it nohaow, heh, heh."

The cat bowed. "Thank you, wino-*san.*"

There was a loud, meaty thump. The old man grunted. The cat looked up to see him falling forward onto the counter. Tomokato backpedalled as the whole flimsy booth fell over. The old man gasped and kicked and died, a knife buried hilt-deep in the back of his head.

The cat crouched, looking for whoever had thrown the knife. But he knew the blade could have been hurled from any of the alleys before him. He retreated slowly in the direction of the street the old man had indicated. When he was reasonably sure he was not being pursued, he turned and headed up the street, which seemed a mere tunnel between leaning, moldy attic-façades.

After a time he thought he heard flapping footbeats behind him. He whirled, saw a dark figure duck out of sight. He turned once more, continued on his way. But before long, he heard footbeats again, more footbeats than the first time. He looked over his shoulder. Five hunched shadows scuttled into alleys, vanished into manholes. He drew his sword, kept going, looking back again and again with increasing frequency. Each time, he glimpsed more skulkers dodging from view. Before long, there seemed to be hundreds of them, and they were fighting for hiding-places to leap into, and the flap of their feet was like the tread of so many eldritch ducks. . . .

He decided to put an end to it. Rounding a sharp bend in the street, he put his back to the wall of a collapsed house and waited, concealed by the gloom beneath an overhanging roof. But if his pursuers were advancing, he did not hear them. He began to relax.

Suddenly there came a soft, padding sound. He tensed, ready to spring.

A dark shape appeared around the bend. The cat shrieked and bounded out, sword whistling in a savage arc.

The shape stopped beneath a streetlight, gasped. Tomokato checked his stroke, snarling an oath.

"Shiro!" he exploded.

The kitten beamed. "Uncle!" he said, and bowed. "I was wondering when you'd get here."

"But . . . but . . . " Tomokato sputtered, "what are *you* doing here?"

"I came to find you, of course," Shiro replied. "I want you to teach me about being a samurai."

"But *how* did you find me?"

Shiro looked insulted. "I may be young, uncle," he said, "but I'm not stupid."

Tomokato pushed his helmet back a bit, and scratched his forehead, looking at the dark buildings around him. Cautiously, Shiro following, he went back around the bend, looking down the street. There was no sign of his pursuers.

"Do your parents know you're here?" he asked Shiro.

Shiro looked down at the crumbling cobblestone pavement. "Well, yes. . . . "

"Don't lie to me, you little fool," Tomokato snarled. "I should put you across my knee right now. . . . "

"But you've got work to do, right?" Shiro asked, looking up and smiling wickedly.

Tomokato gritted his teeth.

"Are you going to chop Wartley's head off?" Shiro asked.

"Maybe. It depends."

"Can I watch?"

"I don't have much choice. I'm not about to leave you alone in this place, so you'll have to

come along. But after that, you go back to your parents."

Shiro's young face soured. "Aw, please, uncle-*san*. . . . "

"Forget it. Now come with me."

Leading Shiro by the paw, Tomokato pressed back up the silent street. The air was laden with a virtual fog of fish smell.

"Doesn't this town smell good, uncle?" Shiro asked.

Tomokato said nothing.

Presently they reached the library. It seemed strangely incongruous in its squalid setting, with its Spanish-Modern architecture and white-stucco walls. Originally a porno house, it had been built with a grant from the National Endowment for the Arts.

They went up the walk. Tomokato sheathed his blade before going in.

The librarian was obviously startled to see them. However, they were no less startled by him. Hunchbacked, green-skinned, frog-eyed, cov-

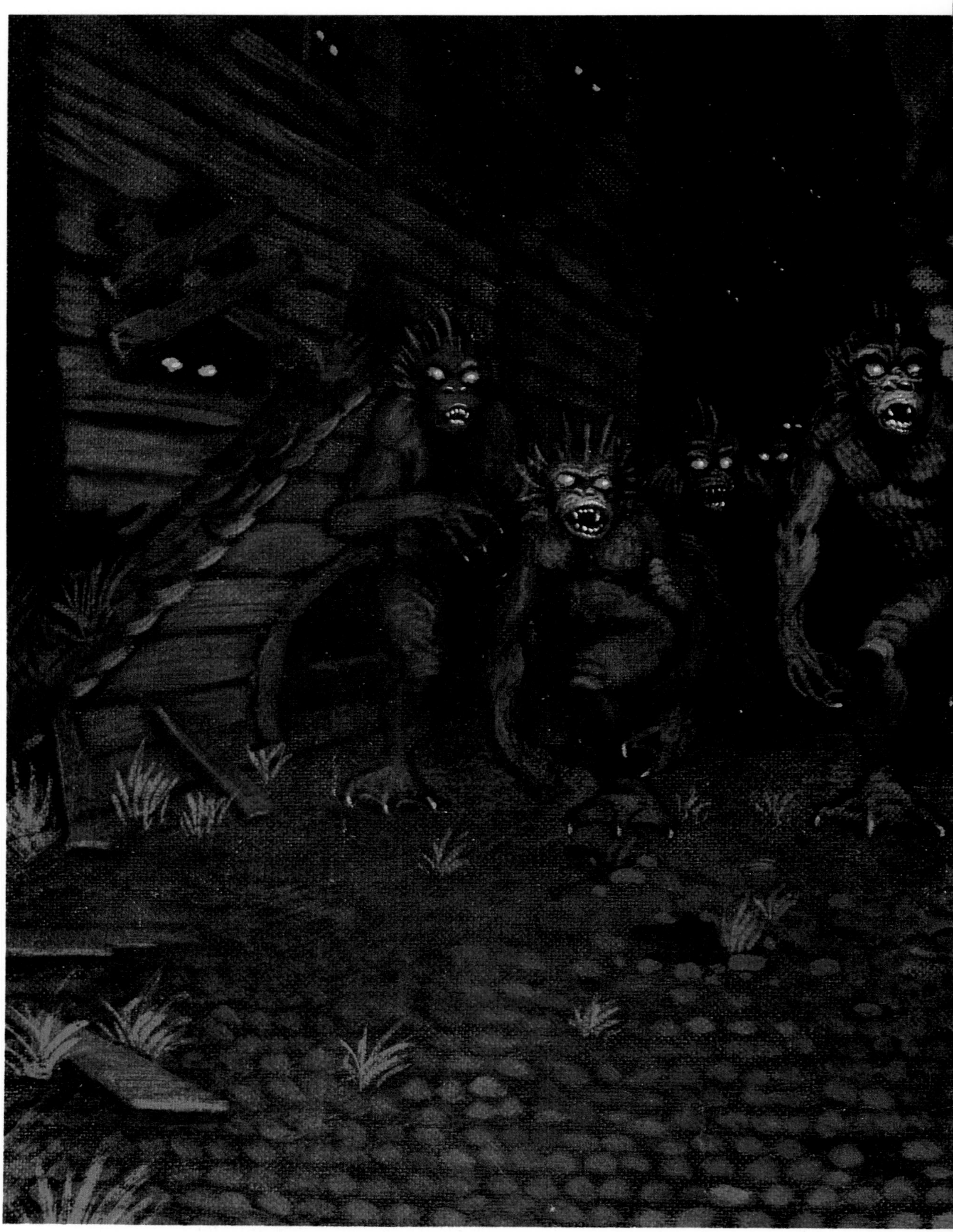

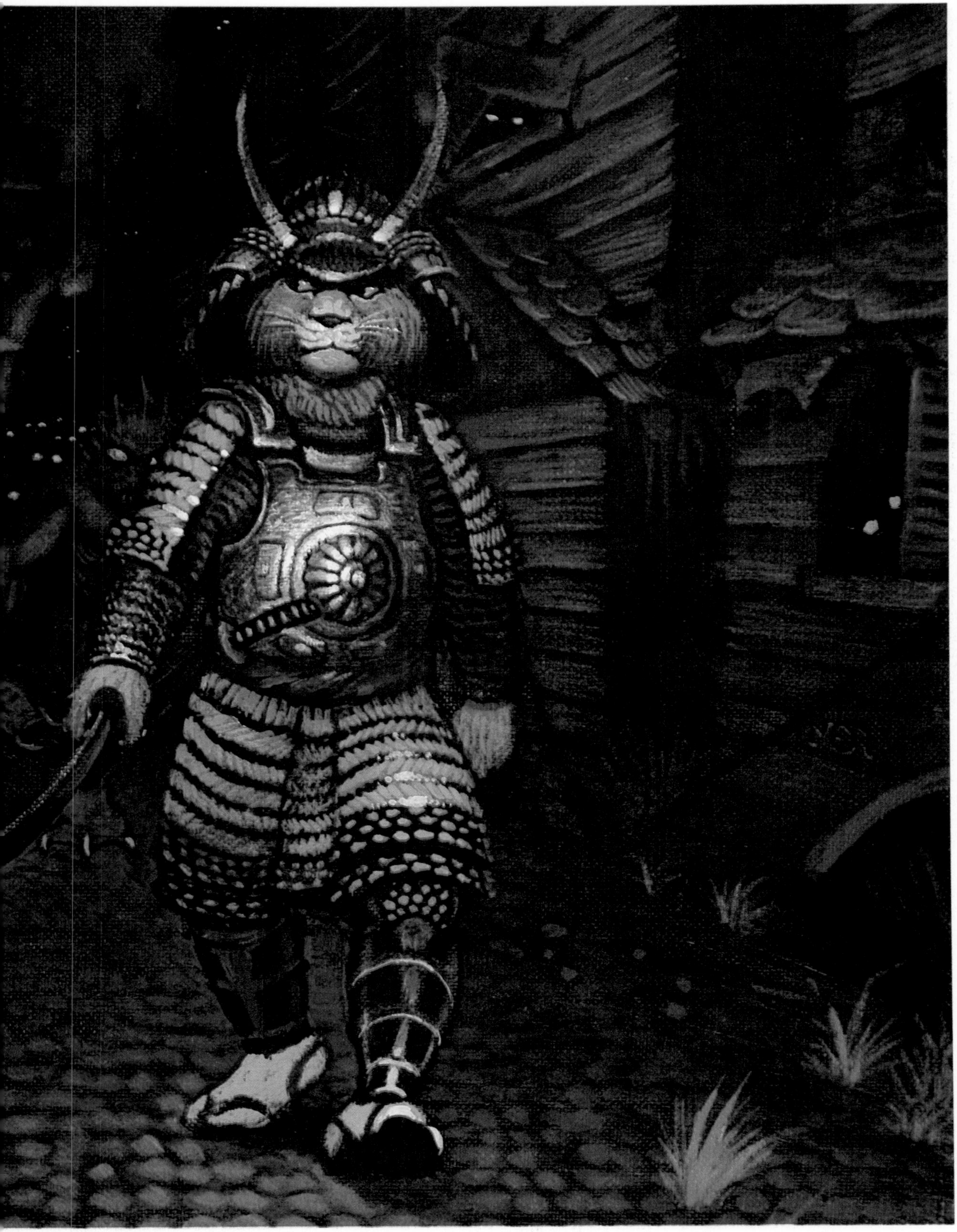

ered with scales, he barely looked human; translucent webs ran between his long bony fingers, and he stank grievously of fish. He was, however, wearing a very natty blazer and turtleneck sweater. Swiftly regaining a modicum of composure, he smiled unctuously at the heavily-armored feline and his nephew.

"From out of town, aren't you?" he gurgled, pulling at a ring in one huge gill-like ear.

Tomokato nodded, eyeing him suspiciously. He wondered if the fellow's appearance was typical for Outsmouth. If so, that certainly explained why the townspeople bundled up so heavily when they went abroad.

"I understand you have a volume here called *The Book of the Dunwich Cow,*" the cat said.

The librarian nodded and waddled out from behind the desk. "It's this way. In the children's section."

Shiro and Tomokato followed him. He removed a huge, iron-hasped tome and set it down on a reading table.

"Has anyone else asked for this book lately?" Tomokato asked.

The librarian shook his scaly head and went back to his desk.

Tomokato looked at the book. He realized he should be thinking about how best to set up his ambush, but he found himself curious about the tome's contents. He decided to read some of it, to

see why Wartley was so anxious to get his hands on it. Sitting down, the cat undid the hasp and cracked the book open. An ancient dry smell rose to his nostrils.

Shiro tugged on his arm. "Are you just going to sit there and read, uncle? When are you going to kill someone?"

"Shh," Tomokato said. "Find a book of your own. After all, this is the children's section."

"Oh, all right," Shiro replied. Going over to the stacks, he picked out an edition of the *Necronomicon* illustrated by E. H. Shepard, and sat down on the floor to read it.

Tomokato, meanwhile, was already into the second page of *The Book of the Dunwich Cow.* The text exerted a weird fascination on him. It told a strange and horrifying story, relating how, in aeons past, the earth had been dominated by terrible beings from another planet. Godlike in their powers, they were called the Real Old Ones, and their cruel dominion over the earth had lasted for hundreds of millions of years — until they were driven out by the more energetic Middle-Aged Ones, a group of Trotskyites from the Pleiades, who were in turn betrayed and defeated by a rival faction within their own Politburo. But the Real Old Ones, though weakened and forced to retreat, never lost their desire to possess the earth, and long after the Middle-Aged Ones and their rivals had been destroyed by the inherent weaknesses in their economic theories, the Real Old Ones were still scheming to gain back the territory they had lost. To that end, by various arcane means, they encouraged humans to worship them, humans who would form an occult Fifth Column against their own species when the day of conquest came. . . .

Tomokato read on and on. He sped ever faster through page after yellowed page. It occurred to him that he was in the grip of a powerful and nameless compulsion, but he had no desire to resist. He *had* to keep on going.

Dimly he became aware that Shiro was standing beside him. The kitten spoke three times before Tomokato heard him.

"Uncle . . . "

"What?" Tomokato demanded, hardly paying attention even then, eyes racing over the pages before him.

"I have to go to the bathroom," Shiro said. "Do you know where it is, uncle?"

"How could I?" Tomokato grated.

"Guess I'll just have to find it myself," Shiro

said, and wandered off.

Within seconds Tomokato had completely forgotten that he had even talked to him, immersing himself ever more deeply in the book.

"The names and natures of the Real Old Ones are these," went the text. "Yog N'goggawoggah and Yoknapatawpha, twin masses of stone-cold cream chip beef that ooze sluggishly in the center of all time and space, are their chiefs, terrible in combat, unappetizing to behold. Their herald and messenger is Stor-Atroomtemp, Lord of the Luke-warm, Cosmic Blight, Master-of-Many-Shapes-and-Interesting-in-None-of-Them. Their publicity is handled by the horrendous Isaac Azathoth, the All For One and One For All, Typist of the Many Tentacles, Sultan of Conceit. The demon-general Athoggua directs their monstrous armies, and is sometimes and mistakenly called Tsathoggua, because whenever he knocks on a door, the folks inside ask, "Who's there?" and he answers, " 'Tis Athoggua." Leaders of the Real Old Ones' naval forces are the frightful K'Chu and Bl'syu, horrors who walked earth's abyssal sea-bottoms in ages past, and will again. Yea, some say they have already returned, vanguard of the attack that is to come, and are even now seducing many humans to their cause, twisting them, reshaping them, enticing them to mate with sea-bed horrors. According to certain whispered legends, the human followers of K'Chu and Bl'syu, and the hybrid offspring of these followers, are known as the Abysmal Ones, and their two chief citadels are the twin cities of Outsmouth and San Francisco; and once a year the terrible submerged island of K'Chu surfaces just outside Outsmouth harbor, and the Abysmal Ones flock to it and make sacrifice to their dread lord, who rises from his muck-and-seaweed-covered coffin...."

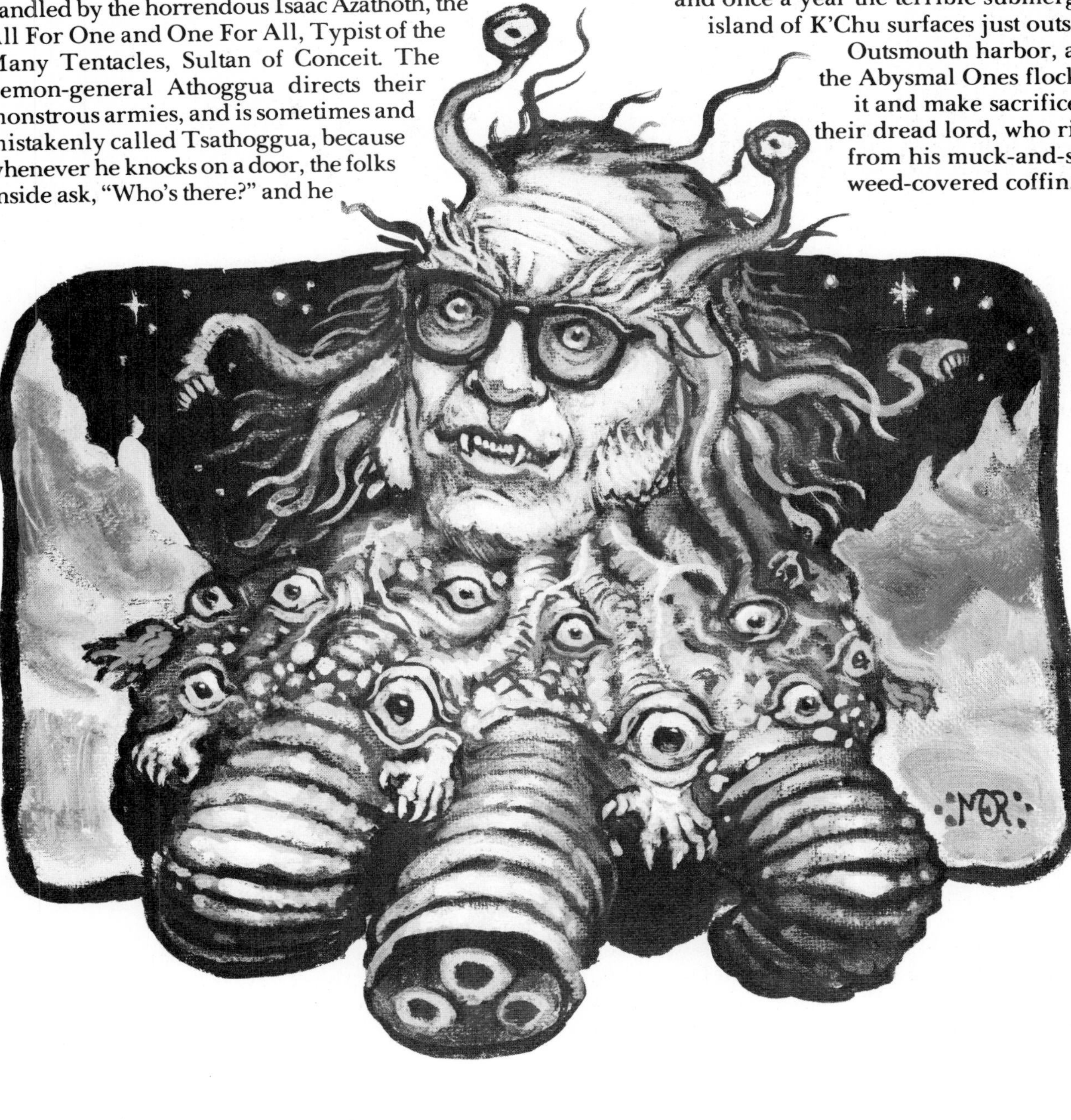

Tomokato had read more than enough; but he could not tear his eyes away from the book. He had learned all he wanted to about the inhabitants of Outsmouth, and about the Real Old Ones, yet still he raced ahead through the book, caught in a spell from which there seemed no escape. Even as he read, he ran his paws along the edges of the book, feeling the piled height of the pages he had not yet seen. No matter how many leaves he turned, the stack of unread pages never seemed to grow smaller; indeed, it even seemed to increase. He was trapped by the book, trapped in a town filled with demon-worshipping fishmen, trapped and unable to resist, snared while his defenseless young nephew was off looking for a

bathroom . . . battling to control the tide of panic rising in his mind, he plunged ever deeper into the bottomless horror of the book. . . .

Over at the front desk, the librarian watched him with some interest, fishy eyes staring. He wondered why an adult would be reading such juvenile pap.

There was a tap at a nearby window. Turning, he saw a tall figure beckon to him from out on the library lawn. He went outside.

The man that greeted him towered at least seven feet above the blighted grass. Light from the windows showed him to be hooknosed, nearly chinless, with very pale, albino-like skin. Long white hair fell beneath the rim of his near-shape-less hat. He was clad in a tight-buttoned, checkered sportcoat that seemed several sizes too small, Bermuda shorts that exposed two psoriasis-plagued knees, and wingtips. Fist-sized bulges appeared and flattened from time to time beneath his jacket, as if large rats, having chewed their way through his body, were now straining against the cloth, trying to get out.

"Well?" the librarian asked.

"You know what you've got in there?" the stranger asked, pressing one of the bulges in his suit down with both hands.

"No, what?"

The stranger led him to the nearest window, pointed in at Tomokato. "That," he said, "is a cat."

The librarian's mouth sagged in horror. Cats were things of nightmare to the fishmen. Devourers, destroyers, felines had been utterly banished from the town generations before. And no living Outsmouther had ever seen one, though the very mention of them was enough to make a fishman all but gobble with fear.

"Reading one of *my* books. . . . " the librarian said tonelessly, shuddering. "I don't believe it."

"Trust me," the stranger said, slapping an arm against a particularly large bulge that had appeared on his side.

The fishman looked at him, struggling to regain his composure. "Well, if he *is* a cat, there are ways of dealing with him."

"Such as?" the pale giant asked, suit squirming in a dozen places.

"I've got this seagoing friend. . . . "

Inside, Tomokato was still glued to the book. The pile of unread pages, as far as he could tell, continued to grow. He was turning the leaves at a blinding speed now, yet still the awful words were soaking into his mind, staining it with their hideous secrets. He felt as if he were being slowly suffocated in a torrent of unmentionable filth, implicated in the festering evildoing of the Real Old Ones, initiated into their unbelievably perverse blasphemies. His stomach churned, his mouth was dust dry; his whiskers crawled and knotted in disgust.

He became aware of a creaking noise. It grew steadily louder. He did not know it was the sound of slowly-buckling wood until the table collapsed, giving way under the ever-increasing weight of the book. The top tilted across the cat's armored knees, and the book slid to the floor. He lost eye-contact with it.

The spell was broken.

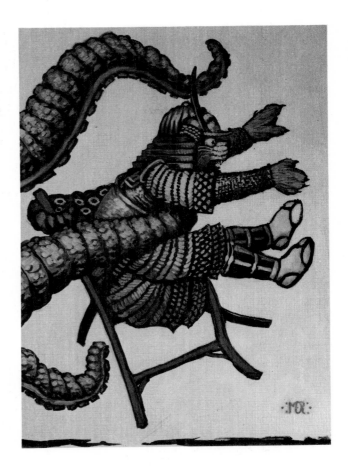

He gasped and panted. Relief surged through him.

It did not last long.

Something thick and rubbery wrapped itself around him, something stinking of long ages of sea-bottom ooze. He looked down. It was a great tentacle, its surface glistening in the lamplight. The arm had slipped about him from behind, pinning him to the seat-back.

He went for his shortsword, but in that very instant the tentacle whipped him backward; his paws shot out as it yanked him between the library-stacks, chair and all, and before he could recover, a second tentacle strapped his arms to his sides. He was dragged out into the parking-lot behind the library and turned around. Off to the side, in the sputtering flashes from a dying street-light, he saw the huge, unstable mass of the octopoid the arms belonged to. Directly in front of Tomokato was a vast crowd of Outsmouth fishmen, the librarian among them. A tall pale man was with them. Tomokato recognized him from a photo he had seen. Wilbur Wartley. The cat glared at him, spitting, showing his teeth. He battled vainly against the living bonds that held him.

"Miaowara Tomokato," Wartley said, and smiled. "I've heard so much about you."

"Murdering maggot," Tomokato snapped.

Wartley sneered. "One man's maggot is another's *übermensch*. But you, on the other hand, are a mere born victim." He folded his arms on his chest. "But how shall we finish you?"

"Sacrifice," said the librarian, with a sadistic, wide-mouthed leer.

"Sacrifice," whispered a hundred Abysmal Ones behind them.

"To whom?" Wartley asked.

"K'Chu," the librarian answered. "Our god. His island rises tonight, just outside the harbor."

"Sacrifice," the other fishmen whispered again.

"K'Chu will appear?" Wartley asked.

The librarian nodded solemnly.

"Splendid," Wartley said. "I've been hoping to meet him for quite some time. That's why I came. I thought I'd find out how in *The Book of the Dunwich Cow*. But it seems I won't be needing it."

"You'll be an honored guest at the ceremony," the librarian said. "K'Chu will be very pleased when he learns how you warned us about the cat. . . . " He paused, suddenly troubled. "I just remembered. There was a smaller cat too."

"A kitten?" Wartley asked. "Don't worry. They're not so dangerous. You can hunt him down at your leisure."

"Very good," the librarian replied. "But in the meanwhile, we should be off to the ceremony. The island will be rising soon."

He turned to the other Outsmouthers. Hats pushed back, faces revealed, they were an horrific, revolting throng, even more misshapen and fishlike than he; and they were certainly sloppier dressers.

"To the boats!" he cried.

The crowd waddled and hopped and glided from the parking-lot, into the thick darkness of an adjoining street. With each house they passed, a dozen more fishmen seemed to join the throng. Still gripping Tomokato, binding him helplessly to the chair, bumping and dragging it along the rotting cobbles, the octopoid was near the front of

the mob. Wartley strode along beside the cat, gloating, pointing out various local monuments, acting like some hellish tourguide, reeling off information he had gleaned from a pamphlet put out by the Outsmouth Chamber of Commerce.

"Perhaps you're wondering why all the houses are made of attics," he said.

The cat's eyes blazed at him, and his whiskers bristled. "Actually," he said, voice seething with slaughterlust and hate, "I was wondering about that, yes."

"When the town was still a normal fishing-village," Wartley began, "the first people who mated with the sea-demons didn't think their offspring would be too popular, once they grew up and started showing their breeding, as it were. The hybrids were kept in attic rooms, shuttered away. But as the number of hybrids increased, so did the need for attic space. And so . . . "

He waved a repellently white hand toward the dormer-piles on either side; it shone like a dead fish's belly in the gloom.

The crowd reached the harbor. The octopoid, along with Wartley and the librarian, went aboard a decrepit old Boston Whaler. The other members of the crowd climbed into various scabrous craft that were beached on the shore or tied up to several weed-grown, crumbling stone quays.

"We town dwellers can't breathe water yet," the librarian told Wartley. "That only comes later, when we're mature, and it's time to go live with Father K'Chu under the waves. But in the meantime, we need boats."

The unholy armada started out to sea. No sails billowed, no oars beat, no engines chugged; many bizarre luminous sea-creatures, half-glimpsed beneath the churning waves, towed the craft swiftly from the harbor.

The moon rose, a leprous green. Its reflected light glowed in a low fogbank rolling in from the East. The sea-creatures drew the boats near the mist and halted. Expectant silence fell over the fishmen. Huge round

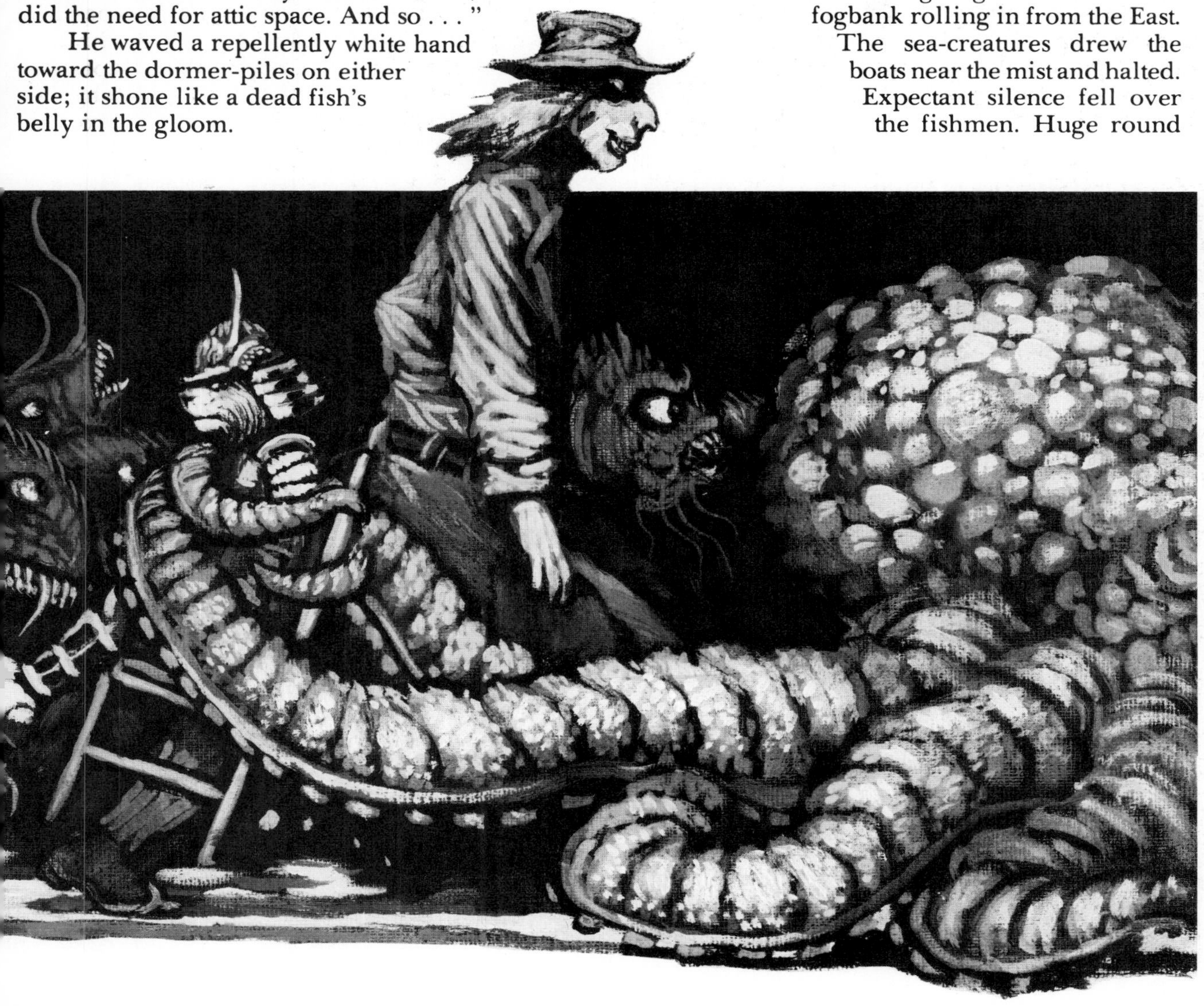

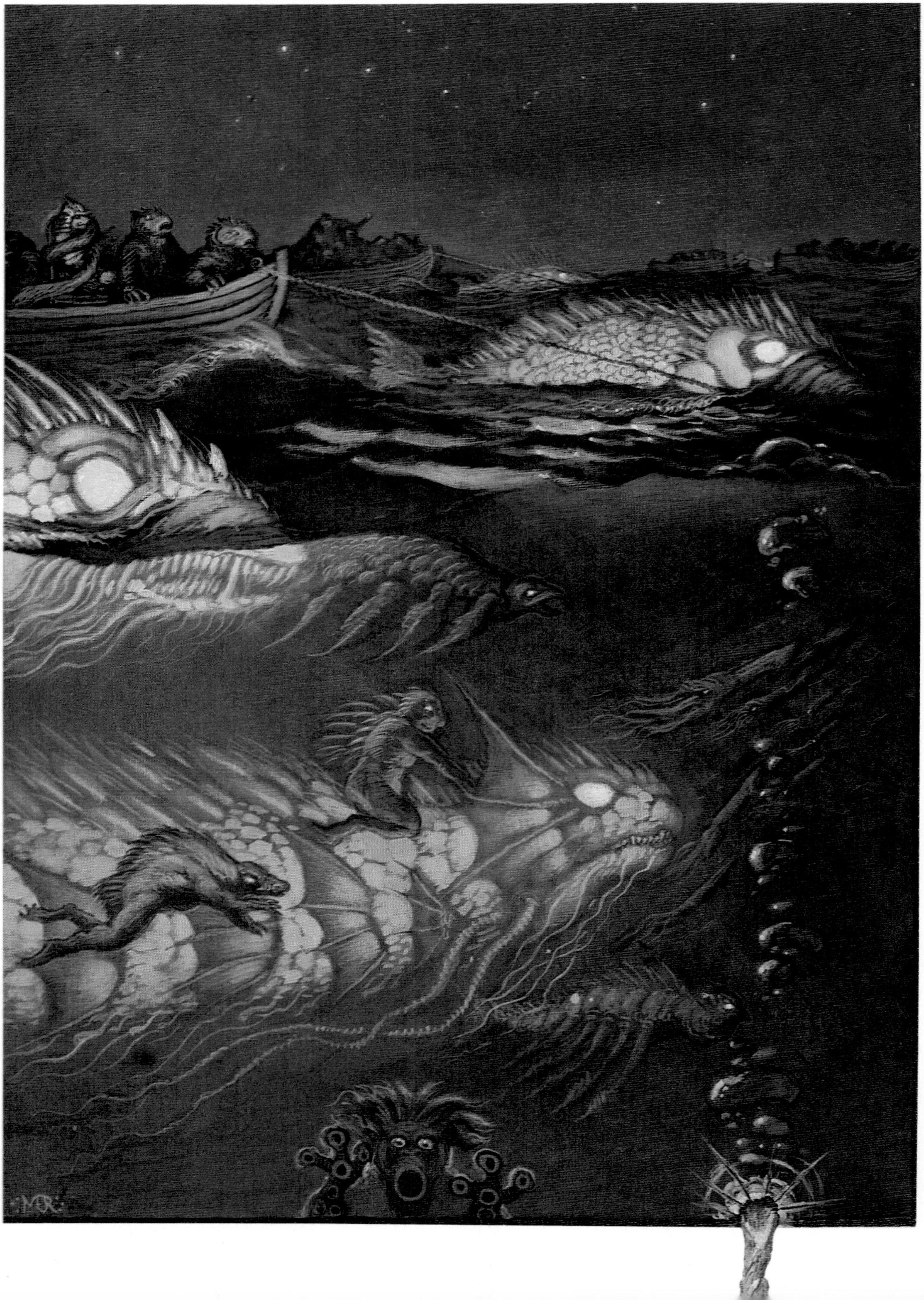

eyes trained on the fog, they gaped and gulped with barely-suppressed excitement.

Out of the depths of the sea came a loud yet muffled rumbling sound, soon joined by a vast hollow bubbling, and a hissing as of a leviathan serpent. A cloud of thick black smoke, shot with bursts of garish yellow-green flame, gushed up out of the center of the fogbank. There was a horrible wrenching noise, as if the arm of some cosmic giant were being pulled from its socket, or as if something unbelievably huge was being ripped from the sea-bottom mud. The black smoke dissipated quickly. The crowns of gargantuan bubbles arched through the roof of the fogbank, then burst ponderously, as though in slow motion. Among the bubbles rose huge, dark, dripping crags, gleaming green, shining in places with faint, multicolored phosphorescence. A powerful wind came bellowing out of nowhere, ripping the fogbank away, fully revealing the peaks of the submersible island. Encrusted with barnacles and pale coral, covered with hanging gardens of kelp, great domed and pillared buildings, manifesting a demonic and non-euclidean geometry, began to appear above the churning foam, water sluicing in green-glinting torrents from their cyclopean stones.

After a time, the upward movement halted. The ooze-slathered stronghold of Great K'Chu loomed in its entirety above the muddied waves. The air was filled with its briny, fishy sea-stench. The smell brought a poignant memory back to Tomokato: Shiro at his side, beaming, "Doesn't this town smell nice, uncle?" Pain stabbed at Tom-

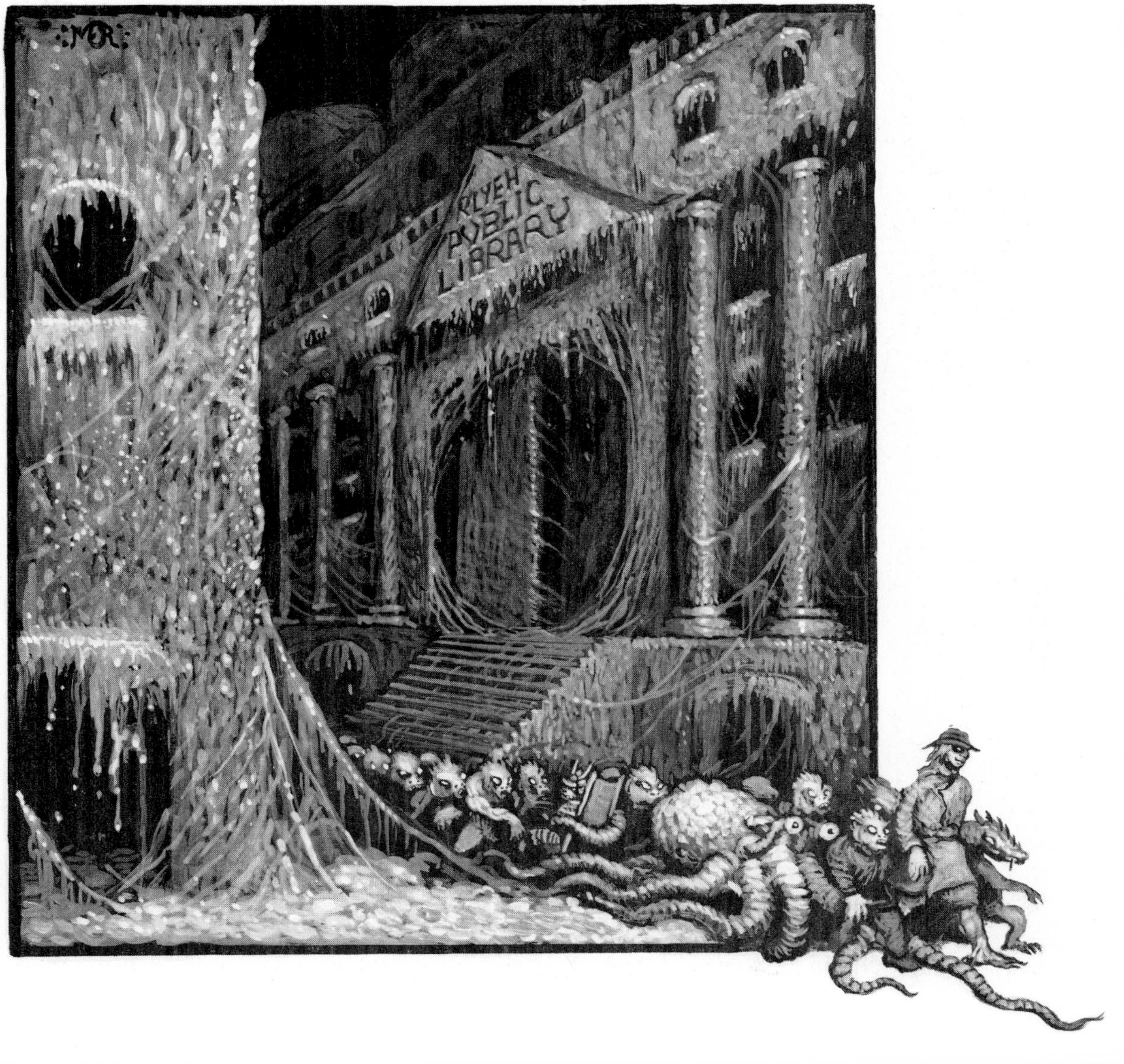
MR
RLYEH
PUBLIC
LIBRARY

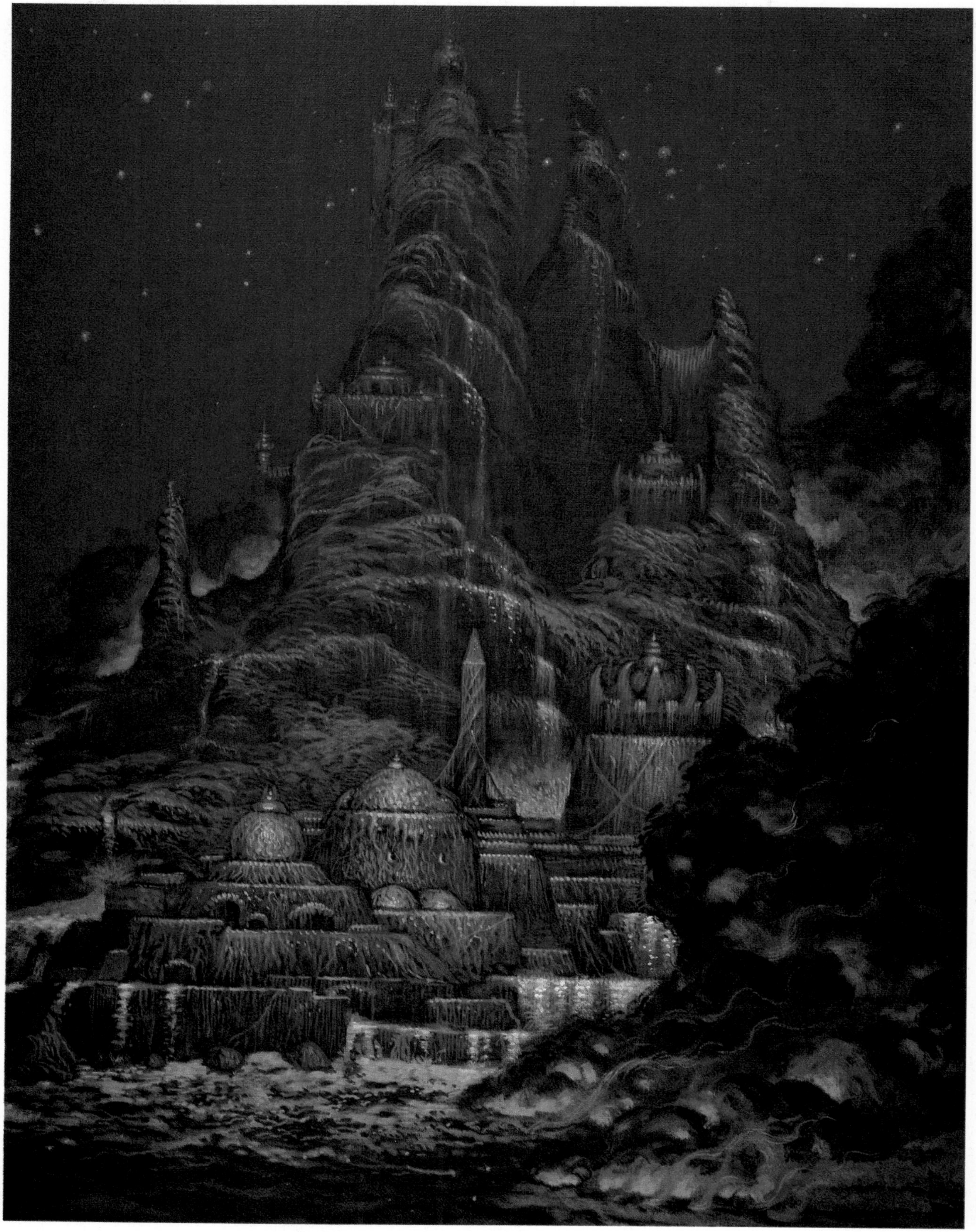

okato's heart as he wondered what Shiro's fate would be. With fierce nobility, Tomokato recognized his own responsibility, acknowledged it fully to himself. He had drawn Shiro away from his home, however unwittingly. He cursed himself for letting the kitten develop such an attachment for him.

The little bastard!

The sea-beasts drew the boats toward the island. As they neared the stinking, silty beach, the fishmen unharnessed the creatures, allowing the craft to coast into shore. Anchoring the boats with grappling-hooks, the Outsmouthers clambered out. The octopoid slithered inland, trailing Tomokato, followed by Wartley. Passing or trampling many dying, flopping fish, the crowd squelched its way towards the city.

And unseen, unheard, a small dark figure came cautiously behind, zigzagging between barnacled rocks and hummocks of weed.

Skirting the wreckage of an old three-masted schooner, the crowd mounted a tall, slippery staircase, entering the city through a huge arch overhung with twitching, gelatinous garland-growths. Ahead stretched a great temple-flanked boulevard. The throng passed along it, pushing toward the mountain-slopes. The splash and slurp of their feet echoed between the dank, unhallowed façades, and their voices went whispering back and forth; but no sounds answered from the dark doors and windows on either side, save the drip of thick oozy water. No longer able to breathe air, the Abysmal Ones who normally inhabited the city had departed before the island began to rise.

The crowd slogged steadily through the city. Everything around them, with the exception of the sunken ships and Nash Ramblers that lay half-covered by the muck, suggested that some horrible culture, completely alien to the earth, had grafted itself upon this submersible isle. There were square traffic circles, flat bridges with no empty space beneath them, obelisks that looked like arches and arches that looked like obelisks, buildings constructed entirely out of negative space, vending machines that dispensed hot and cold running sweat, Easter-bunnies in store-windows wearing sombreros and bandoliers and carrying machetes; even the local McDonald's had inverted arches, and the statue of Ronald outside was cringing under the fanged assault of a Mayor McCheese who was biting at his leg like a man-eating clam. The whole place had the look of a theme-park for

Venusian leeches, which is exactly what it had been until K'Chu had returned from exile.

As the crowd neared the foot of the mountain, they stopped before a vast black-coral platform on which was mounted a titanic stone sarcophagus, seventy feet long. The coffin was heavily enslimed with ages of accumulated muck, but strange glyphs could still be seen on its rim, and along the side of the lid. No sentient being had ever read them; they had been placed on the stone in some unfathomable way by a group of sinister creatures who had left no trace of themselves, not even the glyphs.

At a word from the librarian, the octopoid placed the cat, still bound to his chair, atop an altar-like stone some distance from the coral platform. Intoning words that echoed and bubbled deep within the recesses of his eldritch glottis, the librarian took out a Shriner's cap and strode slowly around the altar, lighting two sparklers, one gold, one silver, swinging them in circles until they burned out. Two Outsmouthers ran up with a tall unicycle, helped him onto the seat; up and back he rode between the platform and the altar, twirling a tasselled baton, sitting again and again on a mystic whoopee-cushion attached to the seat which refilled itself automatically and magically. His prayer gurgled on and on. Mud from the unicycle-wheel splattered up onto his clothes. The other fishmen began to chant slowly, uttering a hideous counterpoint to his prayer. Somewhere in the crowd, a steel guitar twanged soullessly.

Finally the librarian completed his prayer. The chanters fell silent. The steel guitar went on for a few more bars, its haunting chords echoing through the night, and fading mournfully. A sinister hush fell.

Something stirred within the sarcophagus, scraped and thudded hugely, hollowly. Tomokato looked up at the coffin. There was a loud grating of stone against stone as the lid began to slip back, then a burst of deep, thundering laughter. A gigantic warty talon hooked itself under the lid, tossed it aside. Glistening with some mucoid substances, slitted eyes glowing with venom-green malevolence, a bulbous octopus-like head rose above the coffin-rim. Muscle-ringed tentacles five feet thick snaked over the side.

"Hail, O Great K'Chu!" intoned the Outsmouthers.

K'Chu sat up higher in his coffin, then stood. The tentacle-fringed octopus head was mounted on a colossal scaly body that occupied some impossible evolutionary niche midway between dragon and ape. Stunted batlike pinions rose above the monstrosity's shoulders.

Tomokato saw the god's lambent eyes turn toward him. His flesh crawled; a billion acupuncture dwarves sent a wave of tingling horror down his spine; his navel was awash with unalloyed terror. Even so, he readied himself to meet his end. He lifted his chin proudly, forced a smile to his lips. He would die like a true samurai. Not even the soul-blasting horror promised by those slitted octopus-eyes would daunt him.

"Ho, *ho!*" K'Chu bellowed, studying him. "What's this now? Catnip? For *me?*"

The Outsmouthers laughed uproariously. Tomokato winced.

"K'Chu!" came the voice of Wilbur Wartley. The sorcerer, coat bulging and settling furiously, rushed up beside the altar. Tomokato thought he saw a pink tentacle slide over the top of Wartley's collar; but then it slipped back out of sight, if indeed it had ever been there in the first place.

"K'Chu!" Wartley cried again.

K'Chu eyed him, amused by his impudence. The Outsmouthers, still kneeling, were murmuring and whispering, amazed and enraged by Wartley's impiety, waiting for a command from their lord to rise and attack; but K'Chu decided to hear Wartley out.

"What do you want?" he demanded.

"You don't recognize me, do you?" the sorcerer asked.

K'Chu squinted at him, got out of the sarcophagus, moved a bit closer to the edge of the platform.

"Don't come any nearer!" Wartley cried, and whipped out a jewel-studded electrum talisman. "This contains sacred relics. . . . "

K'Chu staggered back as if he had been struck, leaning against the coffin, suddenly sensing the power emanating from the talisman.

"Fingernail parings?" he asked in a shuddering voice.

Wartley grinned. "From *L. Ron Hubbard!* I can destroy you, K'Chu, you and all your brood."

The stench of fear poured in torrents from K'Chu's unclean flesh.

"Name your price," he bawled.

"First, recognition," Wartley said, grabbing a tentacle that snaked out of the front of his jacket, stuffing it back inside. "Then contrition." He laughed. "You still don't know me, eh?"

K'Chu shook his bulbous head, took out a pair of wire-rims and put them on. "Sorry," he said at last.

"Of course, I don't suppose there's any reason why you should," Wartley went on. "You left before I was ever born — *Dad.*"

K'Chu laughed nervously. "My son's name is Kenny, and he goes to Bucknell. You can't tell me . . . "

"It broke mom's heart when you left, you know," Wartley said. "She died calling your name." He drew himself up to his full height, holding the mystic talisman above his head. "I think you owe me and mom an apology."

K'Chu considered it. But he could not allow himself to be humbled before his followers. He had only one choice.

"Kill him!" he thundered to the fishmen.

Wartley heard them snarling behind him, turned as they rose and rushed toward him like piranhas coming off a diet, fanged mouths gaping, eyes burning green, webbed claws lunging.

Red flame burst from the talisman. Bloody lightning snaked toward the Outsmouthers, ripped through one after another, scattering the muck with chunky light tuna. The librarian almost reached Wartley. "Sorry, Charlie," said the sorcerer, and blew the creature's brains out. He began to laugh and sing, leaping about madly as he slaughtered any Abysmal One who tried to get near him, chanting the chorus from *Fish-Heads* again and again. "Eat them up, *YUM!*" he shrieked, voice cracking high as he turned a roly-poly head into a fine spray of catfood.

During the confusion, Tomokato felt the tentacle binding him tighten, as if with a spasm of pain. The octopoid gave a thin, wailing shriek, and its arm loosened and withdrew, freeing him. Tomokato looked about, wondering what had happened, right paw snatching at the hilt of his *katana.* He had a brief glimpse of Shiro jumping down off the altar, clutching a green-stained spike, a long rusty nail taken from some wreck. The kitten had rushed in from the side, stabbed the tentacle, or so Tomokato guessed. But there was no time for guessing now. He spun, drew his sword. The octopoid, already recovering, sent several tentacles questing toward him. He dodged and

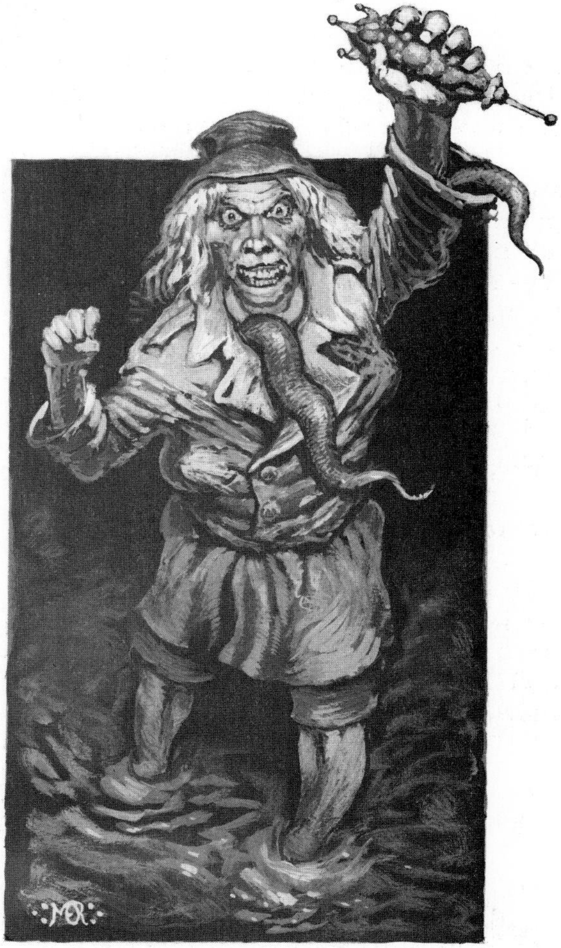
MCR

ducked, avoided them all, leaped toward the monster's head. A single stroke popped its top off. Long pulpy streamers, grey and green, leaped out like abominable party-favors.

Strange brains, Tomokato thought, and jumped down from the altar.

Shiro joined him.

"But how . . . ?" Tomokato demanded.

Shiro just stared at him, panting.

"I know," Tomokato replied. "You may be young, but you're not stupid."

Shiro nodded haughtily.

The battle between Wartley and the Outsmouthers was still raging; and a quick glance up toward K'Chu told Tomokato that the god was watching it closely.

"Hide behind that octopus-thing," Tomokato told Shiro. "Stay there."

"Where are you going?" the kitten asked.

Tomokato pointed to the platform.

"Can I come too?"

"No!" Tomokato cried, and was off, circling

the altar, sprinting toward the platform-steps. K'Chu noticed him, but took little heed, intent as he was on the battle between his followers and Wartley.

It was going badly for the fishmen. Most had been killed, and the survivors began to retreat. Wartley turned, ready to use his talisman on K'Chu. He had been wounded many times, torn by claws and teeth, and he wobbled on his feet. His eyes glinted triumph, but K'Chu sensed that the talisman had lost much of its power. . . .

Crimson light flared, stabbed toward K'Chu. The god's intuition proved correct. The lightning dissipated before it could reach him.

Wartley staggered closer. K'Chu tried a spell. Wartley's talisman was still too strong, and warded most of it off. The sorcerer's left eye exploded in a burst of blue and yellow star-shaped confetti, and flames gushed from his nostrils as his nose-hairs were set ablaze. But that was it. Wartley came closer still, loosed another bolt. It struck K'Chu, sank into him, jolted him, curled his tentacles into an obscene Shirley Temple hairdo all around his head. His mind blurred, but he was not beaten yet. Wrenching a piece of stone from the side of his sarcophagus, he hurled it at Wartley. Never expecting so elementary an attack, the sorcerer did not duck in time. Barely grazing his head, it

stretched him out on his back just the same.

"Finish him!" K'Chu cried to his surviving minions, who surged forward again. Yet even as they neared Wartley, the cat, having bided his time, rushed up to K'Chu's legs, and with a devastating *Teriyaki Kagemusha,* or *The Monk Shows Those Lousy Foreigners a Bloody Thing or Two* blow, he chopped them both through at the ankles. For a moment or two, K'Chu did not realize what had happened. Feeling the pain, he did a short and stumpy tapdance, and fell forward with a thunderous howl, landing on Wartley and the surviving Outsmouthers. There was an ear-splitting crackle as K'Chu's scaly body slammed against the talisman; wreathed in searing snakes of red fire, he bounced upwards, backflipped several hundred yards, and landed in a perfect split, like some immense alien cheerleader. The red fire died. So did K'Chu.

Tomokato descended from the platform. He and Shiro went over to Wartley and the Outsmouthers who had been near the sorcerer when K'Chu fell. Looking at the bodies, Tomokato told himself he would never eat Chef Boy-ar-dee food again as long as he lived.

"Are you going to chop Wartley now, uncle?"

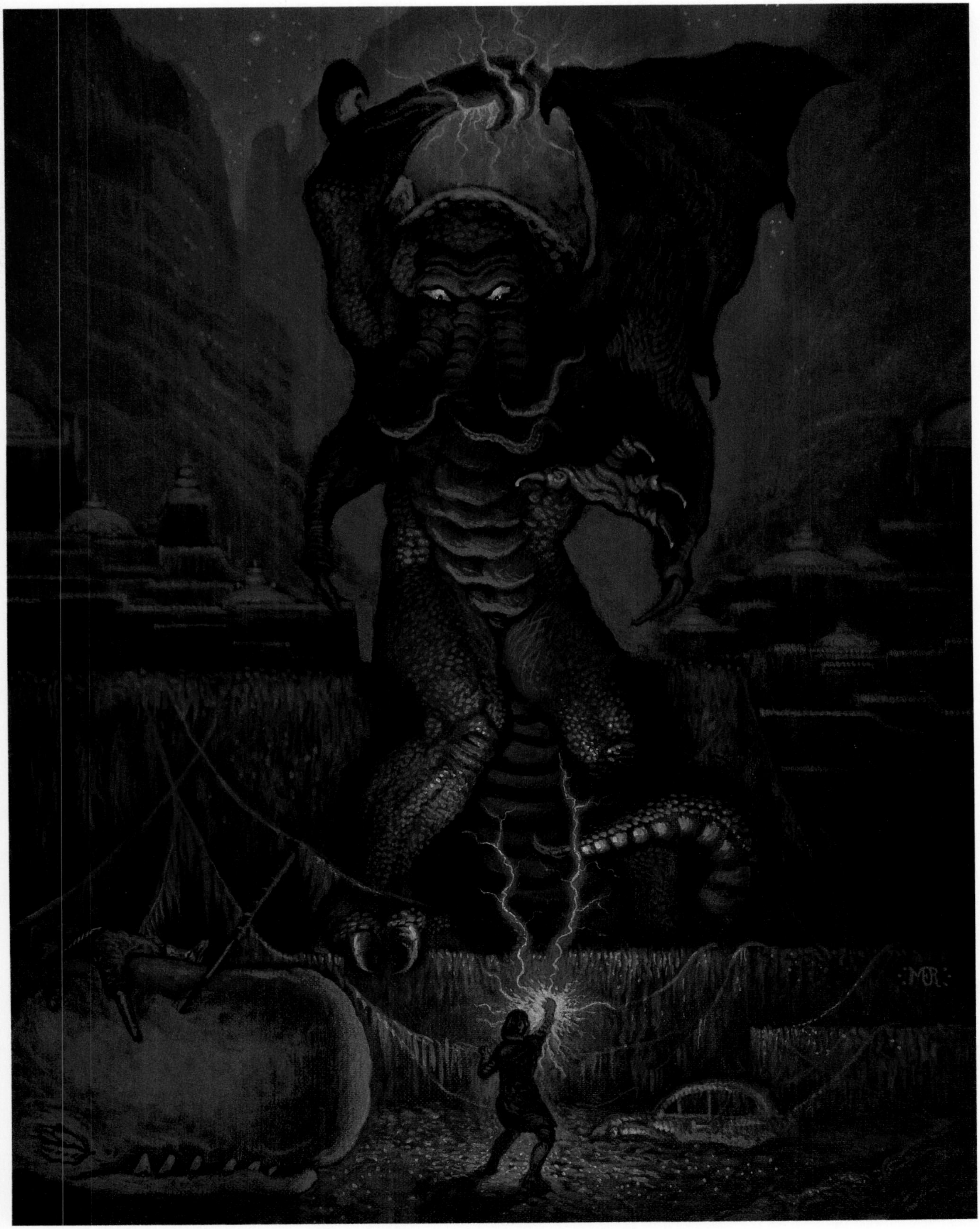

Shiro asked eagerly.

"He's dead," Tomokato replied, not even sure which one of them *was* Wartley.

"What difference does that make?" Shiro asked.

"Come," Tomokato said. They picked their way back toward the shore. Obligingly, the island remained topside. They found the boat Tomokato had come in. He remembered seeing a couple of oars. Freeing the grappling-hook, he put it in the boat. Shiro got aboard, while Tomokato pushed off and climbed in. Getting the oars, he set them in the locks and rowed away from the island. Without much fuss, it sank slowly behind them.

Dawn found them heading due South, some distance from the coast. Tomokato had not stinted at the oars; he did not want to come ashore until he was somewhere near Boston. Shiro was asleep.

Finally, near mid-morning, Tomokato decided to head on in. He beached the craft within the hour and lifted Shiro gently out. But something caught his eye in the boat, something that filled him with horror. He had a vague memory of Wartley taking his shoes and socks off before stepping out onto the muck of K'Chu's island. The articles were still where Wartley had left them, in the bottom of the boat. The shoes were normal enough, regulation wingtips, real roach-spikers. *But the socks were of no human shape!!!*

BEYOND THE BLACK WALNUT

THE HYPERBOREAN LANDS CA.13,000 B.C.
NORDHEIM
ALMURICS-HEIM
ALMURICS-HOLM
SWEDEGARD
DENMARK
COPENHAGEN
PICTISH WILDERNESS
DUBLIN
BARBARIA
THE BIG BODY OF WATER
DEADWOOD
TUCSON
CANADA
SOUTH BEND
ALMURICVILLE
FT. TICONDEROGA
AQUITAINE
PARIS
DELAWARE
THE AUTHOR'S HOUSE
ZINGARA-WENTHESTRIN GARA
CHRYSLER-KORDAVA
OPHAL
ALMARICTON
BAY OF BISCAY
NABONIDEA
ALEXANDRIA

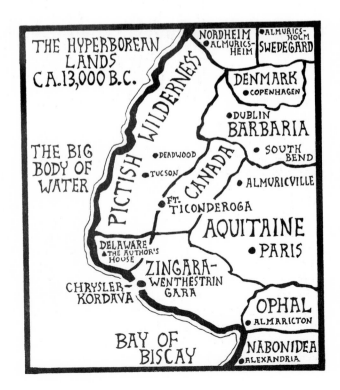

Reaching Boston, Tomokato put Shiro on the Kyoto bus and set off after new prey — Thpageti-Thoth, a Nabonidean Necromancer. Taking advantage of a special half-price samurai fare, the cat flew to serpent-haunted Nabonidea, only to learn that the wizard had not remained there after returning from Japan; Thoth had conceived the mad scheme of travelling far North, into savage Pictland, there to use his magic to unite the Picts under his rule. The cat followed his trail into the Hyperborean countries; crossing Aquitaine, he entered its puppet state, Canada, pausing at Ft. Ticonderoga, the last Aquitanian stronghold before the Pictish border. . . . — *Cat Out of Hell*

The midsummer sun glared down from its zenith, an unblinking red orb. Sweating inside his armor, Tomokato was suddenly aware of just how parched his mouth was as the gate-wards admitted him to the stockade-enclosed parade-ground of Ft. Ticonderoga. Off to the left, opposite the barracks houses, stood a row of timber buildings. Several were fur warehouses, where Aquitanian merchants bought and stored pelts brought in by local trappers. The rest were shops of various kinds. Tomokato guessed he might be able to find someone who would sell him some cold milk. Passing

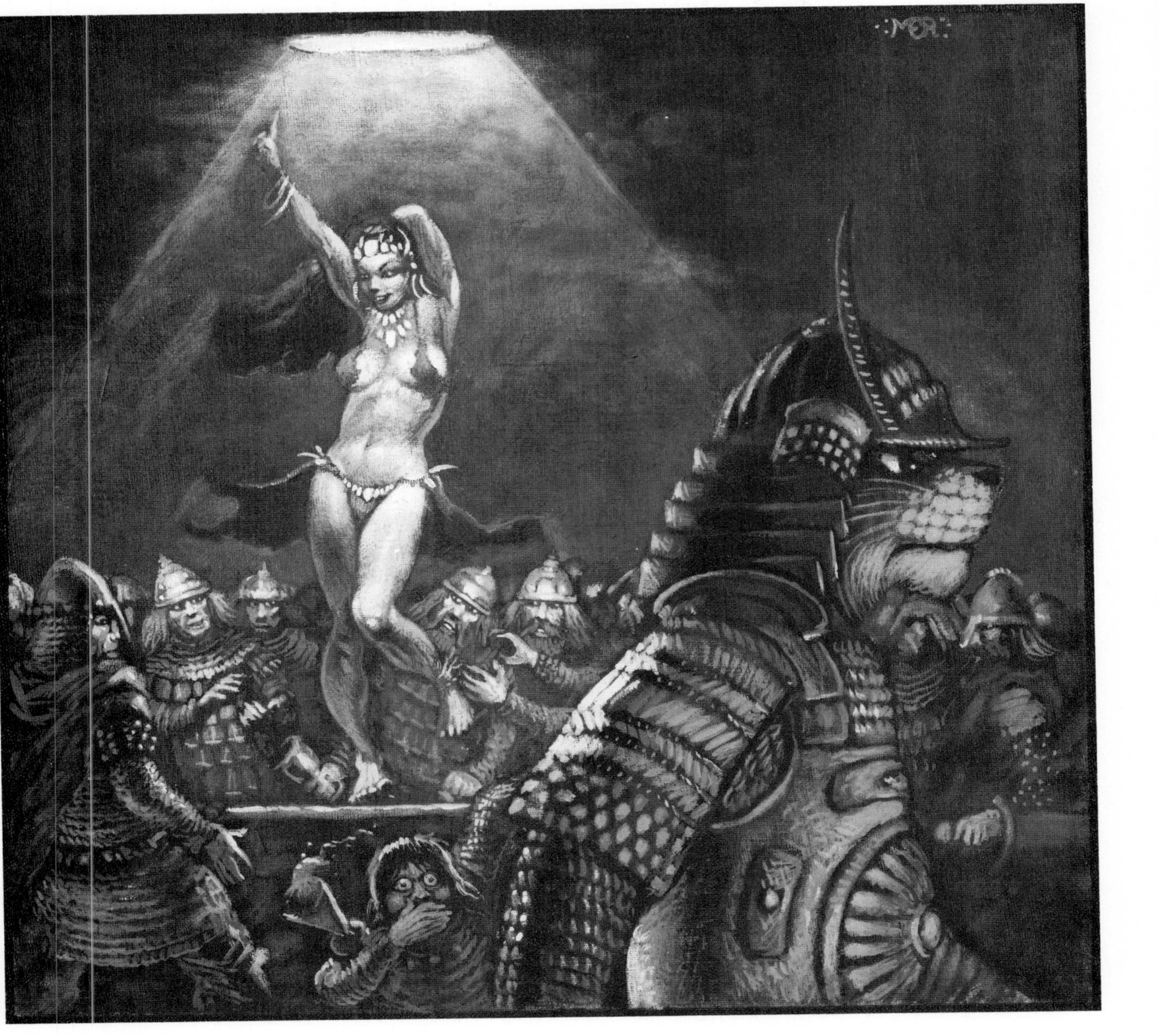

several groups of brown-mailed Aquitanian soldiers (who gawked at his outlandish appearance as he strode by), he found a tavern called *The Slut and Brew,* and went inside.

The common-room was dark and close, and not much cooler than it had been outdoors. The air reeked of sour wine and old sweat. The benches were crowded with roistering Aquitanians, soldiers and merchants both, as well as Canadian frontiersmen clad in furs and buckskins. Off in a corner, an almost-naked dusky-skinned Pictish slave-girl was doing a feverish erotic dance on a table-top, skillfully dodging the clutching fingers of the men who stood round about. Gracefully, yet barbarically, she whirled and writhed to the sensuous disco rhythms of *Hot Stuff,* which thumped orgiastically from a nearby jukebox.

Tomokato went up to the bar. A buxom barmaid in a low cut dress sauntered over, brushing sweat-lank blonde hair from her eyes. Her curiosity about the cat's appearance was plain.

"Where you from?" she asked, shouting to be heard over the music. But even as she spoke, *Hot Stuff* bumped and ground its way to a close. The cat opened his mouth to speak, but looked around without saying anything, puzzled by the complete silence that had fallen over the tavern. Everyone else in the place, including the dancing-girl, was staring at him.

He shrugged and turned back to the barmaid. "I'm from Japan," he said.

"Ah," she said knowledgeably. He guessed she had never heard of it.

"Do you serve milk here?" he asked.

There were snickers behind him. He ignored them.

"Well?" he asked, eyeing the woman squarely. She nodded.

A voice roared: "Since when did you start serving *cats* in here, Zenobia?"

"This is a tavern, not some damn dairy section," bellowed another man.

A chorus of great guffaws broke out. Still the cat fixed Zenobia with his placid stare.

"Would you get me some milk?" he asked.

"Would you get me some milk?" a man mocked, trying to imitate Tomokato's gruff voice.

"Please," said Tomokato.

Zenobia cast a nervous glance at the other customers, but went and got him a saucerful. Bending over the bar, he began to lap the milk up.

There was a racket of benches being pushed back and overturned, and suddenly there were hide-clad Canadians and steel-helmeted Aquitanians on either side of him, and more behind him, by the sound of it.

"You don't get the message, do you, *cat?*" a mailed trooper gritted.

Tomokato sighed, lifting his head.

"I think we'll have to teach you a lesson," said another man.

A brutish grunt of agreement ran through the crowd.

"I'm going to count to ten and pray for self-control," Tomokato said evenly. "If you honorable gentlemen have not retired by then, and the gods haven't granted my request, I'll redecorate this establishment with your stinking, vari-colored offal."

The men who hemmed him gasped with amazement, taken completely aback by the calm self-confidence in his voice. Most took a few involuntary steps backward. The cat was already counting.

"Four . . . Five . . . Six . . . "

A man growled a curse, and a blade began to rasp from its scabbard. Tomokato heard the mob starting forward again.

"Ah well," he said philosophically, and whipped out his *katana*, spinning, slicing the first five men through at the bellies. The upper halves of their torsos hung in air for a brief instant as the lower halves stepped out from under them. Horror and agony and sheer embarrassment flooded the men's eyes. Then the bodies, tops and bottoms, dropped to the floor.

The other members of the mob swore and retreated.

"Get back here!" cried one dying Aquitanian. "He's no big deal, really!"

The others were not convinced. Many were trampled in the rush through the door.

Tomokato wiped his sword off on a dead soldier's trouser-leg, resheathed it and turned

like to recruit you. Aquitaine could use a warrior such as you."

"I serve only myself, since the death of my Lord Nobunaga," Tomokato answered. "And I've set myself a task of great importance."

"What is it, if I might ask?"

"Revenge for my master," the cat replied. "I'm tracking one of his slayers, a necromancer named Thpageti-Thoth. I've heard that he's across the border. In Pictland."

"He is indeed," the Captain confirmed. "And it's quite a coincidence that you want him dead. So do I. He's trying to create a Pictish confederacy to attack Aquitaine's Northern Marches, and he must be stopped. I'm going to send a party North to try and kill him. That's why I wanted you. Still not interested?"

"I can accomplish everything I want to accomplish alone," Tomokato said.

"Maybe," the Captain conceded. "Maybe not. I suspect the Picts have the numbers to defeat even a warrior such as yourself. But even if they don't, you'll still need guides. You're a stranger in these parts, aren't you?"

The cat nodded, weighing the Captain's arguments.

"Perhaps I could use some aid," he admitted at last. "But Thpageti-Thoth is *mine*. Is that understood?"

The Captain nodded. "What's your name?"

"Miaowara Tomokato," the cat replied.

"Mine's Almuric. I'm commander of the fort. Come with me back to my quarters. We can discuss my plan there."

An hour later, after Almuric had finished outlining his scheme, a huge man entered the spacious cabin unannounced, dropping into a chair and kicking off his shoes, flipping one directly into Tomokato's lap. Tomokato winced at the stench and brushed the shoe to the floor; then he eyed the newcomer. The man was heavily muscled, clad in a thigh-length shirt of steel mesh-mail and cross-gartered fur leggings. A helmet flanked by short bull's horns rested on his black-maned head. His eyes were volcanic blue flames in a rugged, deeply tanned face.

"I caught up with the Porka Picts that raided that farm," he told Almuric. "Took 'em just this side of the Black Walnut."

"Any survivors?" Almuric asked.

The man just laughed, as if the question were absurd.

back to the bar where he finished his milk. Zenobia was gone.

Presently there came a loud hubbub outside the tavern. Facing the door, he saw that a large crowd of soldiers had gathered.

"He's in there, Captain," a man cried. "He killed five of our men with one stroke."

A tall man entered, silhouetted against the dusty light. As he drew closer, Tomokato saw that he was armored in silvered scale-mail; the fellow had the hawkish features of an Aquitanian aristocrat. He stopped some distance from Tomokato, looking first at him, then at the semi-circle of bisected corpses.

"You did all this, eh?" he asked.

"Yes," Tomokato replied. "And I could easily do the same to the rest of your men. Please don't make it necessary."

The Captain put his hands up. "I wouldn't think of it," he replied. "As a matter of fact, I'd

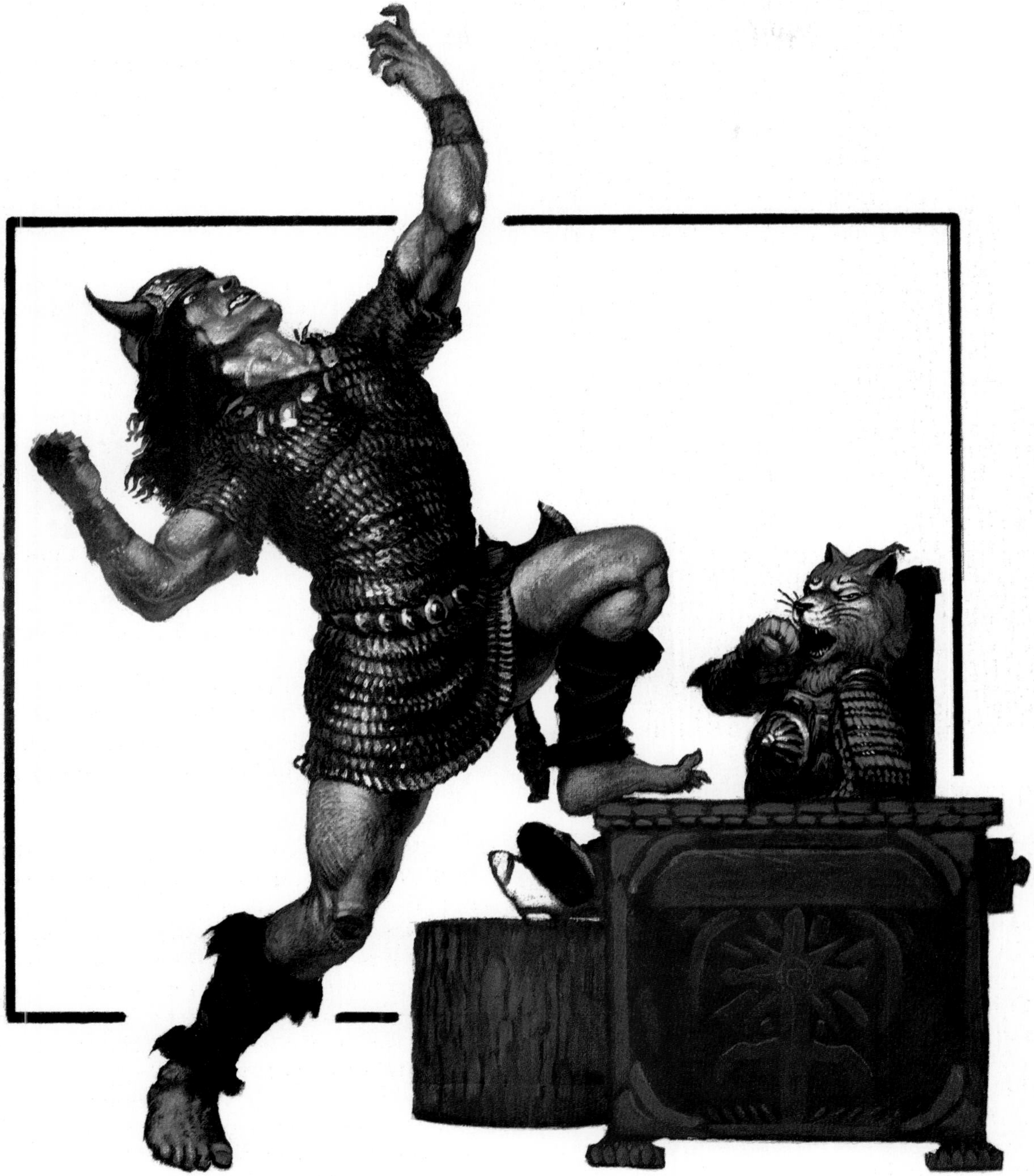

"This is Con-Ed," Almuric told Tomokato. "He's a Barbarian. From Barbaria. He's also my finest woodsman. He'll be leading the expedition tonight."

"Fine," Tomokato said quietly. "Just as long as he leaves the wizard to me."

"I've already promised Thoth to you . . . "

Con-Ed leaped to his feet. "You did *what?*" he exploded. "Thpageti-Thoth murdered my woman, and you promise this scrawny little putty-tat . . . "

"That putty-tat, as you call him, killed five of my best men in *The Slut and Brew,*" Almuric retorted. "With one stroke."

"Crom and Corky!" Con-Ed roared. "You're easily impressed. Don't you have eyes in your head? Can't you smell the stink of civilization on the little snot?"

"You forget yourself, Con-Ed," Almuric said testily. "I'm a civilized man myself."

"No wonder your nose doesn't work," Con-Ed shot back. "Manannan Mac Davis! You civilized dogs are all alike. Sexually depraved, cowardly, effete, robbed of all manhood. You make me sick, prancing around like pansies, spouting philosophy, using circular wheels and toilet paper! It's different in Barbaria. Nothing we like better than belching and fighting. And when we father children, we do it the manly way! None of this hugging and kissing and lovemaking. We grab our women and sweat on 'em. Works like a charm." He paused, nostrils flaring, and struck a dramatic pose, one foot up on Almuric's desk. Muscles crawled and roped and knotted on his arms and neck and forehead. Fiercely he grinned, flexing his teeth. "Barbarism is the natural state of mankind. And in the end, it will always triumph!"

Almuric nudged Tomokato. "He's not as obnoxious as he seems, really."

The cat said nothing.

Toward sunset the members of the raiding-party gathered outside Almuric's cabin: all but one. Con-Ed, never one to be prompt, was off at a louse-cracking contest.

"He's always telling me he can't shackle himself with our civilized schedules," Almuric explained to Tomokato. "He says he's got a little barbarian clock inside him, unfettered and noble and free, a clock that keeps a different kind of time. Once I told him how silly it sounded, and . . . " His voice trailed off, as if some painful memory had given him pause.

"What happened?" the cat asked.

"I heard this little alarm-bell ringing inside his mouth, and he said, 'It's punch the pansy time,' and he hit me so hard that he severed my spinal cord with my nose."

With a shock, Tomokato suddenly realized that the Aquitanian's magnificent hawk-nose was actually protruding — turned inside out — through the rear of his skull. Almuric's 'beard' and 'moustache' were actually hairs on the nape of his neck. Tomokato had been talking to the Captain's back all along.

"Never got over it," Almuric said ruefully. "But here; let me introduce you to the other men." When he had their attention, he said, "Troops, this is Miaowara Tomokato. Doubtless you've heard how he killed those five men in *The Slut and Brew* this afternoon. Well, he's on our side now, and I've promised him Thpageti-Thoth."

He pointed to the first man in line. "Tomokato, that fellow there is named Almaric. He's a Canadian. Fine tracker and woodsman. Played a few seasons with the Maple Leafs."

Almaric gave a great gap-toothed grin, and lifted a vicious-looking, steel-edged hockey stick. "How's it goin', eh?" he asked.

"Man next to him's named Amlaric," Almuric continued. "He's from Normandy. Fought in the French Underground with Bishop Odo. Best man with a chopper you ever saw."

Clad in a knee-length mailcoat, wearing a conical steel helm with a wide nasal, Amlaric was slinging his kite-shaped shield behind his back. He gave a curt nod to the cat, then checked the sight on his Thompson submachine gun.

"That's Amralic the East Anglian there," Almuric went on. "A born killer. Vicious young punk."

Amralic, armored in a scale-mail corselet held together with safety-pins, was a tall, weasly-looking teenager whose spiky hairdo sent orange and purple tufts up through the holes he had deliberately punched in his own helmet. His only weapon was a gigantic Wilkinson sword razor-blade with the words *Hi Mum* written on it in crimson lipstick.

Almuric moved on. "That small, squinty fellow's named Amluric the Armenian," he said. "Bad news after dark. Superb strangler."

Wearing an Armenian army uniform beneath his plundered Vietnamese byrny, Amluric was slowly wrapping a length of Armenian string cheese around his fists. He smiled savagely at the cat, and pulled the cheese taut, looking for all the world like a practitioner of some bizarre dairy-food variety of Thuggee.

Fifth in line was a heavily-built, middle-aged man in a hardhat and muscle-t mailshirt, smoking a cigar and leaning on a massive military jackhammer. He smelled like he had lived next to an oil refinery most of his life.

"That's Al Murik, from Jersey City," Almuric said. "Used to be an enforcer for the Teamsters."

Al Murik dusted ashes from his cigar and belched.

"And last but not least," said Almuric, "we have Al-Muriq, from the United Arab Republic. He's seen a lot of action against the Picts and the Israelis. He's a specialist in military archaeology. Very big on mummies. Finest man with strategic embalming you'll ever meet."

"Salaam," Al-Muriq said, bowing to Tomokato. Undertaker's tools hung from his belt; various bags filled with formaldehyde and pitch were strapped to his body.

Momentarily Con-Ed appeared.

"Well, did you win?" Almuric asked.

"Of course," Con-Ed replied, working at his teeth with an ivory pick. "Let's go."

The other soldiers lined up behind him. He led them toward the gate at a trot.

"Good luck," said Almuric to Tomokato.

"Thank you," Tomokato said, and bowed, then took off after them. The company plunged into the shadowy forest outside the gate, swinging north at a fork in the road.

The last light died redly in the West. Purple shadows crept over the sky. Stars winked forth. The party came to a place where the road narrowed to a white sandy track. Before long it was nothing but a glimmering footpath, hemmed by darkness on either side.

On and on they pressed, deeper into the forest. Experienced night-fighters, Con-Ed and the other men could see like cats in the gloom. So could Tomokato.

After an hour or so, they reached a great clearing. Dimly silhouetted against the starlit sky, a huge rock formation in the shape of a walnut loomed up in the middle.

"That's the Black Walnut," said Al-Muriq to

Tomokato. "It marks the border between Canada and Pictland. From now on, we might run into Porka Picts, so be on guard."

Their pace slowed to a walk. Passing the outcropping, they pushed on into the woods beyond. Save for the sound of their feet, and the jingle of their armor, and the hoots of owls, and the scurry of small animals in the underbrush, and the sigh of wind in the trees, and the shrieks of captured Canadian settlers being tortured by Picts off in the distance, the woods were utterly silent.

After a time, Con-Ed called a halt. They sat down. The Barbarian planted himself next to Tomokato.

"Why do you want to kill Thpageti-Thoth?" he asked the cat in a low voice.

"He helped murder my lord," Tomokato replied.

"And you actually think you can beat me to him?"

"Yes."

"You're mad," Con-Ed told him. "What are you? A house-cat in armor, a mincing mouser. I, on the other hand, am bursting with pantherish vigor, tigerish savagery, leonine courage. I can outrun the deer, outswim the fish. I eat nothing but all-natural foods. I'm the ultimate noble savage, half-slayer, half-Granola bar. How can you hope to compete with me?"

For some time, Tomokato said nothing. "You know," he began at last, "the samurai Kumazawa Banzan once said, 'Ignorance stinks, but barbarism smells even worse.' "

Con-Ed bristled. "Was that an insult?"

"How could it be?" Tomokato replied. "Banzan never knew you."

Con-Ed's wrath subsided.

In the silence that followed, a dozen twigs snapped simultaneously.

"Amluric," Con-Ed growled, "are you snapping twigs again?"

"Nope," the Armenian replied.

"Hot damn," Con-Ed grated.

Immediately a sheaf of firearrows came whistling out of the murk, just missing Tomokato's nose, burying themselves in a nearby tree, setting the lower branches instantly ablaze. From all sides there rang the fearsome war-cry, sounded in thousands of throats, of the Porka Pict Clan: "Th-th-th-th-th-th-th-th-that's all, folks!" and with a flourish of spears and spiked clubs, a churning mob of dark-skinned, all-but naked savages charged in from all sides.

Tomokato and his allies leaped up, closing ranks. Tommy-gun blazing, Amlaric blasted away one-handed from behind his kite-shield. Swarthy bodies spun to the ground, gouting blood. But for each Pict that went down, a hundred sprang to take his place, maddened not only by slaughterlust, but also by the fact that they had to compete so frenziedly just to get a gap to die in; howling, whooping, trampling their own slain, the savages closed swiftly on their prey.

"Tell me," Al-Muriq shrieked in Con-Ed's ear, "what do you think of *those* barbarians?"

"On a scale of one to ten," Con-Ed bellowed, crushing an onrushing Pict's head with his double-bladed axe, "I'd give them a three."

The hideous clamor of close combat ripped the night. Amlaric's gun rattled short vicious bursts. Al Murik's jackhammer pounded and roared. Men wailed in agony. Blades thunked into Pictish flesh. Pictish clubs banged off Aquitanian helmets.

"Bones of the saints," Con-Ed bellowed in his thick Dublin brogue as a huge gout of blood and brains splashed him in the face. "This sure is *fun!*"

The fight blazed on. Tomokato's *katana* whirred and slew. Almaric hacked and chopped with his hockey-stick and Amralic's razor-blade slit throats and opened bellies like a Ronco Deluxe Pict-Slicer. Al-Muriq's needles glittered wickedly in the firelight, pumping quarts of formaldehyde into hapless, swiftly-mummifying savages. Necks snapped by deft twists from Amluric's string-cheese, Pict after Pict bit the dust.

But despite their losses, the Picts would not retreat. They fought like complete fools, but they had the courage of their convictions (most had been convicted many times) as well as the numbers to overwhelm their foes. Amralic went down with a zero through his brain. Almaric was impaled on the upper prong of the six in a sixty-four. Al-Muriq was dashed senseless to the ground by a whistling iron-studded twelve. Shrieking Norman war-cries, spraying his machine gun back and forth, Amlaric swiss-cheesed an oncoming 3.141 and the Picts that held it, only to have his weapon jam; other Picts grabbed up the fallen number as he cleared the gun, and he looked up just in time to get *pi* right in the face. Grinning like demented math teachers, several savages did long division on Amluric and Al Murik, sawing away merrily with knife-edged threes.

Only Tomokato and Con-Ed still stood

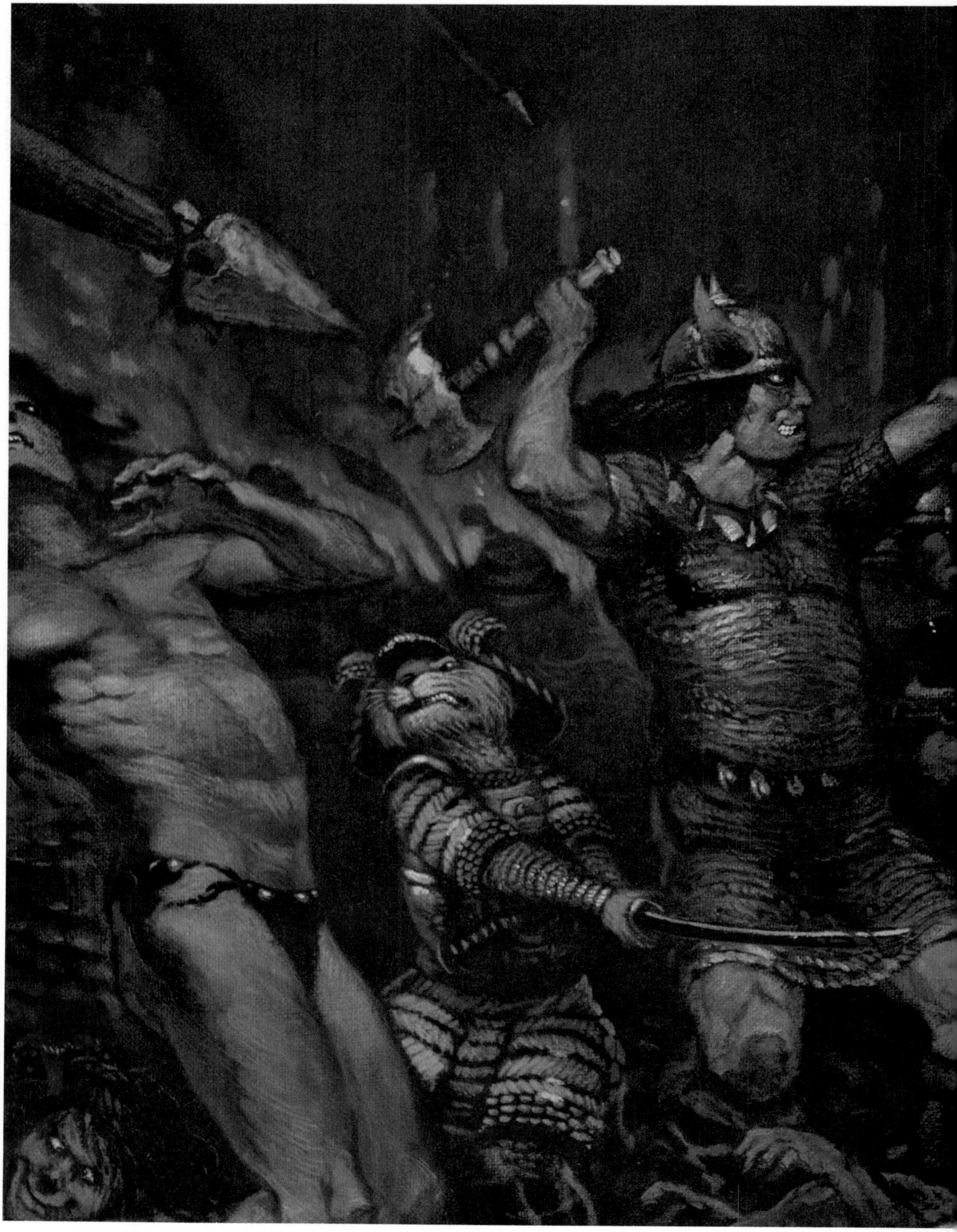

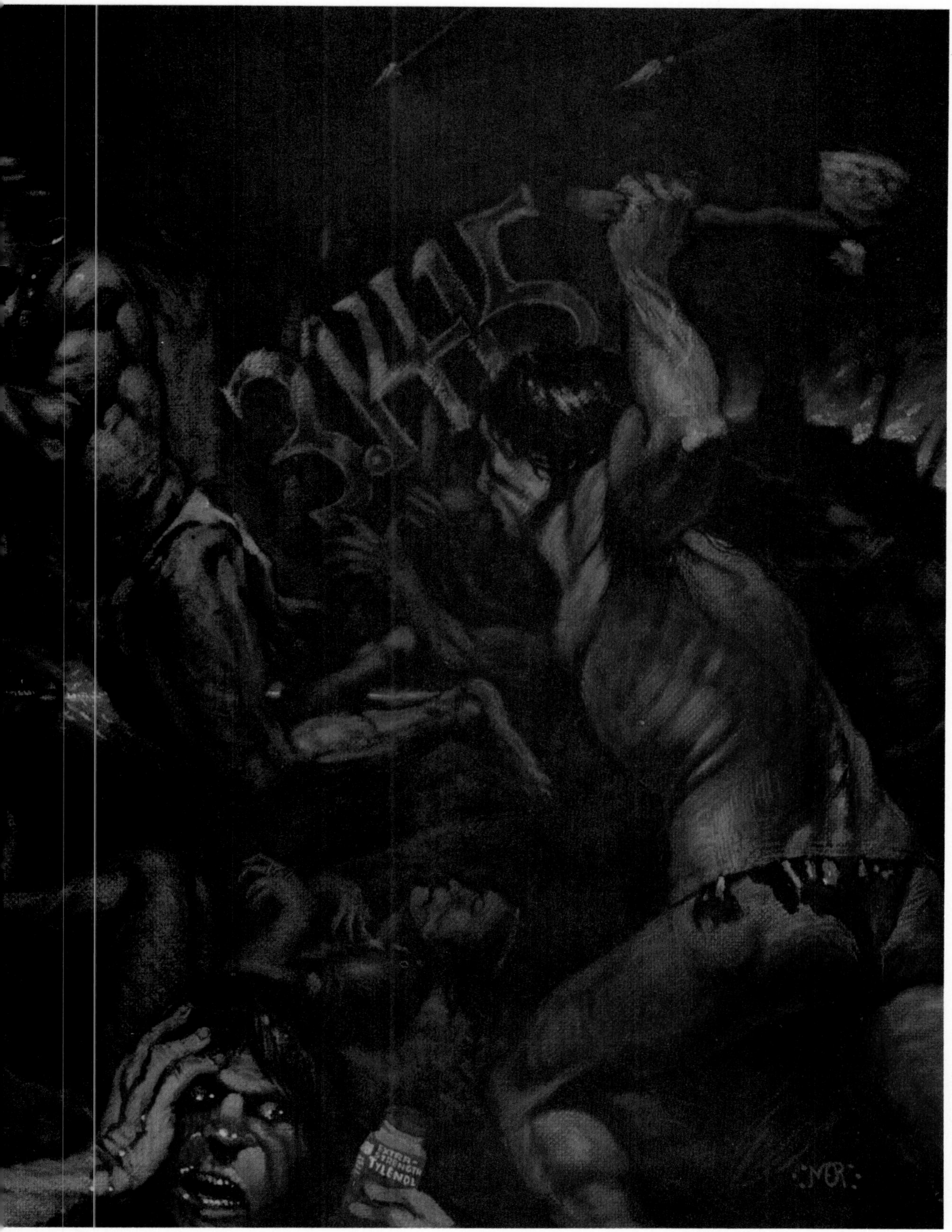
TYLENOL

against the Pictish tide, battling back to back, smiting, slashing, somehow managing to hold the savages at bay, limned crimson in the glow of the ever-spreading fire. They fought magnificently, but knew that, in the end, the Picts' numbers would prevail.

"Let's try to get out of the light, at least," Tomokato cried over his shoulder to Con-Ed.

"Right," the Barbarian replied. Lashing out left and right, they cut a grisly path through the swarthy throng, finally breaking free and dashing full-tilt off into the woods. Stocky, bandy-legged, the Picts could not match their speed. After a time, the sounds of pursuit faded. The fugitives stopped to rest.

"Thinking of turning back?" Con-Ed panted.

"No," Tomokato answered. "I came for Thpageti-Thoth, and I'm going to get him."

"The Hell you will," Con-Ed snapped.

"Believe what you wish," Tomokato answered.

Con-Ed laughed, and his voice softened a bit: "At least you're game, I'll grant you that. Too bad you didn't have the right upbringing. You might have been a real man."

Tomokato did not dignify this with a reply.

After a time, Con-Ed said, "Got your wind back?

"Back?" the cat asked.

Con-Ed muttered something under his breath. Rising, they set off once more, back toward the scene of the battle. Firelight flickered through the trees. They went very close to the blaze. There were no live Picts to be seen, although an advance team from the Forestry Service had already arrived, and was assessing the situation.

"Did you see where those Picts got to?" Con-Ed asked a ranger.

The man pointed. "Off that way. Back toward their village."

"Thanks," Con-Ed said. "Come on, Cat."

Giving a wide berth to the fire, the pair picked up the Picts' trail.

"We'd be going this way anyhow," Con-Ed told Tomokato. "But I sure do love night-time tracking. Keeps me feral."

Eventually they came to the foot of a treeclad, rocky slope, and pressed on up. At the top, the hill flattened as if its crown had been sliced off by a giant knife. On the far side of the shelf-like summit stood a huge Pictish village, hundreds of huts surrounded by great pines. Moonlight shone on the roofs, and the glow of a vast bonfire rose from the center of the settlement. Dodging from tree to tree, Tomokato and Con-Ed stole ever closer to the outer huts. The sound of a great celebration was coming from the heart of the village; drums throbbed, flutes shrilled, saxophones wailed. Bestial voices rose and fell, growling an ape-like rendition of *You Are My Sunshine*.

Tomokato and the Barbarian neared the fringe of the village. The cat wondered at the apparent lack of guards. There were many Picts up ahead, visible in the gaps between the silhouetted huts, but none seemed to be watching for intruders. All were partying, razzing each other with noise-makers, chugging beer.

Yet the village was not without defenses, as Tomokato soon learned.

Con-Ed strode through a crude tripline made from a creeper. To the left, up in a tree, fifteen Pictish sentries were alerted by a bell, and swung down at the intruders on vines, knives clenched between their teeth; on the right, a massive frame studded with yard-long spikes hurtled up from the ground, trailing dirt and streamers of weed.

Responding instantly to the motion they glimpsed out of the corners of their eyes, Tomokato and Con-Ed bounded forward, spinning in time to see the Picts swing directly onto the spikes. Blades clamped in their jaws, the Picts died soundlessly, stuck to the frame like human butterflies impaled by some demonic entomologist, transfixed like asinine similes.

Tomokato and the Barbarian turned once more, going toward the closest hut. A ladder led up to its thatched roof, which was apparently in the process of being repaired. Several large holes showed in the thatch.

"Let's climb up," Tomokato said. "We can see what the celebration's about."

Con-Ed nodded. They scaled the ladder. When they were midway up the roof, Con-Ed halted, pointing to a gap in the thatch. Firelight from a doorway shone into the room below, illuminating a piled hoard of Pictish war-numbers.

"We could set fire to the hut," the Barbarian suggested.

"Not yet," Tomokato replied.

They crawled to the peak. The support-poles shuddered beneath their weight, but the roof held.

Before them, in a vast redlit circle, was a huge crowd of Picts, who by now had formed a tremendous conga line, and were processing savagely around the great bonfire grunting: "One, two, three, *kick!*"

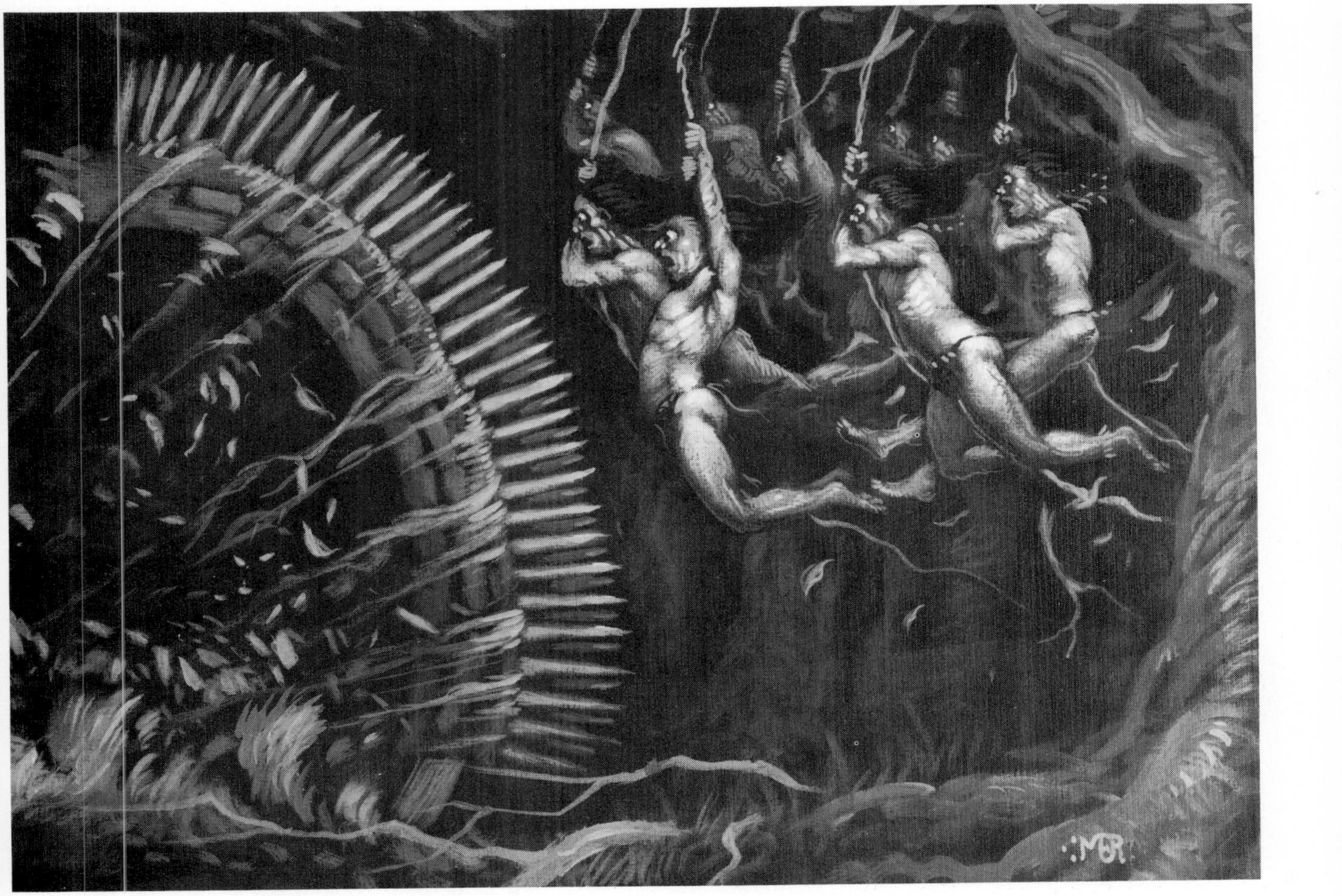

"Crom and Corky!" Con-Ed growled.

"What's wrong?" Tomokato asked.

"Look at 'em! See the ones with the sores? And the others with those size-twenty hooters? Scab and Nose Picts. They were at war with the Porka Clan."

"And now they're in a Conga line with them," Tomokato said grimly.

"Looks like Thpageti-Thoth's plan is working. . . ."

A tremendous blue flash blossomed on the Eastern side of the village. The Picts fell silent and dropped to the ground, grovelling and groaning in superstitious dread. As the blue glare died, a dark-robed man, bald but for a scalplock, was revealed on a timber platform festooned with the skulls of giant serpents and saber-toothed tigers. He raised his wide-sleeved arms, and two luscious Pictish maidens in fur bikinis stepped out from behind him. The audience, which had risen by that time, exploded with lewd comments and wolf-whistles. The girls wiggled to the front of the platform and unrolled a purple velvet banner with the words "Thpageti-Thoth the Magnificent" blazoned in red upon it. They hung it from the edge of the platform, and with splendid flaunts of their near-nude buttocks, went back toward the sorcerer.

"My assistants, Audrey and Maisie," he said. They leaned on him for a few moments, posing sensuously, blowing rosy-lipped kisses at the onlookers before withdrawing from the platform. Returning seconds later lugging a huge, coffin-shaped box, they stood it upright, center-stage. Thpageti-Thoth opened it. There was a man chained inside.

Up on the hut-roof, Con-Ed gritted, "Al-Muriq!"

"Sawing a man in half!" Thpageti-Thoth announced.

Cheers gusted from the audience. He produced a long bucksaw from his sleeve, did various passes over it, closed the door to the coffin;

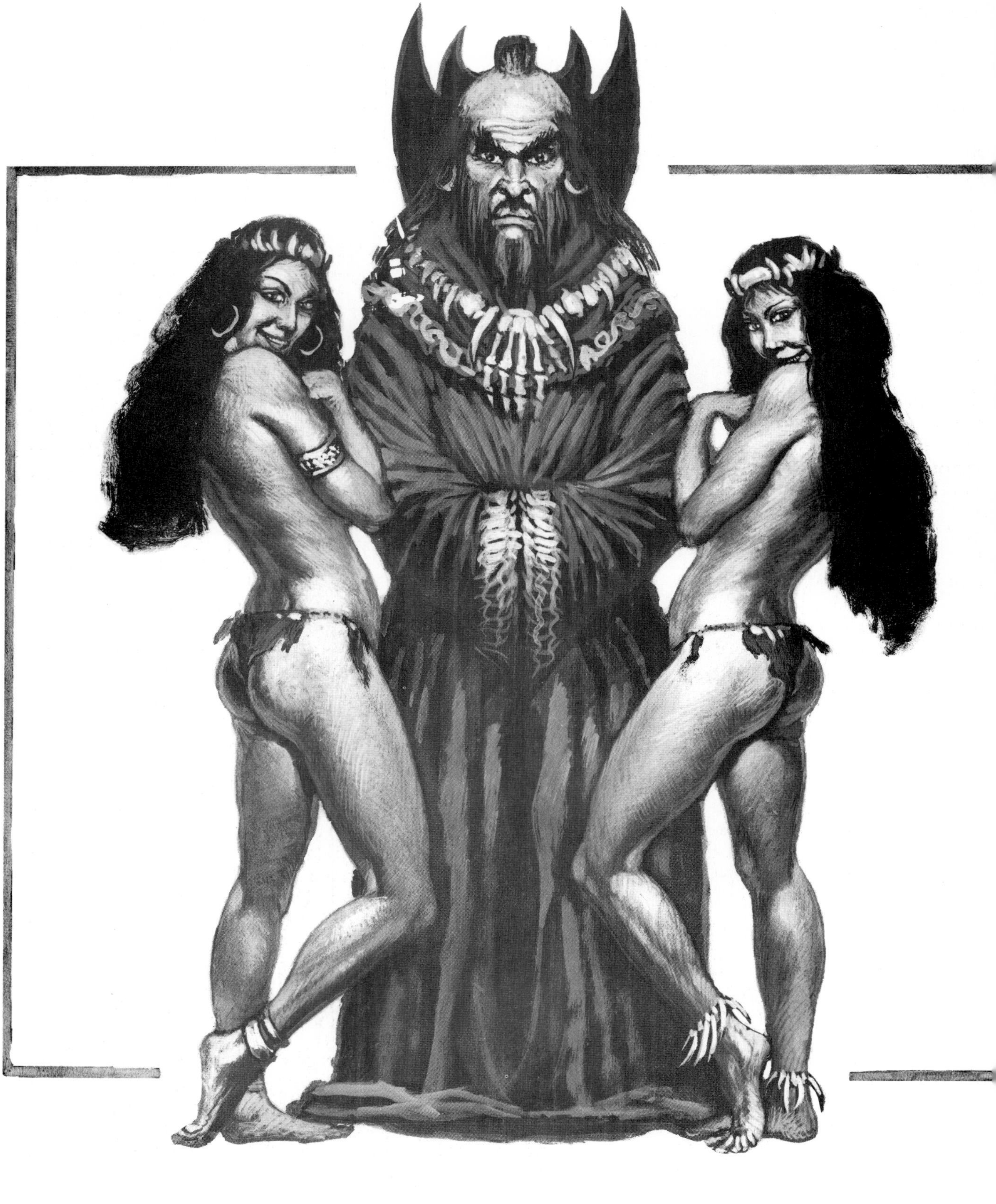

but he left open a small window to show Al-Muriq's fear-stricken face. The sorcerer and Audrey took their places on either side of the coffin, each grasping an end of the saw. To the hideous sound of screams and pleading from Al-Muriq, they began to rip into the wood. Splinters and sawdust flew. Before long, the cries from the Arab died, and there was only the grating buzz of the saw. The blade tore clean through the box, and the coffin's top half fell over. The Picts, who had been silent with wonderment up until then, let out tremendous shouts of delight as a wave of crimson splashed across the platform. Big applause.

"How'd he do that?" Tomokato heard one Pict say to another, shouting to be heard over the uproar.

Thpageti-Thoth and his girls bowed. When the applause finally died, the sorcerer drew up a padded leather chair and sat down, crossing his legs, accepting a mint julep from Audrey while the other girl fanned his face with the fringe from her overstuffed bikini top.

"But seriously guys," he began, "I think you all know why I've called you here tonight. I've been studying my charts, and the portents are good. We march on Fort Ticonderoga at dawn."

The Picts went wild. He raised his arms after a time, quieting them.

"The Aquitanians and Canadians can't possibly stand against our superior numbers. But just to make sure, I'm going to call up a little insurance. A swamp-demon from the Northern Marsh, named Thwack. Nothing can stand before him. I'm going to put my soul in his body; our army will be led by an escapee from Hell, an invincible monstrosity guided by my cunning, a horror that will blast the minds of those who try to resist." He stood up slowly, raising his arms, eyes gleaming balefully, fingers outstretched like vulture's claws.

"Are we or are we not going to kick ass?" he cried.

The Picts roared the affirmative, trembling with eagerness to fling themselves onto the warpath, aching to bathe their hands and faces in Aquitanian blood, to paddle their tootsies in hot steaming gore, to humiliate captured Canadians in hockey before they tortured them to death. . . .

When the tumult died, Thpageti-Thoth intoned a long mystical formula. Producing a short, cylindrical object, he blew into one end, sending a weird sound ringing into the night, an arcane blatting that was almost indescribable, but was most nearly like a loud and eldritch duck-call.

All faces turned Northwards.

Presently there was a flapping as of gigantic wings, distant at first, but coming swiftly closer. Two red spots, like burning eyes, appeared in the sky. Into the firelight flew a monstrous titan shape, half-muskrat, half-mallard. It swooped widdershins three times around the center of the village, then veered off toward a tall pine-flanked stone pillar that reared up behind the huts on the northern side of the settlement, a pillar that had often been used as a place of human sacrifice. The demon landed on its crown, flashing a smile on which only God Himself could do the bridgework.

"All set?" Thpageti-Thoth cried to the creature.

"Ready if you are," Thwack bellowed.

The sorcerer dropped his hands to his sides, tilted his head forward and screamed. A cloud of glowing greenish vapor gushed from his left ear. Soulless now, his body crumpled limply to the platform.

The vapor sped across to Thwack. He inhaled it with a deep drag. His pupils dilated instantly.

"Any of you guys got any munchies?" he called to the Picts. "Doritos, maybe?"

"No Doritos," they replied. "How about some acorns?"

Thwack considered it, shook his head. "No thanks."

Watching from the rooftop, Con-Ed nudged the cat.

"We've got to kill that demon somehow," he said.

"We'd better deal with Thpageti-Thoth's body first," Tomokato replied. "We don't want his soul going back into it."

Con-Ed nodded. "But we'll need some sort of diversion to get to that platform. . . . "

Tomokato pulled up a pawful of thatch. "We were going to burn this hut anyway. And once the fighting starts, the Picts won't be able to use their numbers against us."

"I've got tinder and flint," Con-Ed said.

They descended from the roof. Con-Ed lost no time lighting his tinder, using his axe as a striking-iron. Within moments he had a small blaze going in the roof. Taking clumps of burning straw, Tomokato started other fires along the eave. The flames ate hungrily at the roof, popping and spitting. Large swaths of thatch began to fall in, collapsing on the war-numbers beneath.

"Time to go," Con-Ed said.

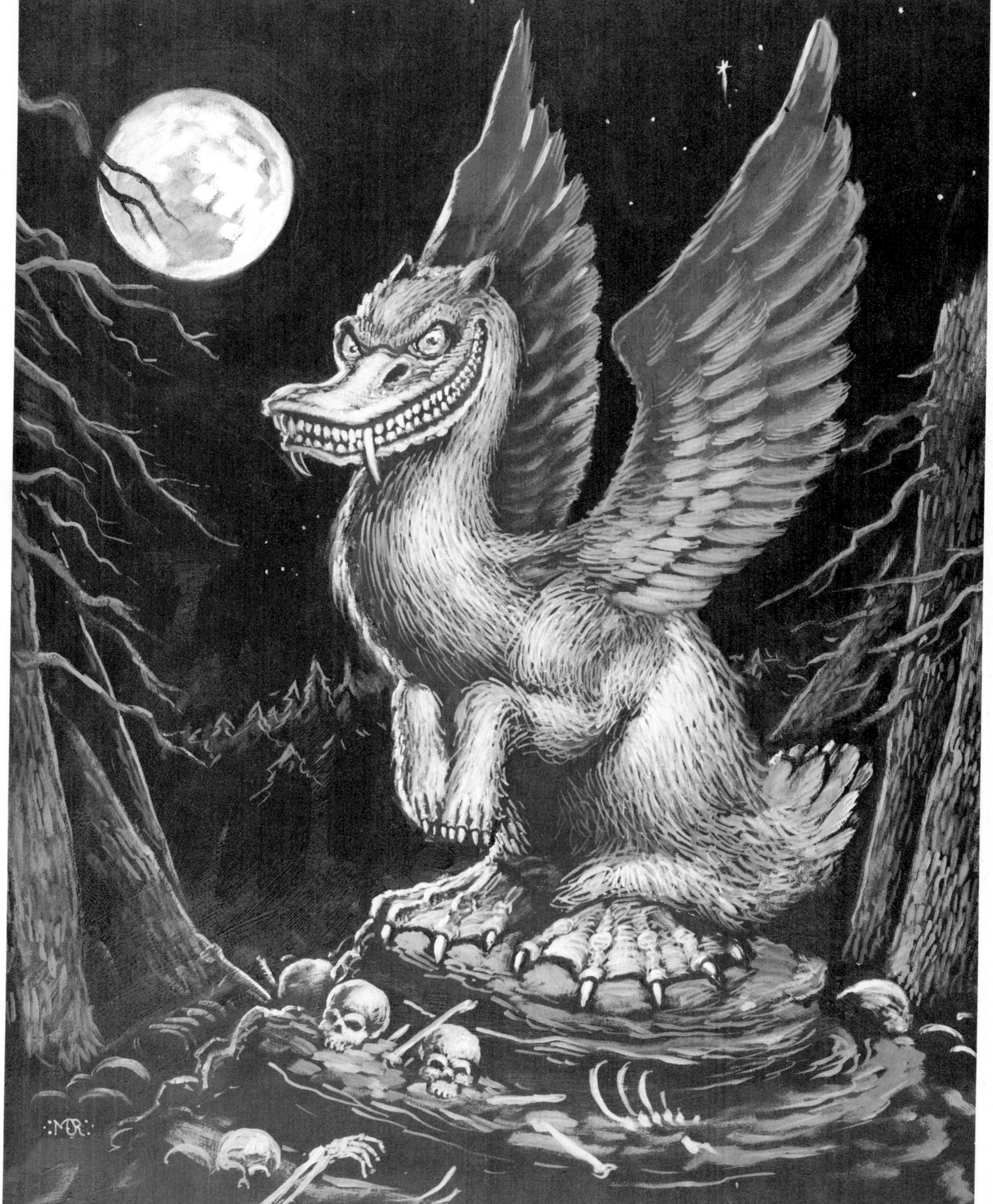

He and Tomokato dashed around the fringe of the village, making their way to the eastern side. They could hear a rumbling, quacking voice addressing the Picts: Thpageti-Thoth speaking from Thwack's horrific duckbill. But before long that was drowned out by another sound, cries from the savages as the burning hut was noticed.

Tomokato and Con-Ed sped toward the center of the village, coming out between two racks hung with shrunken heads. As they expected, the area of the platform was deserted; the Picts were massed over by the flaming hut. Fully half its roof had caved in by then. A hastily-formed bucket-brigade seemed to be doing little good.

Suddenly the numbers within exploded, ripping the hut apart, sending an orange fireball mushrooming into the night, flinging ripped Picts through the air. Survivors scurried for cover.

"Exploding numbers?" Tomokato asked Con-Ed over his shoulder as they ran toward the platform.

Con-Ed blinked. "Is there another kind?"

They reached the stairs, bolted to the top. As they neared the sorcerer's supine form, it occurred to Tomokato that Con-Ed would not allow him the privilege of first chop; a split instant later, he felt a tremendous shock against the side of his helmet, and found himself flying over the edge of the platform. The Barbarian had struck him from behind. Blackness billowed out of the back of Tomokato's mind as the ground surged up at him, and he lost consciousness.

Head aching, he woke a minute later. Getting slowly to his feet, he drew his sword and went back up onto the platform. His vision was clearing swiftly, and he saw that Con-Ed had rearranged Thpageti-Thoth's body rather extensively. The Barbarian was gone.

"On the platform, you fools!" Tomokato heard Thwack quack thunderously. "The Cat! The Cat!"

Tomokato spun. All the Picts in the world seemed to be converging on the platform, brandishing spears, stone axes, spiked clubs. He drew his *wakazashi*, knowing he would have to fight two-bladed, one cat against a savage, screeching horde. On they came, like a swarm of huge army ants, maddened, bloodthirsty. . . .

Con-Ed, meanwhile, had slipped outside the village once more, running toward the rocky pillar on which Thwack still perched; the demon was watching the Picts converge on Tomokato. A tremendous clamor arose as the savages and the cat locked in battle. Thwack did not hear Con-Ed scrambling up toward him until it was too late. Even as he turned, the Barbarian caught him with a whistling Herculean cheap-shot, axe biting deep into muscle and bone, crippling the demon's right wing. Even so, Thwack's first impulse was to leap skyward; Con-Ed vaulted onto his back as the demon bounded up from the pillar. Thwack arced down toward the village, landing with a crash, belly-first in a storage-hut full of nuts and roots. Miraculously unhurt, Con-Ed rolled clear into a heap of thatch, then followed, growling, as the demon burst out through the front wall of the hut. Shaking free of the debris that covered him, Thwack turned with appalling speed, swept his good wing around. Con-Ed leaped back, and the stroke barely grazed his chin, but even so he was pummeled off his feet, and his mouth filled with the hot, rusty taste of blood, and it was a few seconds before he realized that his head had not been batted clean off his shoulders. He shook his head, spitting gore, blinking as Thwack surged over him, snapping. The Barbarian's axe was still in his cabled fist, and he lashed out with all his might, driving the edge deep into Thwack's bill.

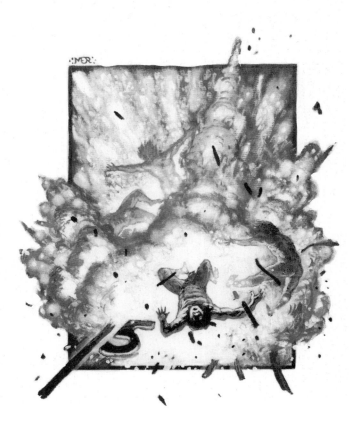

There it lodged. The demon loosed a quacking bellow and jerked backward, wrenching the helve from Con-Ed's hand. With his muskrat-like paws, Thwack ripped it free almost immediately; at the same time, Con-Ed grabbed a splintered pole from the ruined hut, and leaped to his feet, dashing forward, jabbing the sharp, jagged point at Thwack's chest like an insane harpooner, shrieking in rage and triumph as the thrust went home. Black ichor jetted along the shaft. Thwack screamed, yanked the pole out, but held onto it, hefting it and the axe. Ebon blood streamed thickly from his nostrils and mouth, but his demonic vitality was unquenched, and his eyes burned with the livid red of glowing steel. He struck at Con-Ed with the pole, catching him full in the side. Most of the impact was absorbed by the Barbarian's mail, but several of his ribs cracked, and he hurtled sideways. He barely got to his feet before Thwack lashed out again, just missing him. The Barbarian circled to the right, Thwack following, waving the pole and axe, grinning hellishly, licking the blood from his lips. . . .

Con-Ed tripped, falling across a corpse. As he sat up, he realized that the sounds of battle from the village's eastern side had died; even though the demon was hard upon him, he chanced a look over his shoulder. The whole eastern end of the village was littered with swarthy corpses, most of them ferociously mutilated. There was not a live Pict to be seen. The only thing standing was Tomokato. The cat was only a few feet from the barbarian, blowing on the nails of his left paw, which held a bloody, slightly-curved shortsword.

Con-Ed heard Thwack closing in. He looked around in horror.

An armored blur streaked past him. Steel blinked in several murderous lightning slashes as Thwack's massive darkness loomed near. Large chunks of the demon started falling away: first one wing, then the other, then the great hind-legs, and finally the head. The immense turkey-like torso stood upright for a brief second. A crack formed down the middle of it, and the halves opened like a pineapple chopped by a machete.

Tomokato looked down at his victim's head for a moment, then came back by Con-Ed, who was utterly stupefied by the cat's effortless victory over the demon — not to mention his annihilation of the Picts.

"You shouldn't be surprised," Tomokato said, wiping his swords off on Con-Ed's right leg. "I come from a superior culture, the civilization of

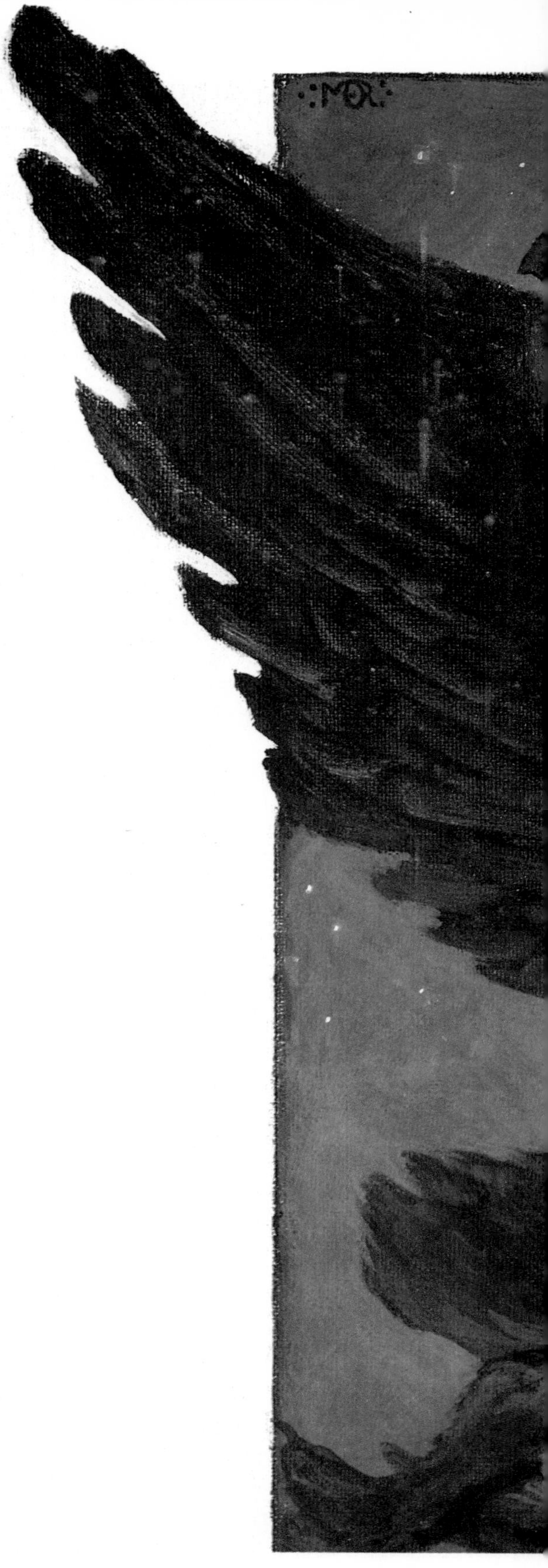

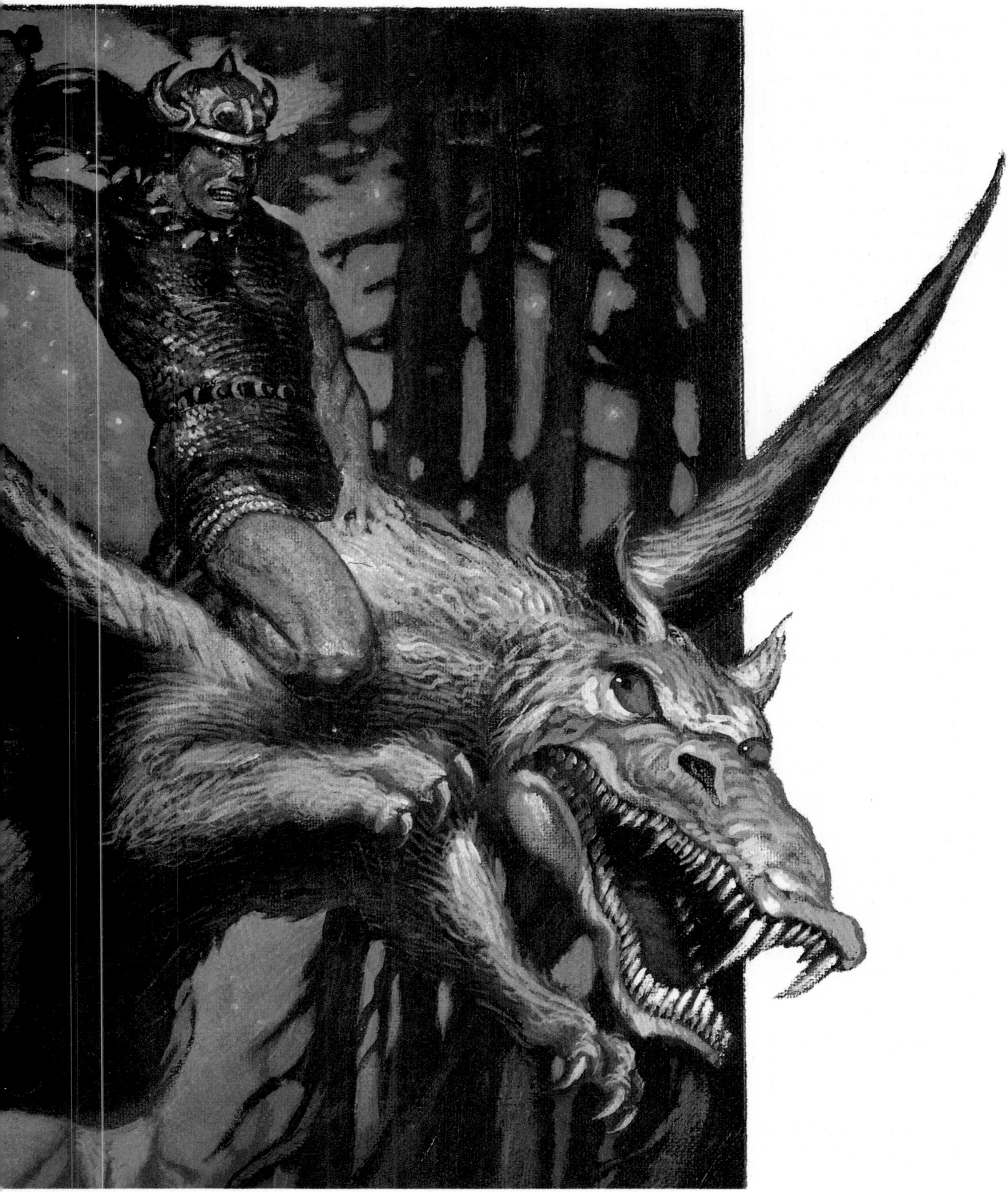

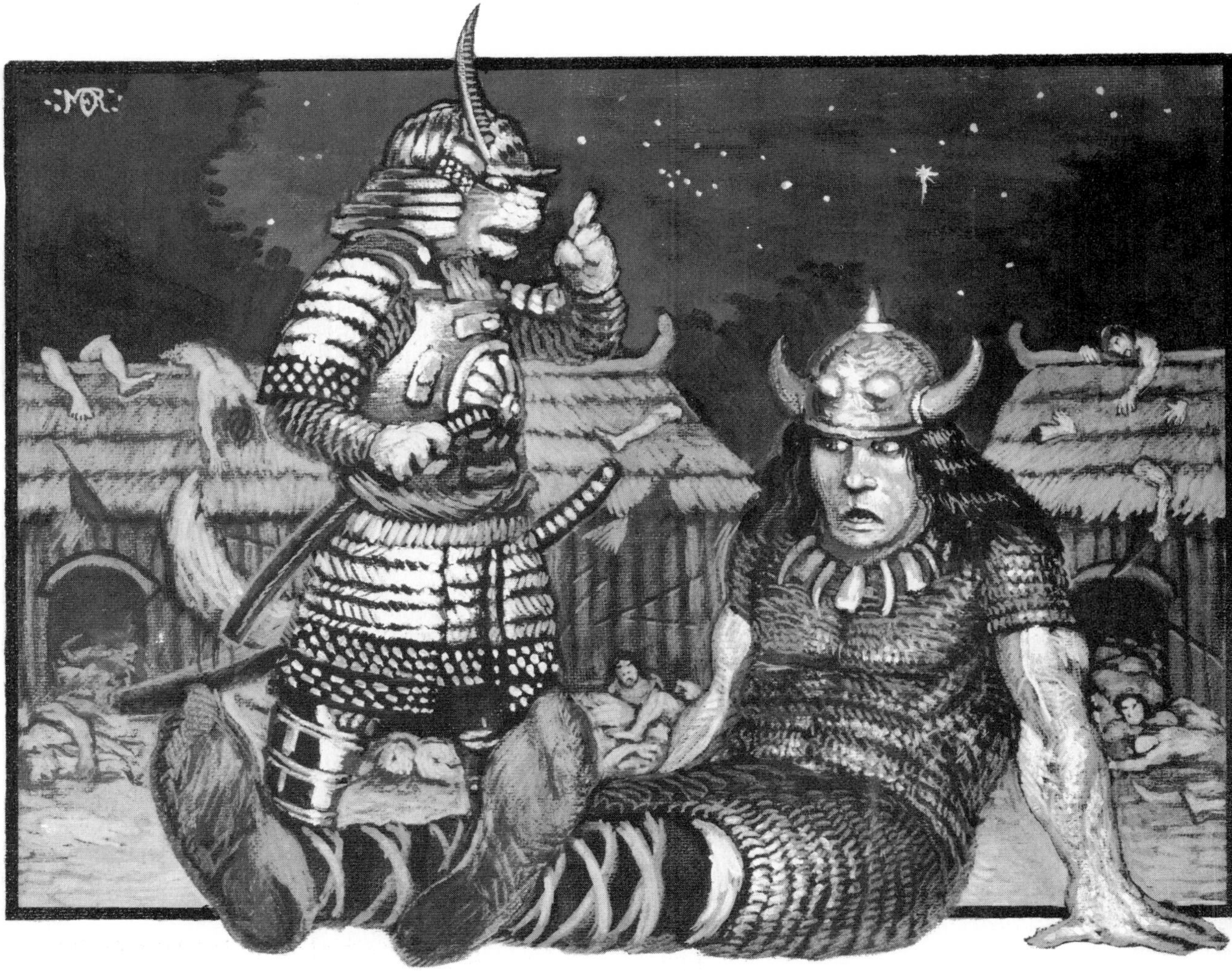
MER

civilizations. That's why I conquered where you failed. You are but a barbarian, and barbarism is but the whim of circumstance. One cannot imagine barbarians truly mastering the delicate and graceful art of the sword, let alone learning enough understated good taste to utilize transistors or devise truly splendid video games. Japanese culture is Divine, Eternal. In the end, it will always triumph."

Clicking his swords neatly back into their scabbards, the cat turned on his heel and strode off in quest of his next victims, the Jormunrekssons, leaving Con-Ed to contemplate this wisdom.

AGAINST THE GODS

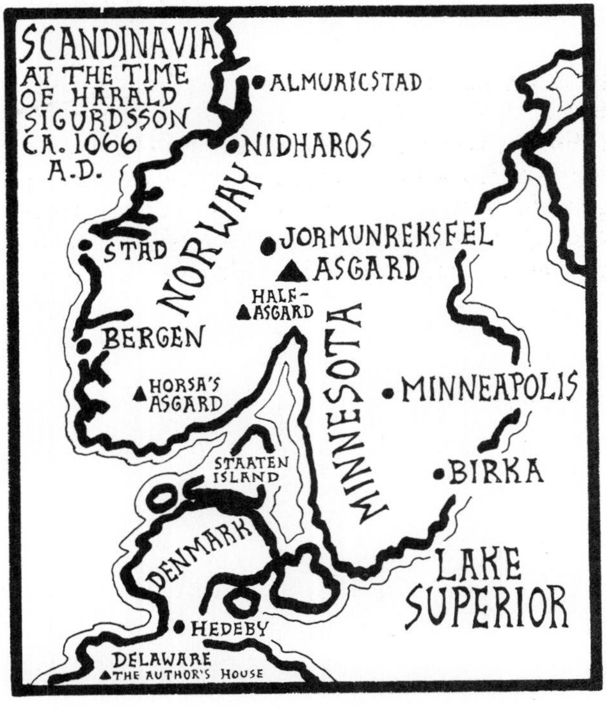

SCANDINAVIA
AT THE TIME
OF HARALD
SIGURDSSON
CA. 1066
A.D.
ALMURICSTAD
NIDHAROS
NORWAY
JORMUNREKSFEL
ASGARD
HALF-
ASGARD
STAD
BERGEN
HORSA'S
ASGARD
MINNESOTA
MINNEAPOLIS
STAATEN
ISLAND
BIRKA
DENMARK
LAKE
SUPERIOR
HEDEBY
DELAWARE
THE AUTHOR'S HOUSE

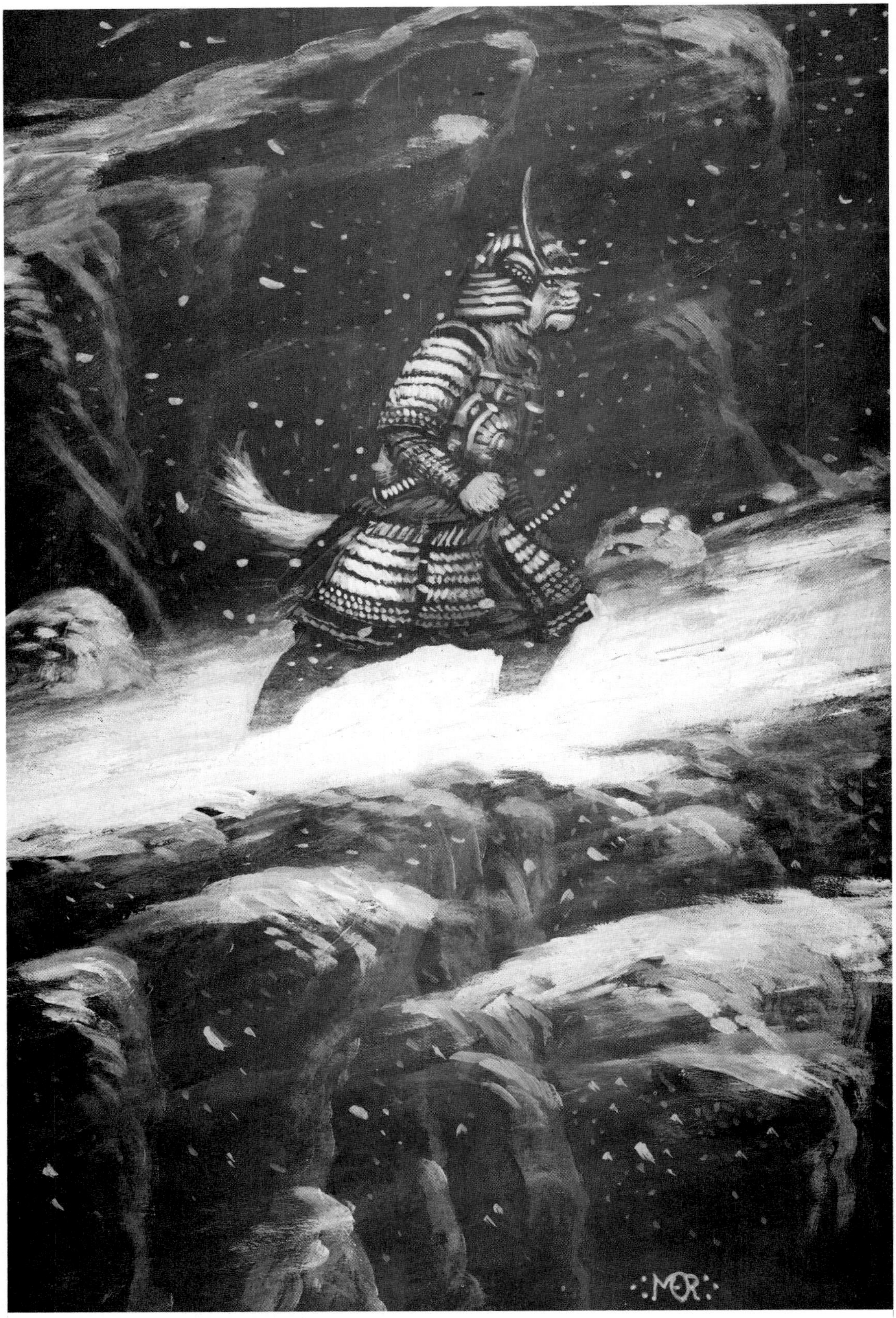

Heading back into Canada, Tomokato booked passage on a tourist barge heading east on the St. Lawrence Seaway. Reaching the Atlantic, he sailed for Norway in search of Ketil and Halfdan Jormunreksson, two vikings who had participated in the killing of Nobunaga. Landing at Nidharos in late fall, he found that the mountain passes were already blocked with snow, and that he could not reach the Jormunreksson's inland stronghold until late Spring; he settled for spending the Winter with King Harald Sigurdsson (Hardraada), who repeatedly tried to enlist him in an expedition to England he was mounting. But the cat would not be stayed from his course, and when the thaw came, he set off after his prey. . . .

— Cat Out of Hell

The sky was slate-grey, and snow was beginning to fall; striding along the cliff-flanked mountain road, clutching a cloak to his face, teeth chattering, Tomokato wondered how a midsummer afternoon could be so cold.

It's only because you're so high up, his common sense insisted.

Then why's it so raw down in the valleys? a voice replied in his mind. *It's been getting steadily colder for the last two months, highland and low, and now it's starting to snow again. . . . Something's happening. Something unnatural. Those voices you keep hearing in the wind. Those figures you've seen riding in the sky these past three nights . . .*

He tried to keep his mind off such thoughts. He tried to think about the task at hand. He was closing in on the Jormunrekssons, of that he was sure. Bad directions had sent him wandering fruitlessly through the Norwegian mountains looking for the brigands' stronghold. But he had been set on the right path by a war-party that King Harald Sigurdsson had sent out to quash a backwoods jarl, and now he guessed he would be in sight of Jormunreksfel within the hour.

The road climbed steadily along the grim, dark-grey mountain wall, zigzagging back and forth. It was a tremendous feat of engineering, and the cat was amazed that the people of such a backward land could have built it; he half believed the tale he had heard at the farmstead where he had spent the night, a tale that said the road had been constructed by the old gods, whose fortress, Asgard, was said to stand atop one of the mountains nearby. The road, which had originally been much longer (so the legend went), had run from Asgard to the sea, but had been mostly destroyed by the giants, so there was no longer any direct route by which mortals could reach the home of the gods.

Up and up the cat slogged, and the snow grew ever deeper, falling with preternatural speed and fury. But after a time, it stopped, and the wind died. A strange hollow silence descended over the mountain, as sinister in its own way as the wailing voices that had seemed to ride on the gale. The sky hung low and close above the ragged stone-ridges.

The cat reached a snowy gorge, the pass which he had been making for. The road ran along its floor, descending on the mountain's far side. Tomokato pushed through the gap, halted at the top of the slant, looking out over a misty, treeclad valley. A tremendous rocky wall loomed on the far side, flecked with snow, veined with glaciers that looked tiny with distance. Tomokato could see only the mountain's buttressed feet; everything above was wreathed in cloud. Even so, he had never seen such a vast pile of stone. He wondered if it was the mountain that Asgard was supposed to crown.

He started down the slope, paused as a faint braying of horns broke the silence. He thought he saw a fringe of cloud rip loose from the lowering leaden ceiling, and dip toward the valley-bottom, even though there was no wind. It seemed to take on the form of a dark rider, galloping downward for a time, then upward, as if following the contours of invisible hills; behind it came a ghostly company of smaller, mistier riders. The first wheeled and swept back toward them, brandishing what looked like a mighty axe. They scattered, fleeing back up into the clouds. The first rider wheeled once more, and sped off on its way, vanishing from Tomokato's sight behind a ridge that arched up from the center of the valley-bottom. A spurt of flame licked up above the stony keel, and there came a rolling burst of laughter, which seemed to turn into new howls of wind; the snow began to fall once more. Tomokato shivered with a chill that was more than mere cold, trying to fathom what he had just witnessed. He resumed his descent.

Far below, atop a great outcropping, he made out the shape of a small wooden fortress. Jormunreksfel.

It took him the better part of two hours to reach the bottom of the mountain, where the road vanished amid a tumble of boulders. Through scurrying rags of mist and snow, he could still

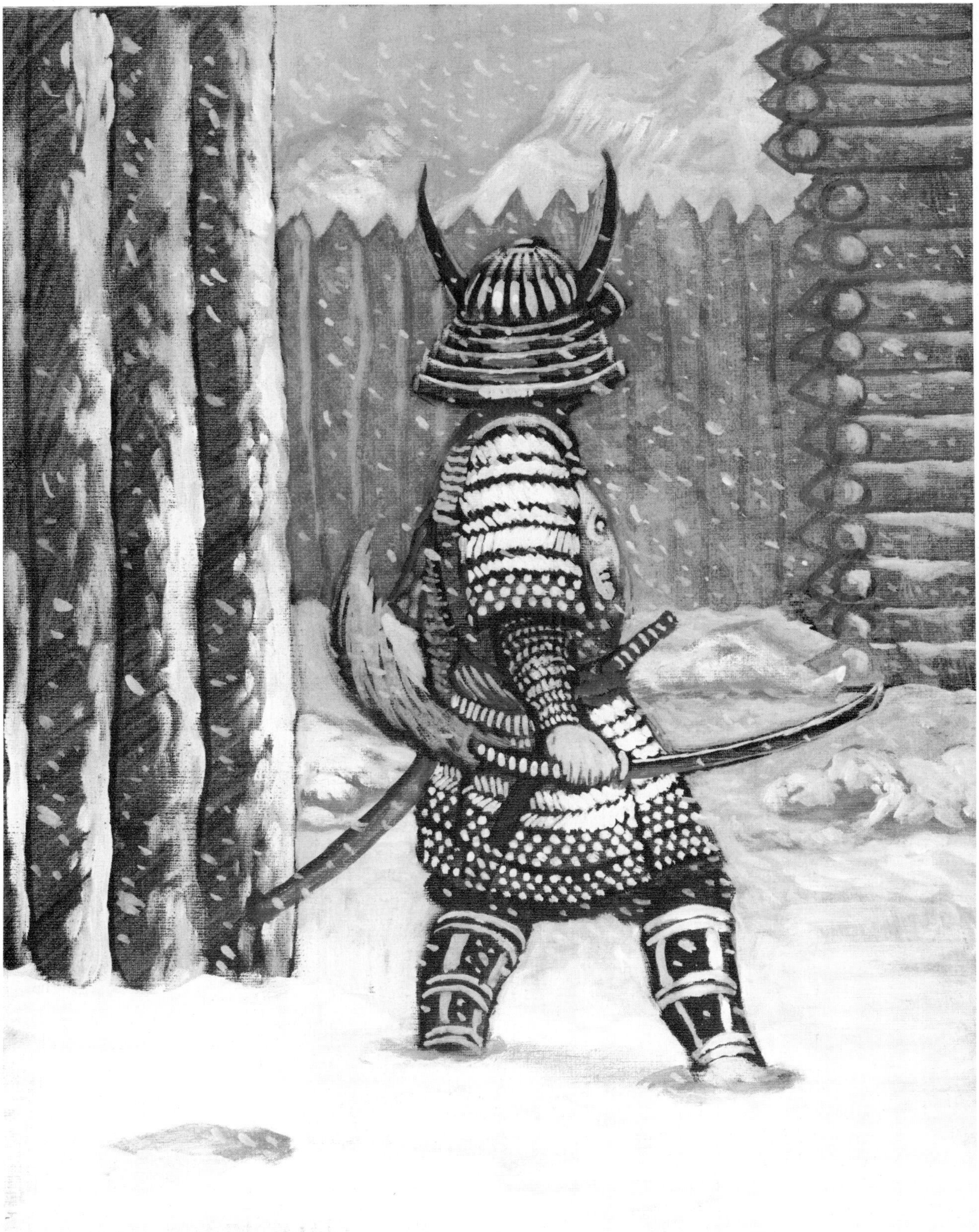

make out the stronghold atop its crag, and made toward the outcropping. Coming to its foot, he found a broad, carven staircase, partially sheltered from the blizzard, and started up. Nearing the fortress's gate, he found it hanging from its hinges. Inside the courtyard sprawled dozens of bodies, man-shaped hummocks in the snow. He entered slowly, sword drawn.

"What do you want?" screeched a fleshless voice from an arrow-studded blockhouse on the courtyard's far side.

"I'm looking for Ketil and Halfdan Jormunreksson," Tomokato replied.

"I'll tell you where they are," rang the voice, "if you promise me two things."

"Which are?"

"Not to hurt me. And not to strip any of those bodies. The loot's mine! Odin knows I took enough from those bullies, bowing and scraping. I wasn't even their thrall, though I might as well have been: . . . Promise me!" A long white hand jabbed out of a window in the blockhouse, pointing a skeletal finger at the cat.

"I promise," Tomokato answered.

The unseen speaker cackled. "Very well then. Halfdan and Ketil are dead. They fell to fighting one another, with all their men. Halfdan started it. He was always the worse of the two . . . treacherous to the end. Used every foul trick in the battle. Never could have done so well against a fighter like Ketil — never heard of a swordsman to match that one. . . . They fell not two feet from where you're standing, saxe-knives in each others' throats."

Tomokato looked around. There were no bodies so close.

"Where are they now?" he asked.

"The Valkyries took them," the cackler replied. "I saw it myself. They flew off with them to that great mountain yonder, across the valley. The root of Asgard. Halfdan and Ketil are feasting with the gods now, waiting for the last day."

"Last day?"

"Ragnarok. The Weird of the World, when the giants and monsters will storm Asgard, and slay the gods, and the universe will fall in blood and fire. It's coming even now. The Fimbulwinter has begun. Snow in Summer. Riders in the skies. Brothers at each others' throats. A sword age, a wolf age, a wind age. . . . " There was another burst of cackling, utterly senile, utterly demented. "I'll survive, though. I'll buy my way out with the gold from these bodies. I'll bribe even the Mid-

gard Serpent and Surtur the Fire-Giant. . . . "

"If I climb up to Asgard," the cat broke in, "I'll be able to find Halfdan and Ketil?"

"Ketil at least," the voice replied. "Halfdan might be with the giants, for all I know."

"Thanks for the information," Tomokato said, turned, and strode from the fortress, leaving the madman alone with his treasures and the twisted dead. Laughter shrilled behind him. Wind whistled between the timbers of the stockade.

He went back down the steps, setting out across the valley floor. Trudging through the snow, he came to the mountain's feet toward sundown. Finding a small cave, he spent the night in it, making a bed from pine-boughs, and a fire from branches.

Morning came still and steel-grey and chill. He started the ascent. At first it was not difficult, but before long he came to a sheer icy wall, mirror-smooth, that was rough going even for a cat. Hacking out pawholds with his *wakazashi*, he managed to reach a height where the cliff-face was more

hats and cigars, and wore vests and spats. They seemed to take an extreme interest in him, and flew by several times before winging upward, toward the peak.

Some time later, shortly after finishing his lunch, Tomokato rose, did several deep knee-bends to get the kinks out of his legs, and prepared to resume the climb.

A rumbling sound reached him. He craned his head back. The clouds were breaking up. The rumbling grew, becoming like an earthquake in the sky.

"Try to storm Asgard, will you, mortal?" thundered a great voice. "Then face the wrath of Thor!"

Down through the ragged, hurrying scud came the careening shape of a golden chariot drawn by two shaggy, bear-sized goats, and manned by a massive redbeard in helm and mail who had a tremendous war-hammer cocked behind his head. He flung the weapon, which was transformed into a snaking, crackling streak of lightning as it sped towards Tomokato.

The cat ducked. The lightning just missed him. He drew his *katana*, watched as the lightning circled, boomerang-like, back up towards Thor, becoming a hammer once more in his hand. As the chariot rumbled past the pillar, the god struck out at Tomokato, who parried with a mighty blow. Howling with rage and frustration, Thor reined the goats around, climbed heavenward, and drove back down at the cat like a celestial avalanche. Again he hurled the hammer. Tomokato deflected it, and the mountain rang with the crash of impact, sparks sleeting from his steel. The lightning returned to Thor.

The god circled without attacking for a time, as if wondering what to do next. But he was evidently a divinity of habit; finally he simply hurled the hammer again.

Wearying of this harassment, Tomokato decided to put an end to it, and struck directly at the oncoming bolt. There was a blinding flash of white light as the streak was sheared in two. The bisected lightning coalesced into the tumbling, plummeting halves of a shattered war-hammer.

Thor yanked his goats to a screeching halt, skidmarks from his chariot-wheels marring the vault of heaven. The goats, amazed by the cat's deed, looked back over their shoulders at the god, who by now had one of his hands clapped over his mouth, and was pointing the other accusingly at Tomokato.

manageable, even though it was still glazed and slippery. Up and up he climbed, driving himself on with sheer willpower, penetrating the clouds. He covered three miles the first day, and four miles the next, emerging finally into bright, bitter sunlight. He blinked at the heights above, which shimmered with a weird, elvish iridescence. He climbed up long chimneys, negotiated impossible overhangs. Nothing could deter him.

On the third day even the heights were shadowed in cloud, and the cold was savage. Toward noon, he leaped from the main cliff-face to a pillar-top that looked like a good place to rest and have lunch. Breath smoking, he sat down on the icy stone and broke out his food and cooking-gear.

He was halfway through his ramen noodles when he heard the beat of wings, and noticed two large ravens flapping toward him. One was thin and lanky, the other squat and fat. Both had bowler

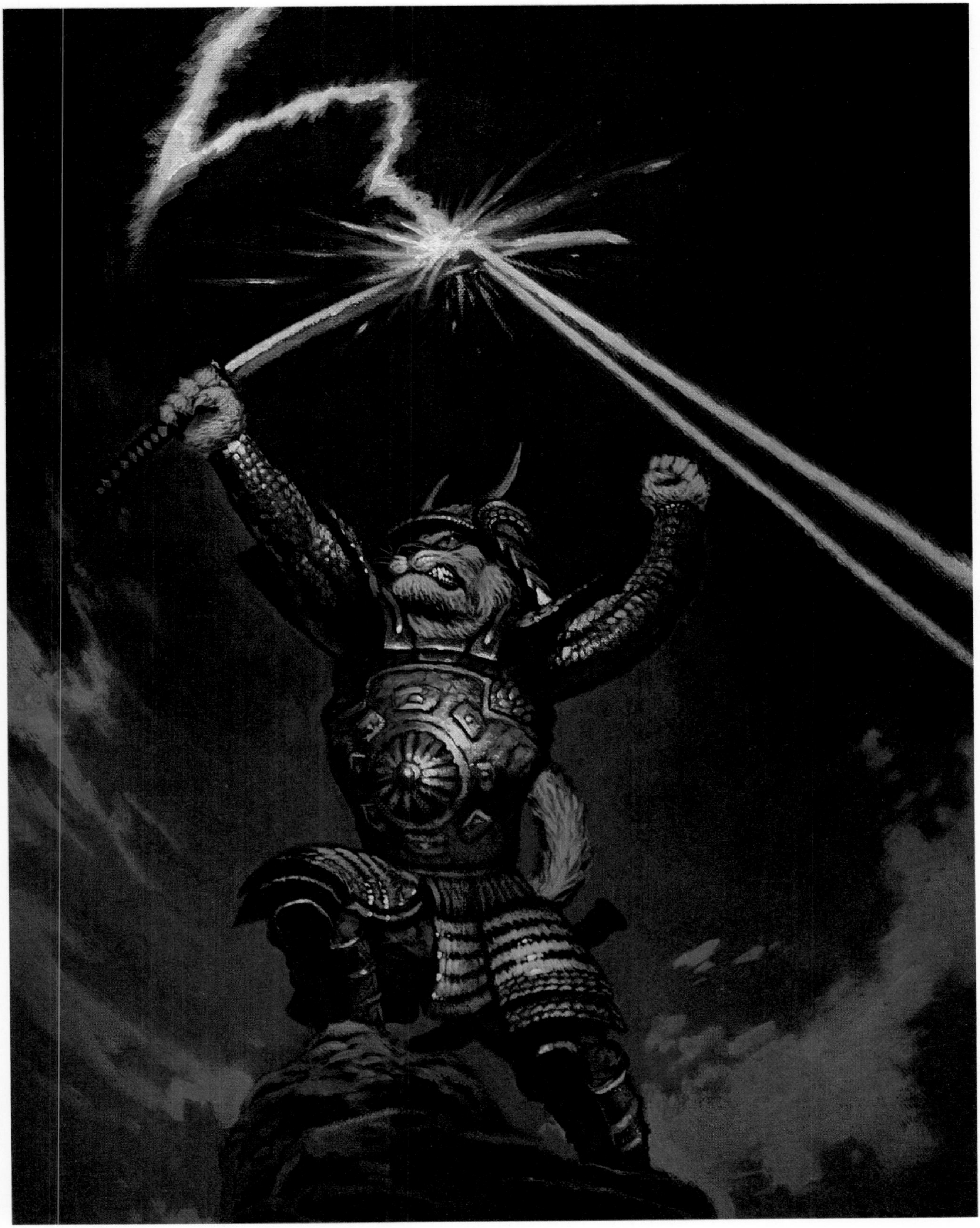

"You broke my *hammer!*" he shrieked at last, between his fingers.

Tomokato shrugged.

"You won't get away with this!" Thor blustered. "I'll carve the blood-eagle on your back, you little bastard! I'll drink your heart's blood from your own skull! I'll *sue!*"

"My lawyer's name is Tsotumo Yakamura," Tomokato answered calmly, unflappably. "He's in the Kyoto white pages."

Thor bellowed an oath, reined about, and rumbled back up toward the mountain-top.

Tomokato watched him dwindle in the distance, then leaped from the crag back over to the main cliff-wall. Ever upward he pressed, finally reaching the weathered, half-crumbled ruins of a road, much like the one he had trod on the other mountain. All but destroyed as it was, it provided more than enough walking room for a cat; he made much better progress. Before long he came to the mountain's top, and found himself confronted by vast cut-stone walls. A great tower-flanked barbican stood in the midst, but the gate beneath it had been completely sealed with granite blocks. A huge board was bolted to the blocks, with runes blazoned on it in faded, cracking red paint:

Gate closed for repairs. Use front door. A series of arrows pointed to the right. Tomokato followed them. He wondered why there was no shooting at him from the battlements. The inhabitants of Asgard had certainly known he was coming. But perhaps the ringing sounds of battle that kept reaching his ears had something to do with it.

As he strode along, he heard an astonishingly loud shriek. Looking up, he saw an armored warrior, back turned to him, standing atop a battlement. The man was riddled with arrows, and seemed to be pointing to his head again and again, almost as if the archers had missed a spot, and he wanted their oversight corrected. Momentarily he stopped screaming, bellowed *thanks!*, resumed his shriek, and pitched backward from the wall. As he spun end over end to the stones, Tomokato noticed that his face was written with a strange kind of exultation, and also that there was an arrow buried fletching-deep between his eyes. The fellow hit the ground with a great echoing thump. The sound (and the scream leading up to it) seemed peculiarly magnified, as if there was something about the acoustics of this place that led to extremely dramatic sound effects.

Tomokato continued on his way. He noticed

that the sounds of battle from within were getting steadily more ferocious. Finally, rounding the base of an enormous tower that stood somewhat out-thrust from the walls, he came upon the front gate. It was warded by a single warrior, cased in mail, nine feet tall; he did not see Tomokato, since he was watching the carnage inside the walls, shouting encouragements to the men battling within, flinching whenever he saw a truly murderous blow being dealt, gesturing with one mailed fist. Tomokato came up behind him, looking at the combatants beyond. There seemed to be two teams, one with red armbands, the other with blue; but the teammates seemed almost as willing to kill each other as their nominal opponents. And despite the blood spewing everyplace, and the severed heads and arms flying through the air, and the internal organs flopping like dying plucked crimson chickens on the pave, everyone seemed to be having a wonderful time. All appeared to have devoted a lot of study to the theory and practice of flamboyant dying, squeezing their wounds to wring every last bit of gore out before they fell, bleeding at the mouth with astounding gusto, sliding animal bones up under their armor to give their opponents' weapons extra crunch

when they struck, as well as large bladders of artificial blood for extra splat. They took gigantic bounds when they were hit, shrieking, roaring really clever dying words; many of the wounded deliberately climbed up on the battlements and hurled themselves off, or waited until a sword or axe would send them down in magnificent scarlet-streaming swan-dives.

Covered with blood, face lit with childish delight, a burly hero disengaged himself from the fighting and ran over to the gate-ward, shouting to be heard over the preposterously loud battle-racket: "Ten marks on the blue, Heimdall."

"You got it, Svipdag," Heimdall answered, and recorded the bet in a little black book.

Svipdag turned to run back, then said over his shoulder, "What's that cat doing behind you?"

"Cat?" Heimdall demanded, turning.

But Tomokato had already slipped past him and Svipdag, rushing into the courtyard. A horn brayed behind him, and instantly all the fighting ceased. Heimdall's voice split the silence:

"Condition Red! Intruder Alert! Get that Goddamn cat!"

Tomokato drew his *katana* and *wakazashi*, waded into the byrnied giants who were already

closing ranks against him. Snarling bearded faces hemmed him close. Swords and axes lashed at him. Spears licked at his throat, and arrows pierced the *Kuwagata* of his helm. But his swords whirled and spun, wheels of death, and neither armor nor flesh nor bone withstood him; he ripped through his opponents like a screaming cannonball, splitting helms, shivering roundshields; on either side of the bloody lane he cut, three ranks and more, men toppled, slain by fragments of steel and splinters of wood from the armor and shields he shattered. He crossed the courtyard, reached a doorway, looked back briefly at the grisly results of his fury and skill. Appalled by his ferocity, the surviving warriors were holding back, their faces pale with awe and dread.

"What a stud," they intoned in a low leaden chorus.

Footbeats rolled up the corridor toward him. Three men were charging at him. Wiping and sheathing his *wakazashi*, he raced to meet them. Three two-handed *katana*-strokes whistled keenly, and the men went down. But there were more behind them, pounding single-file along the passage. Tomokato continued his headlong rush, taking them one at a time, a sprinting butchershop,

a rampaging Japanese *abbattoir*, carving and slicing with the preternatural precision of a Benihana chef. The hall behind him was littered with corpses, minced like so many tempura shrimp.

He burst into a huge audience chamber. Guards surged at him from all sides. He laid them out in a matter of seconds, then looked around. There were no other takers.

Clad in a sky-blue mantle, a gigantic whitebeard sat calmly in a towering throne at the far end of the hall. A spear was across his knees; on his shoulders perched the two ravens that had spotted Tomokato on the mountain-crag. Thor stood off to the side, looking agitated.

"That's the one!" he cried, pointing at Tomokato, who was advancing slowly across the floor, blood dripping from his sword. "That's the one who broke my hammer!"

"Who's in charge here?" Tomokato demanded.

A small figure in helm and mail appeared from a doorway on the left, and made toward the throne, byrny-hem dragging on the floor. "He is," it piped, struggling to lift a mail-weighted arm in the direction of the whitebeard.

"I know that voice. . . ." Tomokato muttered

to himself, pausing.

"That's Odin," the small figure continued. "King of the Gods."

Tomokato, hardly heeding the words, started as he recognized the voice. Rushing forward, he plucked the helmet from the dwarfish shape.

"Shiro!" he cried.

"Uncle-*san!*" Shiro answered. "Glad to see you finally made it. I still want you to teach me about *Bushido,* you know."

"But how did you get *here?*" Tomokato said, exasperated.

"I saved up my allowance," Shiro replied.

Tomokato groaned.

"Ahem," Odin said.

Tomokato looked up, studying the god's face. It was set and impassive. The right eye was missing, its lid sagging limp over the empty socket. The other glittered with strange, inscrutable purpose.

"I take it you know my retainer there?" Odin said.

"He's my nephew."

"He's also one of my most fearsome warriors."

Tomokato was incredulous. "Really?"

"He works great wonders through sheer an-

noyance."

Tomokato shrugged. Perhaps it did make sense after all. . . .

"In any case," Odin said, "what can I do for you?"

"I've come to kill Ketil and Halfdan Jormunreksson," Tomokato answered. "They aided in the slaying of my lord Nobunaga, and I demand vengeance. Call them in here, or I'll take this fortress of yours apart, and you with it."

Shiro laughed with delight as he heard the threat. "Splendid, uncle!"

Odin gave him a frigid stare.

"Yes, I know I'm your retainer," Shiro explained. "But he is my uncle, after all."

Odin returned his gaze to Tomokato. "I doubt you could kill me, cat," he said. "My death won't come till Ragnarok, the last day, and only the Fenris Wolf can inflict it. Likewise Asgard won't fall till then. But as I love to watch a good fight, I'll summon Ketil; though you may find him too much to handle."

"I'll take the risk," Tomokato answered. "But what about Halfdan?"

"He's not here. When the Valkyries brought him, he decided he'd rather fight on the side of

the giants. The last I heard, he was over the Rainbow Bridge and into Jotunheim."

"All right then," Tomokato said. "I'll settle for his brother — for the time being."

Odin nodded his grimly regal head, and picked up the microphone for his P.A. system.

"Attention, attention," he began. "This is Odin, Lord of the Hanged. Ketil Jormunreksson, report to the Throne-Room, on the double."

Ketil arrived before long, shouldering his way into the hall, which was already partially filled with warriors who had followed the cat (at a very respectful distance) from the courtyard. The viking, clad in a scale-shirt and a rivetted spangen-helm, bearing a tremendous rune-warded linden roundshield and a huge gold-hilted sword, approached the throne. Blue eyes shone beneath the rim of his helm. His beard and moustache flamed red. He stood well over seven feet tall, broad-

shouldered, long-limbed.

Odin indicated Tomokato with a nod. "Where were you when this cat hacked his way through the courtyard, Ketil?"

"Out back. Had a little altercation with Gunnar of Hlidarend and Bodhvar-Bjarki. Took me a while. I decided to even the odds and let 'em both try me at once."

"With Bjarki in bear-shape?" Odin asked. Bjarki was a famous shape-changer.

"Of course," Ketil said. "Smeared 'em both anyway. Why'd you call me here?"

"The cat says you killed his lord," Odin answered. "He wants vengeance."

Ketil grinned good-naturedly at Tomokato. "Hoo now. Does he really? Must be Miaowara Tomokato, I think."

Tomokato bowed.

"And you're going to be sorry you ever met

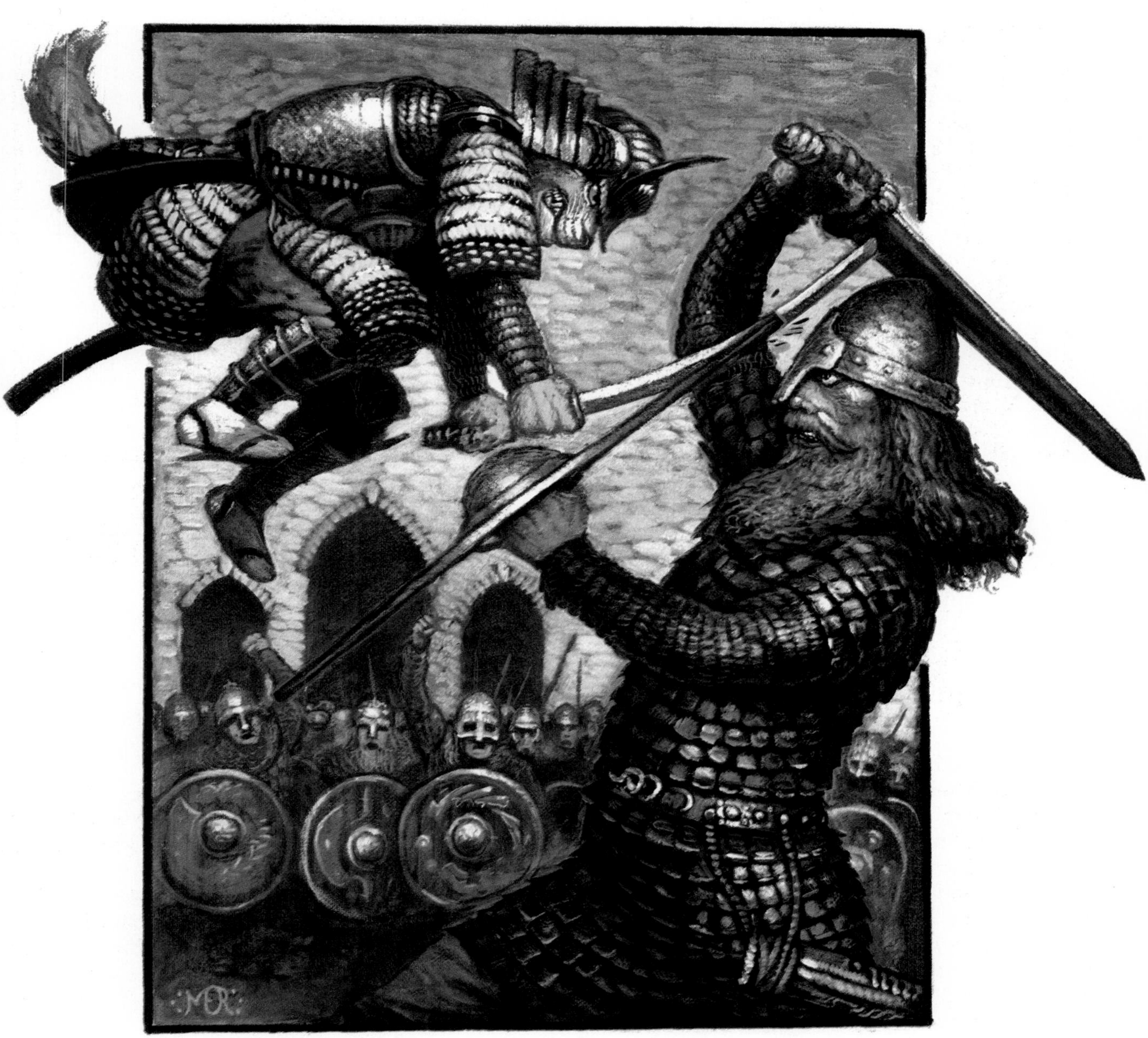

him!" shrilled Shiro from someplace.

"We'll see," Ketil said, and began swinging his sword lazily to and fro, backing slowly away from the cat, raising his shield.

Tomokato followed, growling low in his throat, padding towards him. Shrieking, spitting, he leaped, sword singing down at Ketil's head. Ketil dodged. The *katana* hissed through empty space. Landing, whirling, the cat struck mightily at Ketil's legs. With astonishing speed and agility, Ketil launched his armored body upward, bounding over the blow. Tomokato bounded up too, hacking at his neck. Ketil parried the blow with his shield, and brought a murderous stroke against the side of the cat's helm. Tomokato spun sideways through the air, head over heels, landing on his feet, a glaze of numbness spreading over his mind. He felt blood crawling down his scalp, but he guessed his helmet-plates had held under Ketil's blow. The viking, meanwhile, gave him no chance to rest. Ketil pivotted and bore down roaring, sword looping in a vicious whistling figure-eight. Tomokato jumped over the first slash, ducked beneath the next. He managed to land a blow against Ketil's side, cutting through armor to the flesh beneath, but not piercing the ribcage. Ketil shouted with pain, kicked him in the chest, sent him rolling across the floor. Clattering to a halt, turning, Tomokato fought back up to one knee just in time to fend off a glittering slash aimed at his shoulder. Ketil's sword spanged away, sprang back keening. Rising, Tomokato took a shallow cut below the knee that ripped through his lacquered shin-guard, and replied with a wicked slice that bloodied Ketil's right forearm. Ketil retreated, panting. Tomokato watched him warily, holding back for the time being, surprised by Ketil's skill and strength. Never before had he fought an opponent of such mettle.

Ketil shouted and barrelled in again, laying on mightily. Tomokato snarled, meeting the onslaught stroke for stroke. They feinted and parried and smote, oaths and curses exploding from their lips. Back and forth they pounded. Steel blazing, belling, they circled and slashed. The cat reduced much of Ketil's shield to splinters, tore great rents in the viking's scale-shirt. Ketil wounded Tomokato several more times. The floor was splattered with the cat's blood. Still Tomokato fought on, disdaining the pain, hacking, slicing. Finally he managed to knock the mangled shield from Ketil's all-but numb grip. Ketil responded with a blow that flipped the cat backwards to the floor, breastplate dented, wind knocked out. Ketil moved in for the kill, raising his brand. Gasping, the cat jerked up into a sitting position, and lunged, slamming the *katana* up under Ketil's mail-scales, driving it into his body. Ketil staggered back, grunting with pain as the cat wrenched his blade free. The viking swayed and fell. His eyes rolled up.

Tomokato got painfully to his feet. Looking down at his fallen foe, he eyed him with both respect and regret, sorry that he had had to slay such a valiant warrior. Shouts and applause rang from the bystanders, but he was oblivious.

After a time, Odin rose to quiet his followers, and strode down toward the cat, trailed by a sullen-looking Thor.

"Miaowara Tomokato," he said, "never have I seen such a display of swordsmanship. You're obviously a hero of the first magnitude, to have slain Ketil Jormunreksson, and I extend to you this honor — to fight by my side on Ragnarok, when the gods and giants will meet for the final time, and the universe will burst asunder." He paused. "The pay's really good. I'll match any offer."

Tomokato shook his head. "My quarrel's not with the giants," he panted, "only with Halfdan Jormunreksson. And after he's slain, I have other murderers to track down."

Odin smiled coldly, ruefully. "Pity," he said, reading the determination in the cat's eyes, realizing there would be no point in trying further to persuade him. "In the meantime, though, you should enjoy my hospitality — for tonight at least. One thing we do know how to do here in Asgard is party."

The idea did not much appeal to Tomokato, not only because of his ascetic preferences, but also because he did not want to set a bad example to Shiro. Still, a look out a nearby window told him that night was coming on. The torches in the hall had been lit.

"I'll stay the night," he said, "provided you tell me how to find Halfdan in the morning."

"Of course," Odin said.

"But he broke my hammer!" Thor whined behind him.

"Shhh," hissed the King of the Gods.

Tomokato felt a great heavy hand come down on his shoulder. He turned to find himself staring up at the friendly, smiling face of Ketil Jormunreksson!

"It was an honor to be killed by you," the viking said.

"But... but how..." Tomokato sputtered.

"Asgard's a wonderful place," Ketil answered. "Tailor-made for heroes. We spend the days hacking each other to pieces, then come back to life when night falls, and feast until dawn — and so it'll be till Ragnarok."

Tomokato muttered a curse, stepped back, clapped both hands to his hilt.

"Come now," Ketil said cheerfully, "what good will it do for you to fight me again? Even if you win — and you might not — I'll only come back to life. And consider this: you've fulfilled your obligation. You killed me. What more do you want?"

Tomokato eyed him narrowly, chewing his lip, pondering the Norseman's arguments.

"I bear you no ill will," Ketil went on. "I admire you too much. Shouldn't we be friends?"

It makes sense, Tomokato thought. He shrugged and bowed. "Indeed we should, Ketil-*san,*" he agreed.

Ketil roared laughter and clapped him mightily on the back.

"Uncle!" Shiro cried in horror, running up to Tomokato. "Let him have it!"

Tomokato looked hard at him. "You know, Shiro," he said sternly, "if you want to become a true samurai, you must realize that a warrior's glory lies in fulfilling his duty, not in killing."

Shiro got a pained look on his young face. "Yeah, but killing's the fun part."

"Your nephew's going to go far," Ketil told Tomokato solemnly.

"All right then!" cried Odin nearby. "Let's get down to some serious drinking! Roll out the barrel — "

"And we'll have a barrel of fun!" thundered the gods and heroes, as they obviously had a hundred million times before. Colossal oaken benches swung down from the walls like elvish Murphy beds, and were thronged in a second. Gigantic aluminum kegs appeared from nowhere, and were soon gushing rivers of Michelob *kvass* and Budweiser light mead into hundreds of beakers gripped in eager hands. Cooked hogs dropped with great heavy splats on the trestle-tops, and were instantly assaulted by thrusting, wrenching fingers, and gleaming saxe-knives. The hall rang with song. Roistering and belching and puking, the feasters slammed their fists on the benchboards to the beat of a raucous new-wave version of the theme from *The Vikings.*

Sitting side by side, Tomokato and Ketil had places close to Odin at the long trestle-table that had appeared before the god's throne. Shiro stood guard at Odin's right hand, Norman-style helmet tilted far back on his head so that he could see, paws gripping the helve of a huge two-handed broad-axe that wobbled perilously back and forth. Tomokato took no drink, and at his request, Shiro was given none either; but in a very short time, everyone else in the hall was thoroughly, horrendously sloshed. That was when the entertainment began.

First came the championship dying finals. Elrik Bloodaxe was a heavy favorite, but Ragnar Lodbrok came from behind with an Imperial Jugular Gush, sweeping the top honors. And all the while that was going on, Hrolf Kraki was talking to Thor, who was still sulking; finally he persuaded him to do his famous Trestle Table Leap. As soon as Odin finished handing out the dying medals, Hrolf ordered a group of dwarvish thralls to set up the ramps, while Thor went to get his chariot; before long, the Thunder God came rumbling in through a service entrance, to the immense delight of the crowd, who hadn't seen this stunt in at least a hundred years. He drove his chariot up one of the ramps, whipping his goats furiously, bellowing "Allaho Akbar!" as his vehicle sailed airborne, careening over the heads of hero after hero. But he had too much *kvass,* and had miscalculated; the chariot missed the far ramp by several hundred yards, and plunged, goats and all, into a crowd of feasters with a sickening crash. The hall trembled with the storm of cheers and applause which followed.

Once the mess was cleared up, the chamber went suddenly dark. Then, from a side-archway, there came a cluster of many small lights, which moved steadily toward Odin's throne.

"One, two, three!" yelled a voice. A tremendous chorus started up:

> *"Happy birthday to you!*
> *Happy birthday to you!*
> *Happy birthday, Lord of the Ha-anged,*
> *Happy birthday to you!"*

The torches came back on again. Odin rose tearfully from his seat, staring down at the huge birthday-cake, studded with several million candles, that had been laid on the table before him.

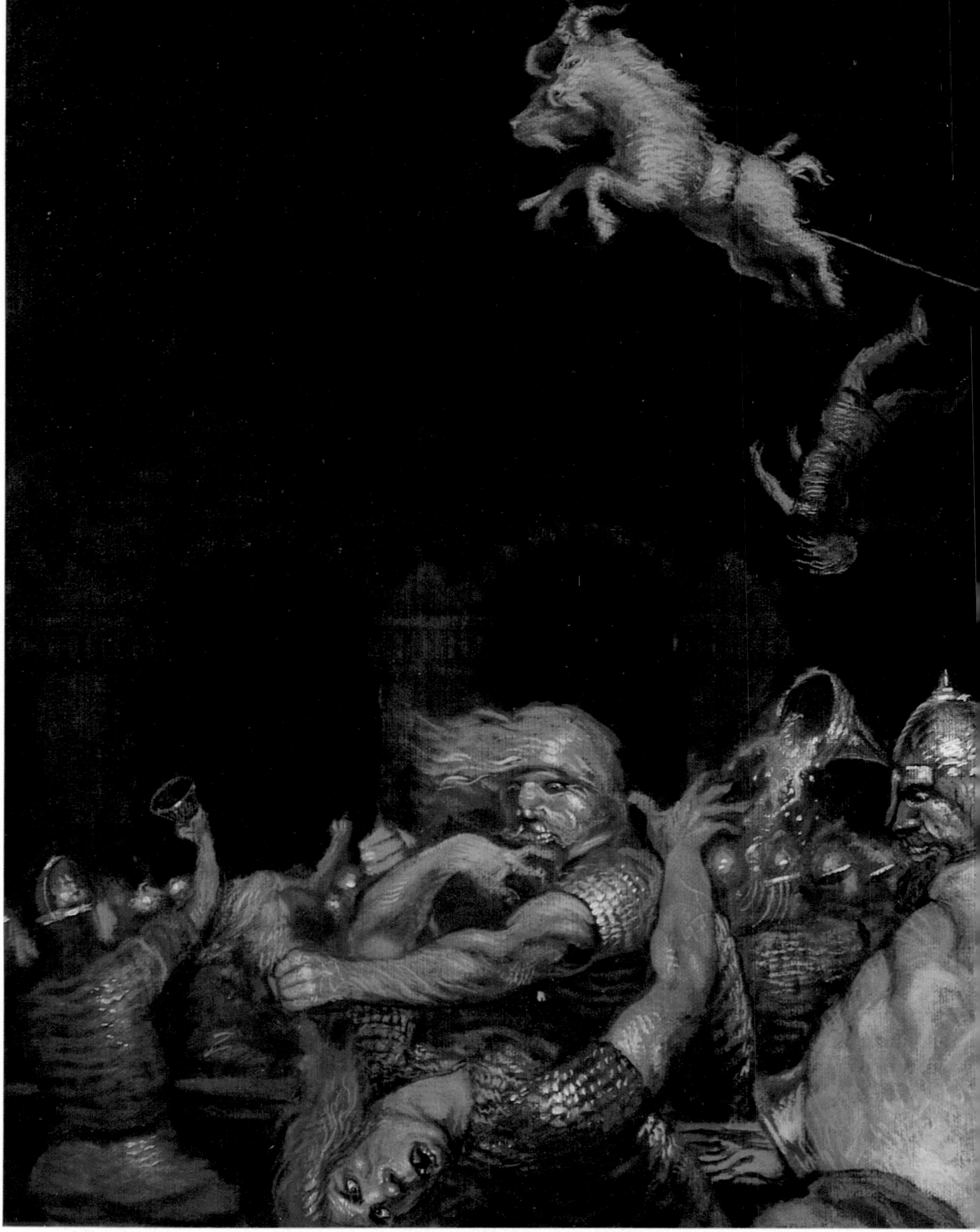

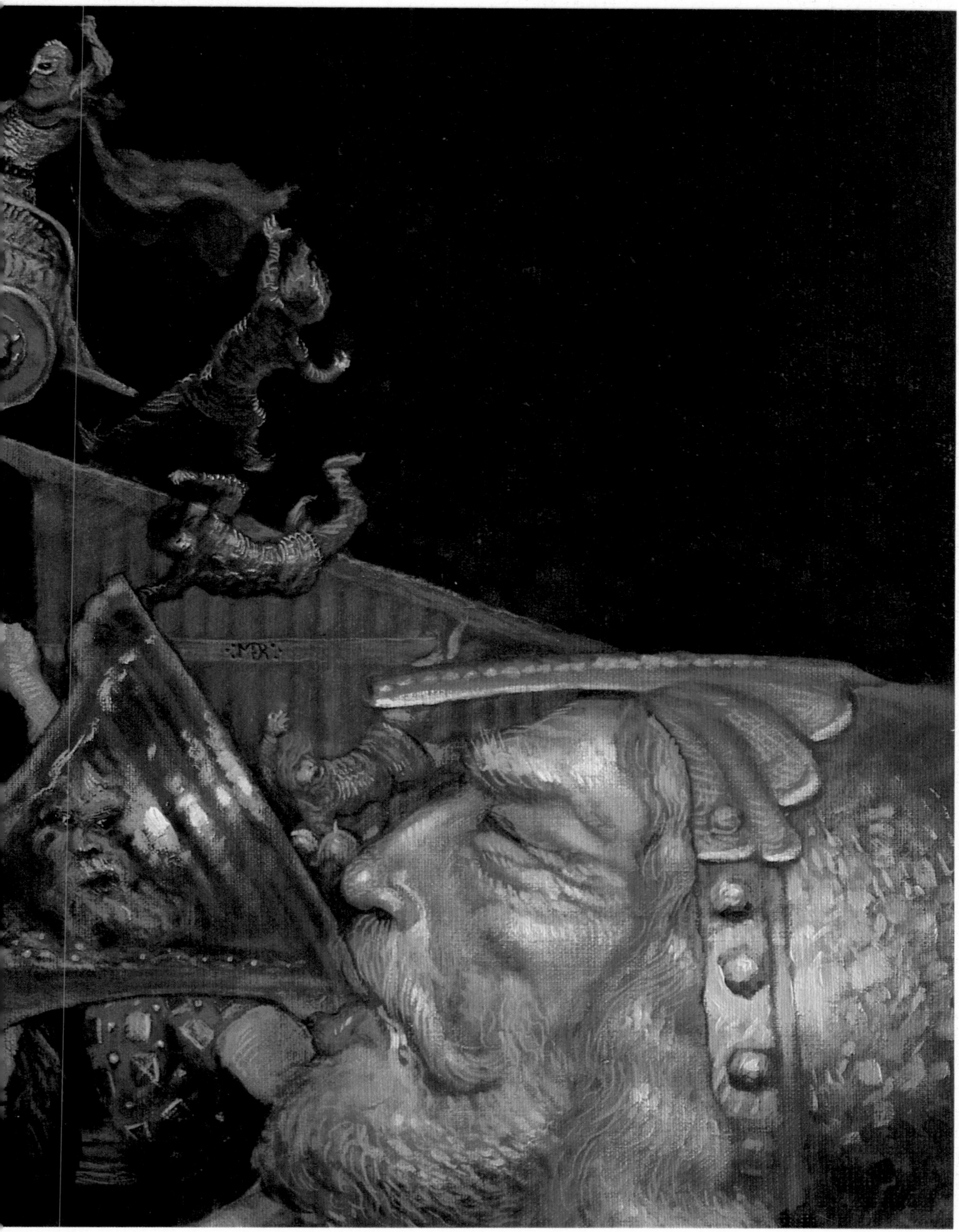

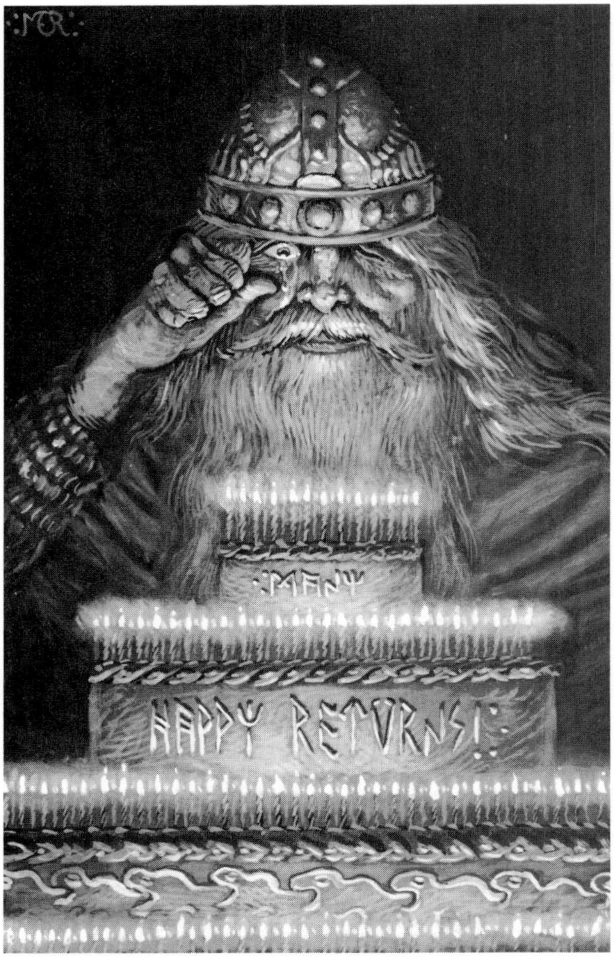
MANY
HAPPY RETURNS!

"I just don't know what to say," he began after a while. "This is really quite a surprise." He dabbed at his single eye.

"Blow out the candles!" clamored a thousand voices.

He drew himself up to his full height; the ravens fluttered on his shoulders, ashes cascading from their cigars. Leaning forward, he blew. The candles winked out like stars on doomsday, all in one shot.

The god Tyr strode up next to Odin, weaving a bit under the influence, proferring a gift-wrapped package with the prosthetic claw that had replaced his Fenris-eaten right hand.

"We passed the hat around the other day," Tyr said. "Took up a little collection."

Odin covered his face with his hand. "You shouldn't have."

"Ah, go on," Tyr urged.

"Well, why not?" Odin said, suddenly greedy. He grabbed the package, ripped it open. His face lit with delight when he saw what was inside. He took out a piece of paper and waved it. "A gift certificate to Walden's!"

"The one in Niflheim Mall," Tyr said. "We figured you'd get a big kick out of it, with your boundless thirst for wisdom and all. This way you won't have to go hanging on any more trees or popping your eyes out. For a while at least."

"Thanks a bunch," Odin said. He waved to the throng of heroes and deities, beaming. "Thanks a whole lot, guys!"

"Don't mention it," they cried.

He laughed and sat back down. The entertainment resumed. A middling-sized dragon was set loose, and Odin and Tyr and Halfdan the Black got their horses and rode about the hall hunting the beast down, to boisterous encouraging shouts from the feasters. Fritzie and June, the Valkyrie Sisters, did some Wagnerian duets. Odin, in high spirits, followed that with a rendering of Wotan's final number from the *Götterdamerung*. . . .

On and on the feast roared, deep into the night. Keg after keg was emptied. Hundreds of tons of roast pork were devoured. Heads reeled, minds grew sluggish and voices hoarse. One by one, the roisterers began to nod and fall asleep.

As the night drew on toward dawn, Ketil nudged Tomokato.

"Hoo, there, cat," he said in a slurred voice. "You haven't had a drink all night."

"I don't drink," Tomokato replied. "It's no good for the health. Also, it sets a bad example for my nephew." He looked round at Shiro. The kitten was curled up in Odin's lap, asleep. Drowsy, Odin was still awake, but refused to stir, unwilling to disturb his retainer.

"You should relax a bit," Ketil told Tomokato. "This was one hell of a party. Better than most, even for Asgard. . . . Sure hope the giants don't come tomorrow morning. We're all going to have unbelievable hangovers. . . . " He sagged forward onto the table, head clunking against the boards. Smiling stupidly, he sank into slumber.

"Good night, my friend," Tomokato said, yawning. Leaning back in his seat, folding his paws on his breastplate, he too dozed off.

It was the beam of sunlight that woke him, shining directly into his face. He opened his eyes, squinting, looking sidelong at the window through

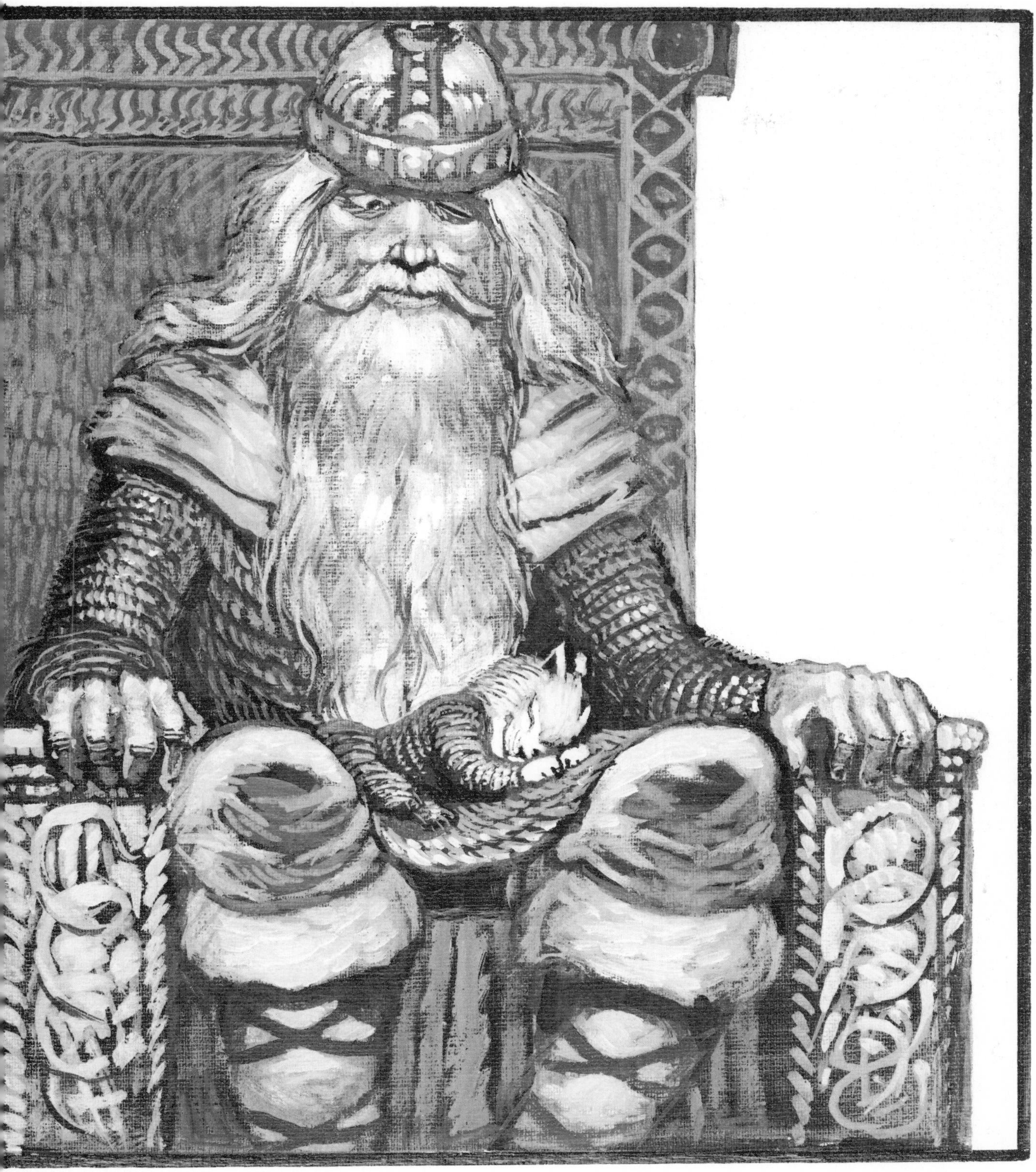

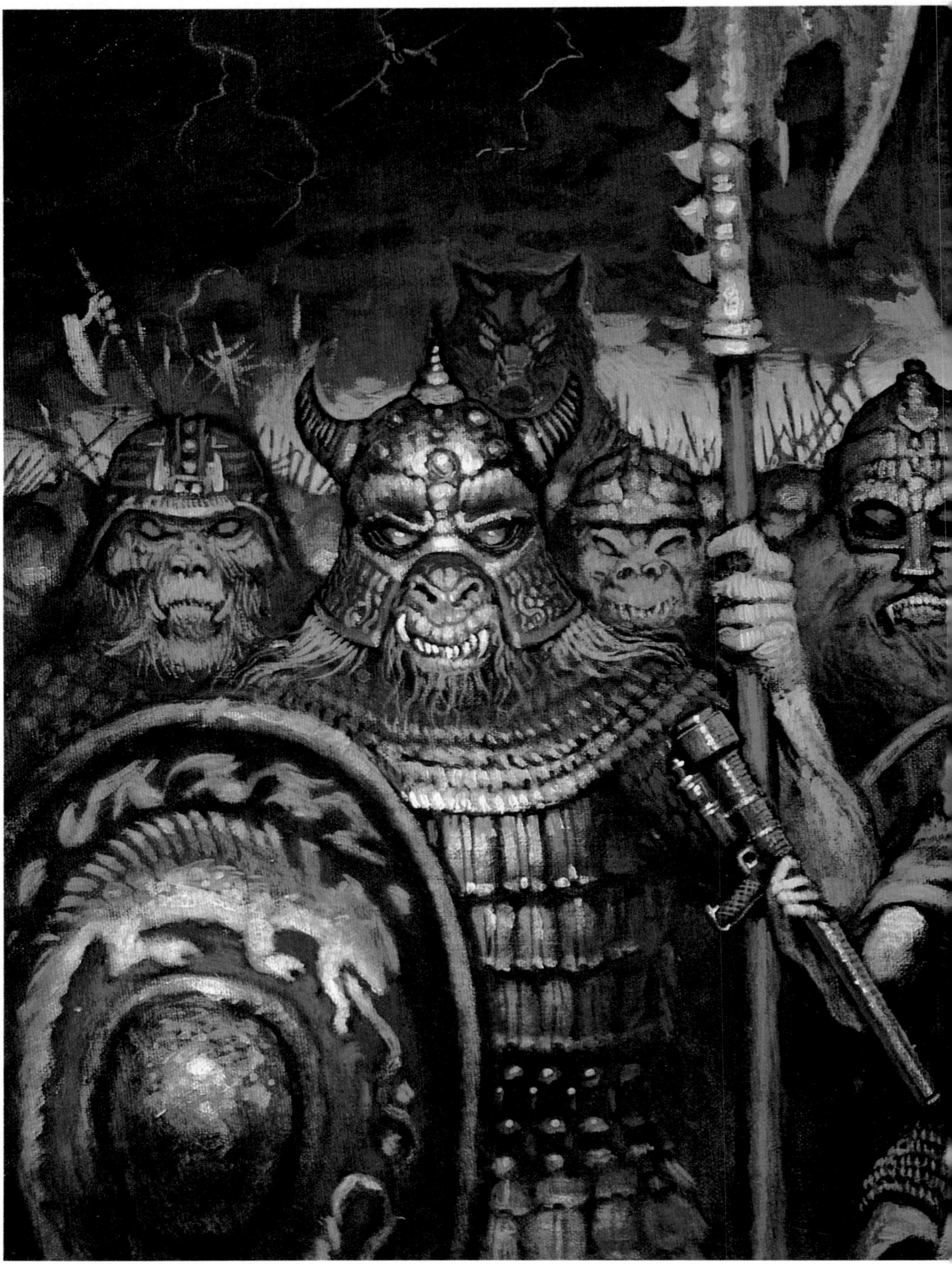

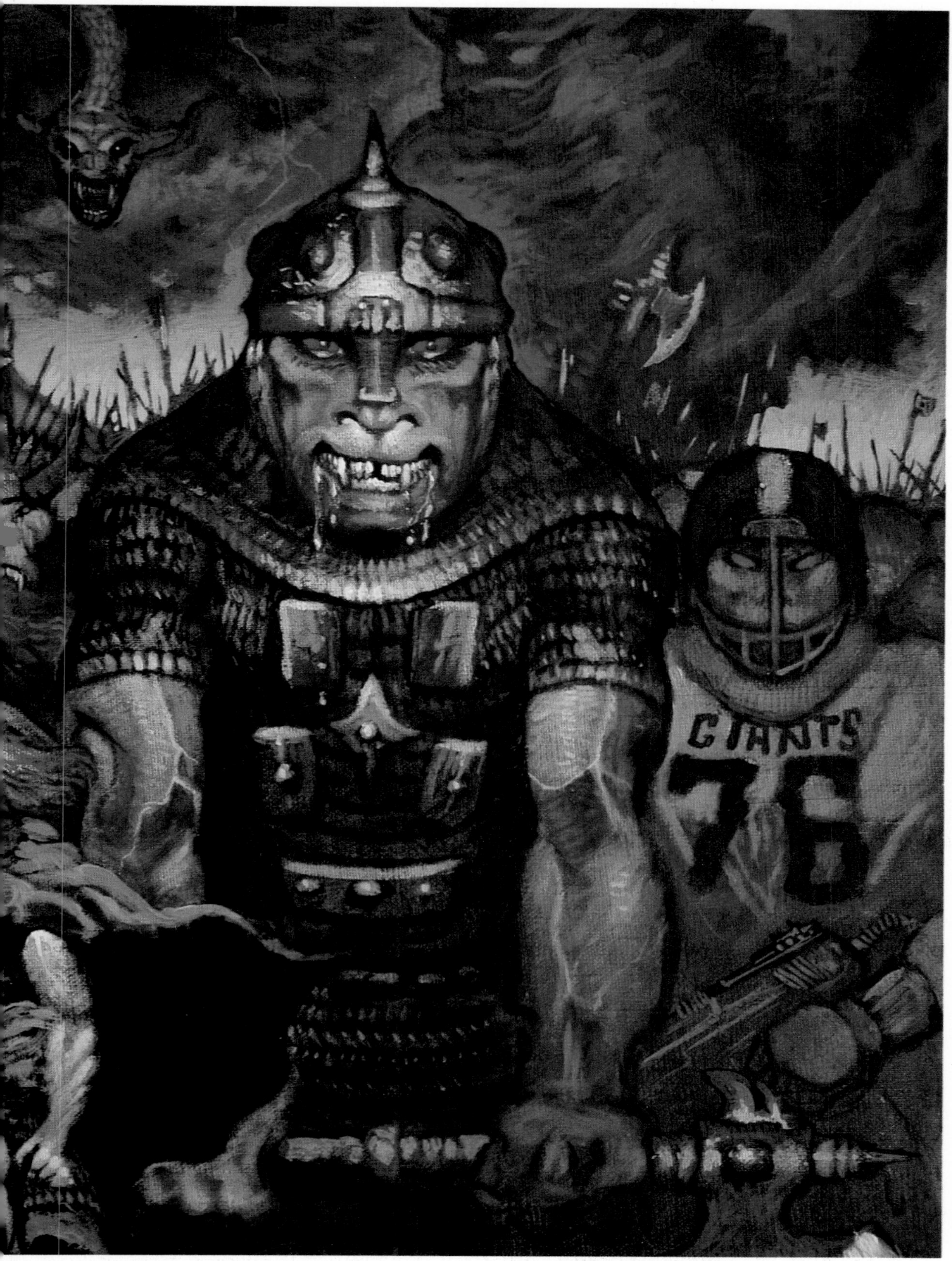
GIANTS
76

which the beam was coming. A very bright, but very cold-looking sun gleamed outside. Rags of mist fled across it, blurring its outline, followed by a dense wall of blue-black cloud that shut out the chilly glow altogether. A low growl of thunder reached Tomokato's ears.

He looked around the hall. The place was littered with sleeping revellers. None stirred.

The thunder rumbled again. He heard Shiro stir beside him, a dry jingle of sliding mail.

"Uncle?" the kitten said from Odin's lap. "I had a bad dream. . . ."

Tomokato looked at him, then at the King of the Gods. Odin was utterly out. The cat noticed that the deity's ravens were not perched on his shoulders. Tomokato wondered where they were; but not for long.

There came a sound of hurrying wings. He turned. The ravens had swept in through the window, and were speeding toward him, cigars hanging from the corners of their mouths, streaming smoky contrails.

"Odin!" they cried. "My Lord, wake up!" They circled desperately around the throne, shouting, trying to rouse the god. He remained in his stupor. So did the other gods and heroes, despite the ravens' echoing cries.

"What's wrong?" Tomokato demanded.

"The giants are coming!" the birds answered. "They're marching on the Rainbow Bridge even now, Surtur, the Midgard Serpent, the Fenris Wolf. . . ."

"And Halfdan Jormunreksson?" Tomokato asked sharply.

"He's with them too. The only human in their army. . . ."

Tomokato stood up, smiling. Halfdan was being delivered directly into his hands.

"Can I go with you, uncle?" Shiro asked, jumping down from Odin's lap, collapsing under the weight of his armor as he hit the floor.

"No," Tomokato snapped, and headed from the hall, picking a swift path over and between the besotted hulks snoring in his path. Within minutes, he arrived at Asgard's front gate. Off to the side, he noticed Heimdall's serene, bearded face sticking up out of a small mountain of crumpled malt-liquor cans; ahead stretched Bifrost, the Rainbow Bridge. Beyond Bifrost seethed a solid wall of blue-grey cloud. It was very dark and thick, but from time to time, he thought he could make out things even darker moving slowly, ponder-

ously, inside it. Except for the intermittent rumble of the thunder, there was no sound, save perhaps for a horrible high-pitched distant laughter that he was not even sure he heard — at first. Gradually, almost imperceptibly, the laughter grew louder, and lower in timber. It became plain that it was being sounded in many, perhaps hundreds, perhaps thousands, of throats. It swelled steadily in force and depth, becoming at last a volcanic roar that made his ribs vibrate, and his heart labor, and his ears throb with pain.

Lightning flashed, ripping at the cloud-wall ahead, piercing it in spots. He thought he could make out huge, misshapen faces leering out through the gaps; but before he could be sure, the holes would always close. The laughter grew louder and louder, reaching a titanic crescendo. . . . Then silence fell, ringing and terrible. Not even the thunder growled.

He felt wind sweeping in from the North, a fierce cold wind, yet utterly quiet. The cloud wall was swept away. Lining the clifftop on the far side of Bifrost, rank and rank after rank, stood a soundless host of giants and monstrosities, horrors without number. Talons twitched on the hilts of great, serrate swords, on the helves of gargantuan morningstars, on the triggers of outsized Lewis machine guns and *panzerfausts;* two-headed dragons manned titan crossbows from the hatches of immense steam-powered tanks with spike-studded treads. Voiceless lightning shone from grotesque armor, gleamed on curving fangs. Lurid fire glowed in eyes deep-sunken beneath overhanging gristly brows. Savage hooked spear-blades waved slowly back and forth above the inhuman horde, as did long black banners marked with grim red runes of death. And rearing out of the midst of that terrifying army were three monstrous shapes, huger by far than any of the rest. . . .

Fenrir the Wolf. Hel-Hound, Odin-Slayer.

The Midgard Serpent. The Doomsday Noose that lies looped about the Earth, Thor's Bane.

Surtur the Fire-Giant. Slayer of Worlds, the Ultimate Destroyer.

"Looks like you've got your work cut out for you, uncle," said Shiro at Tomokato's side.

"I told you to stay behind," Tomokato said.

"But I did. All the way here."

Iron horns blared on the other side, belling forth a single strident note. The giant ranks parted. Out onto the bridge rode a tall man dressed in blue and black, mounted on a pale, skeletal horse. As he drew closer to the cat, Tomokato noticed a distinct resemblance to Ketil. The rider halted some distance away, hand upraised in a token of parley.

"I am Field Marshall Halfdan Jormunreksson," he cried, "Herald of Reichsführer Fenrir Lokisson, and Special Attaché to our beloved Chancellor and Führer Surtur Von Muspellheim. I bring you one message, and one message only. We of the Greater Jotunheim Co-Prosperity Sphere demand the unconditional surrender of Asgard and all other territories now claimed by the so-called Aesir and Vanir, territories which rightfully belong to those of Pure Blood, who are now painfully short of *Lebensraum.* We will give you ten minutes to deliver our message and bring back the reply."

Tomokato never stirred.

Halfdan looked at his watch. "You'd better get moving, lackey," he advised.

"I'm no lackey," Tomokato replied. "I serve no master, though I have one to avenge: My Lord Tokugawa Nobunaga."

Halfdan smiled wickedly. "Miaowara Tomokato," he said. "Fugu Otoko told me about you."

"But not enough," Shiro yelled, "or you'd have killed yourself long ago!"

Halfdan ignored him, still eyeing Tomokato. "I take it you're not going to deliver our ultimatum," he said.

"Get back inside the walls," Tomokato told Shiro, and drew his *wakazashi* and *katana* in a blaze of steel.

Halfdan barked a scornful laugh.

Tomokato responded with a wild shriek and sped toward him. The viking wheeled his mount around and galloped back toward the giant lines. He disappeared inside a gap in the shieldwall before Tomokato could catch him.

The cat never slackened his headlong, screaming rush. A troll in lorica armor and a dragonhide forage cap bellowed an order. Guns and crossbows trained on Tomokato. Slugs and darts began to fly. Tomokato plunged straight on into that whistling barrage; his blades whickered and spun, deflecting bullets and quarrels and arrows and spears, shearing through casting-axes and boulders tied to tree-branches, brushing aside fire from flame-throwers, disarming cruise missiles in midair. Even before he reached his foes, a huge swarth of them had been cut down by

the debris and shrapnel ricocheting from his blades; over their bleeding bodies he leaped, slicing, slashing, lopping off a clawed hand here, a pinion there, ripping the front wheels out from under a mail-sheathed *Schwerwehrmachtschlepper* filled with Jotunheim Waffen SS. An ice-giant charged him; he severed its truss. Grappling with a triple hernia, the creature toppled backward with a shriek, crushing a battalion of dwarf giants from Spitzbergen.

Monstrosity after monstrosity fell to Tomokato's blades. Multicolored gore flew by the bucketful. Before long, the entire landscape for miles around looked as though it had been doused in a thousand varieties of plastigoop. Swords and axes whipped in at the cat were instantly parried. His swords seemed to be everywhere at once. A platoon of the First Muspel Grenadiers drove in at him, thrusting with fifty-foot long sarissas; bounding into the air, dodging and twisting, he avoided each razored spear-point, allowing the grenadiers to impale a troop of arachnoid Teutonic Knights who were even then thundering in on him from behind. Full steam ahead, the battleships *Bismarck* and *Tirpitz* closed from left and right, bows ripping through the rocky ground as though it had been butter, sending stone fragments flying. Tomokato twisted aside, and they veered to avoid colliding with each other. Dashing back toward the *Tirpitz*, hewing a bloody path through trolls and dragonmen, he went up the anchorchain like a monkey, both swords clenched between his teeth; racing along the rail, he came up amidships before the two battlewagons could pass each other; yelling and screaming, he attracted the attention of the gunners on the *Bismarck*, and clambered back over the side on a rope just as the *Bismarck's* turrets cut loose, blasting all-but pointblank into the *Tirpitz's* superstructure. Thoroughly annoyed, the surviving gunners on the *Tirpitz* replied in kind. Tomokato was some distance away, performing unwanted surgery on a Kraken, when both ships' magazines went, taking fully a third of the giant army, reaping misshapen soldiers with fire and shrapnel and concussion.

Still there was no shortage of foes for Tomokato. He was the whirling, slashing center of a maelstrom of carnage for well over an hour. But at last the giants and monsters began to retreat, dragging their mangled tanks and motte-and-bailey fortresses behind them.

Tomokato eyed them, drawing deep breaths, staying where he was for the moment, gathering his strength for a new charge deep into their ranks. He spat out some of the troll and dragon blood that had splashed into his mouth. Oddly enough, the mixture tasted rather like Russian dressing.

Looking over the heads of the monstrosities before him, he saw that Fenrir and the Serpent and Surtur had not moved; they seemed to be conferring among themselves. Surtur nodded to the wolf; Fenrir started forward, rushing heedlessly over followers and allies, the earth shaking under his tread, crushed bodies exploding into the air around him as he ran. Tomokato readied himself to receive his charge, blinking sweat from his eyes. Bursting through a wall of gigantic Icelandic Airlines stewardesses armed with Lochaber axes, the wolf launched himself high into the air, arcing down at the cat, jaws spread. Tomokato's steel hissed and flashed; darkness settled horribly over him as the jaws scooped him up. The wolf gulped him down as though he had been nothing more than an oriental hors d'oeuvre.

The onlookers saw Fenrir turn, grinning. Rising back on his massive hindlegs, he raised his paws over his head in a gesture of victory. A hurricane of cheers rose from the giant host.

His grin faded. A look of puzzlement and

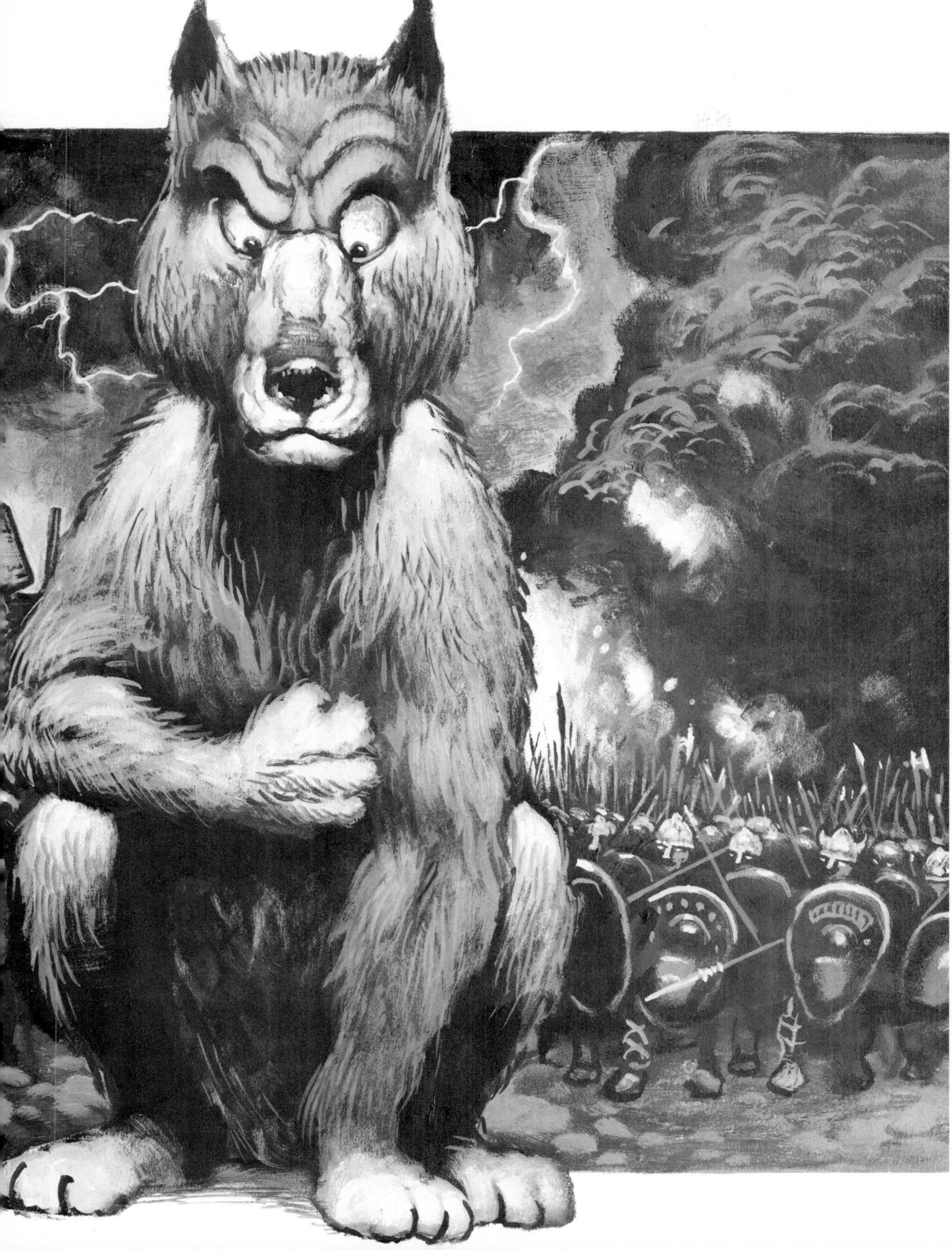

slight discomfort replaced it, almost as if he had felt a twinge of indigestion. He lowered his paws, put one to his stomach. The look of discomfort twisted into a grimace. Loosing a ferocious howl, he toppled on his flank. An instant later, Tomokato chopped his way out of the wolf's belly in a crimson explosion, running forward to escape the stench of the half-digested Alpo that filled Fenrir's stomach.

The giants swore and muttered with dismay, but the Midgard Serpent was not cowed. Its titanic hiss reached the cat's ears, and he looked up to see it moving to the attack, slithering ponderously forward through the giant ranks. Tomokato turned and climbed up on Fenrir's gigantic corpse, taking his stand atop the wolf's shoulder. Loop upon loop, the snake rumbled closer and closer, horned head swaying, huge round eyes staring balefully, soullessly, mouth wagging open like the gate of Hell. Unhurriedly it coiled itself around Fenrir's corpse, head circling ever nearer to the cat. Tomokato pivotted slowly, watching it warily. Finally, its snout not twenty feet from him, it paused. He could feel the foul pulse of its breath on his face, saw greenish venom drooling thickly from its fangs. The serpent gave something that sounded like a hissing laugh, and jerked its head back, staring down at Tomokato from a great height. One droplet at a time, it began to spit venom at him. He dodged and ducked and leaped. When the droplets struck Fenrir's hide, they swiftly ate large smoking holes in it.

The serpent continued this game for some time, until the dead wolf was fairly well pitted. Then, without warning, the great head shot downward, jaws gaping, not to swallow, but to impale and poison. . . .

Tomokato's *katana* glittered as it sheared the air, severing the serpent's fangs. Two more blinding strokes slashed deep into the monster's lower jaw. Hissing in agony, the snake jerked back, trailing venom from its tooth-stumps. Convulsively it opened and shut its mouth several times in quick succession; venom sloshed into the wounds in its jaw. The serpent was not immune to its own poison, as Tomokato had guessed. The deadly fluid seared the reptile's blood, spreading through its body. A long spasm shuddered down the great scaly trunk, and the huge tail thrashed and beat; the horned head sank down, eyes glazed with approaching death.

Climbing back atop Fenrir's corpse, Tomokato heard a roar of rage and hate, and looked out across the giant army. Surtur was coming, a vast dark shape wrapped in flame, sweeping a fiery sword from side to side, pounding thunderously forward, his demoralized underlings trying to scurry from his path.

Tomokato looked back over his shoulder, spotted a swastika-marked ammunition truck he had disabled in his first charge. It was surrounded by craters from cannon-shells. He ran down toward it, clambering over the coils of the serpent. It galled him to retreat, but he knew he could not hope to stand against Surtur's fire. . . .

The burning giant followed juggernaut-like, bellowing, footbeats falling with bone-jarring thumps. Tomokato reached the truck, turned. Surtur closed in, cocked his sword back to strike. Tomokato planted his feet, snarling up at him. The giant's blade whooshed down, trailing long boiling sheets of flame.

At the last moment, Tomokato dashed aside, streaking for one of the shell-holes with all the speed at his command. Surtur could not check his blow; the fiery sword ripped through the ammunition truck, and there was an earth-rocking blast just as Tomokato dived into the crater. Fragments of truck rained down all around him, and several pages from an old issue of *Penthouse*. Surtur sounded an immense howl.

When the debris stopped falling, Tomokato uncovered his head and rushed to the rim of the crater. Flames extinguished by the explosion, Surtur was wobbling like a drunken man, sword trembling in his hand. Now that the fire was out, Tomokato could see that the giant's blade was nothing but one of those cheap Indian-import jobs they sell in the Pier One stores; devoid of his blaze, its owner was even less imposing, two hundred feet tall but preposterously skinny, clad in a set of asbestos Doctor Dentons. But the giant's head was the silliest thing about him, a wide-eyed cartoon-chipmunk head, topped by a little baseball cap. Staggering round and round, Surtur caught sight of Tomokato and stumbled in his direction, raising his sword. Tomokato sped toward him, dodged a clumsy slash, and circled round behind. Sheathing his *wakazashi*, the cat snatched up a fallen AK-47 and let fly one-handed, raking the buttons from the giant's Doctor Denton flap, which swung open. Realizing what had happened, Surtur promptly died of embarrassment, crashing to the ground with a thump like an SS-20 creaming Copenhagen.

Gunsmoke drifting past his face, Tomokato

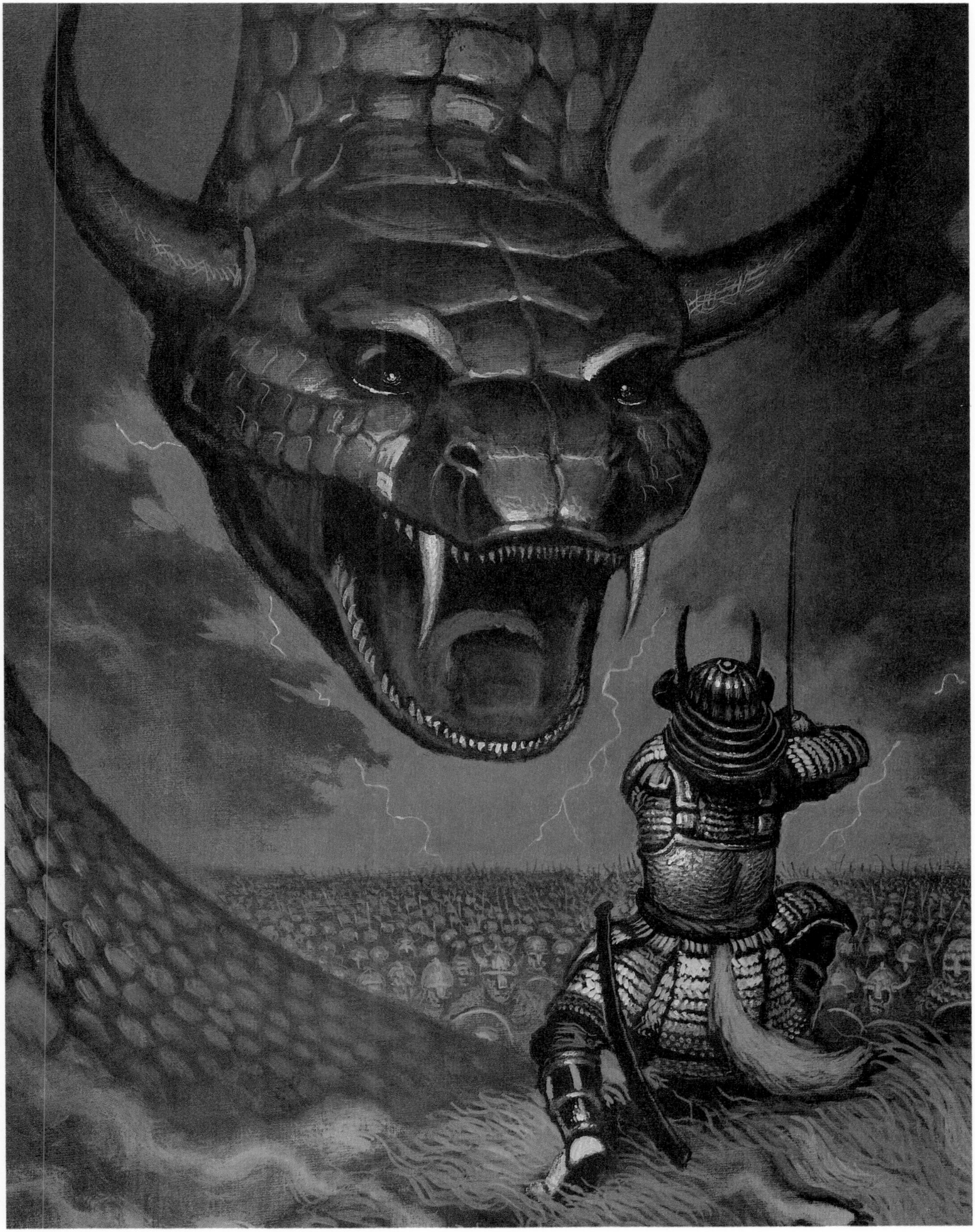

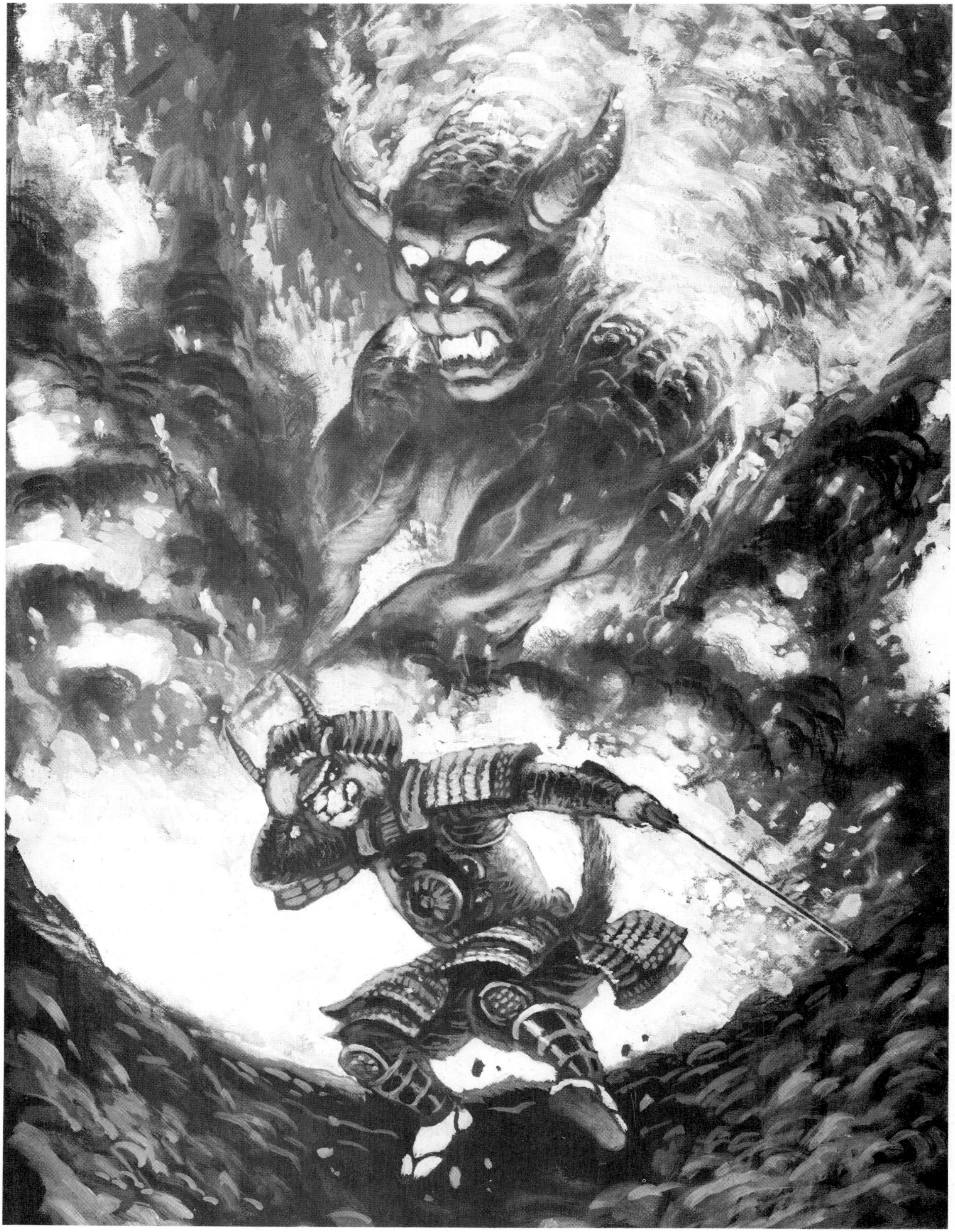

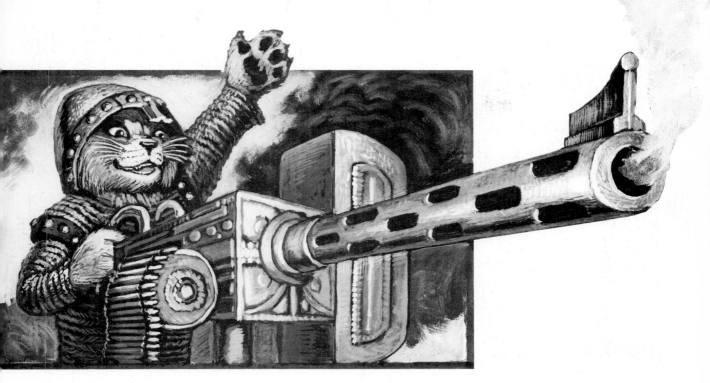

lowered his arms to his sides. Dropping the rifle, he allowed himself a few moments of rest.

Hooves pounded behind him. He whirled. Halfdan Jormunreksson was bearing down on him, shouldering a small Grail rocket-launcher. Tomokato readied his *katana* to deflect the shot; Halfdan fired deliberately low. The ground in front of the cat bulged skyward in a surge of flame and smoke, and a savage shock hurled him backward off his feet, stones clanging from his helm and breastplate. Only his armor saved him. His sword was knocked from his paws. He landed hard.

Halfdan rode through the smoke, grinning. Tossing the rocket-launcher aside, he whipped out a Walther PPK, aiming it at the cat.

"Say goodbye, kitty," he jeered.

But it was not his gun that spoke.

A machine gun rattled. Crimson-spurting holes stitched up and down Halfdan's body. Tattered and torn, he rocked sidways from the saddle trailing long splashes of blood, enfiladed by a screaming salvo of steel-jacketted slugs. He hit the ground and flattened out as if there wasn't a single bone in his body. The skeletal horse clattered off.

Tomokato got up, looked over where the gunfire had come from. Shiro waved at him from the top of a crippled tank, one small paw still on the butterfly grip of a huge, smoking, heavy machine gun.

"How'd you like that, uncle-*san?*" he cried, obviously very pleased with himself. His helmet slid down over his eyes.

Tomokato smiled in spite of himself. "Very much, thank you," he called, and turned back toward the giants, who were watching him in stunned silence. He was feeling a bit on the weary side, but he decided he would have to deal with them; he couldn't let them attack Asgard, not with the gods and heroes still sunk (like as not) in their drunken stupors. Ketil was his friend now, and Odin had shown him a good deal of hospitality.

He started toward the monstrous legion at a trot, the conqueror of Fenrir and the Midgard Serpent and Surtur; the giants wailed and yelped and turned tail, fleeing madly, casting away their weapons. They dashed into a low-hanging cloudbank. He followed.

Before long, he heard their cries growing suddenly fainter, and after that, many sounds like watermelons striking a hard pavement. He slowed down, proceeded more cautiously. Momentarily he found himself on the brink of a sheer precipice which had been hidden by the fog. As far as he could tell, the giants and monsters had all run over the edge in their panic, and those watermelon

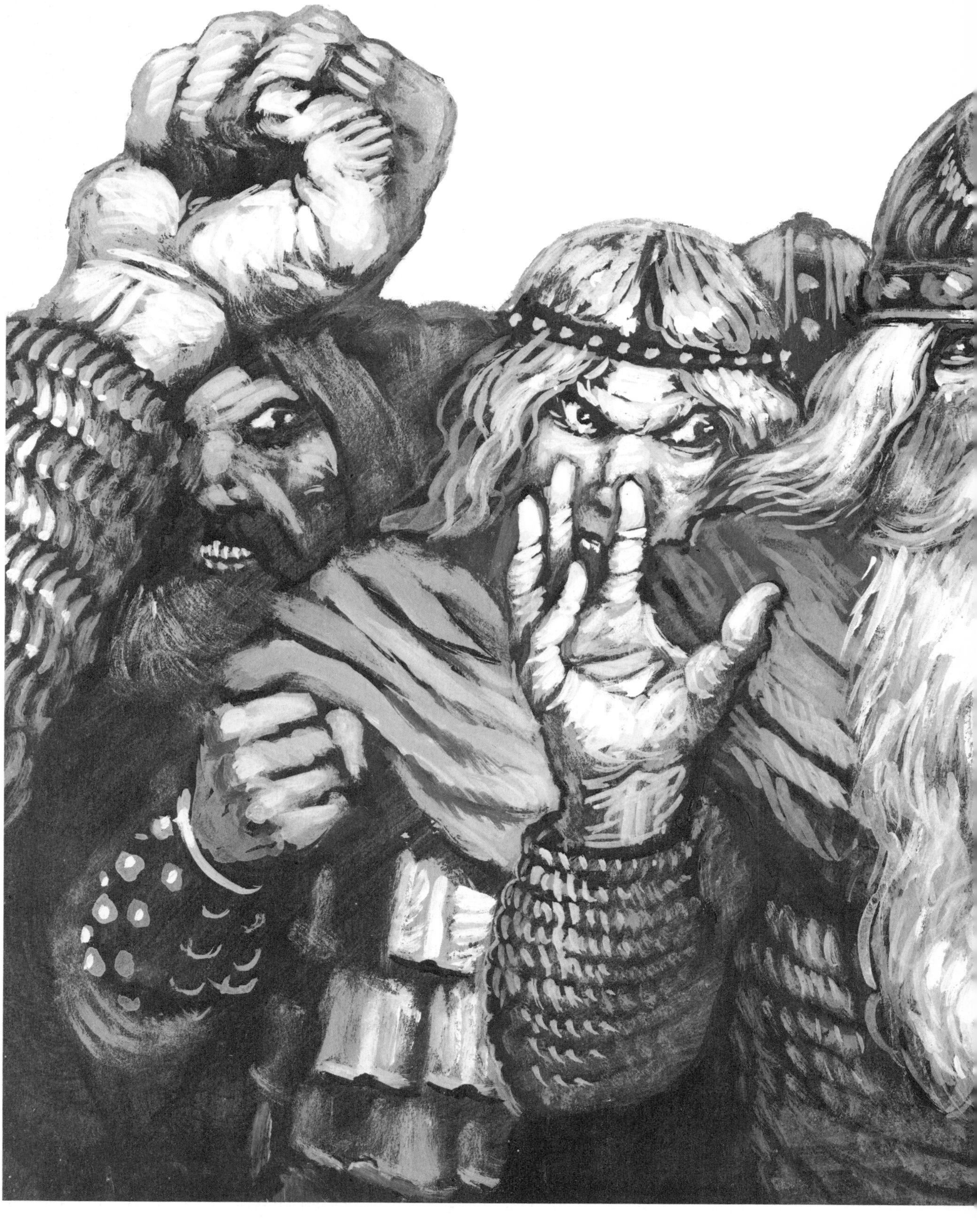

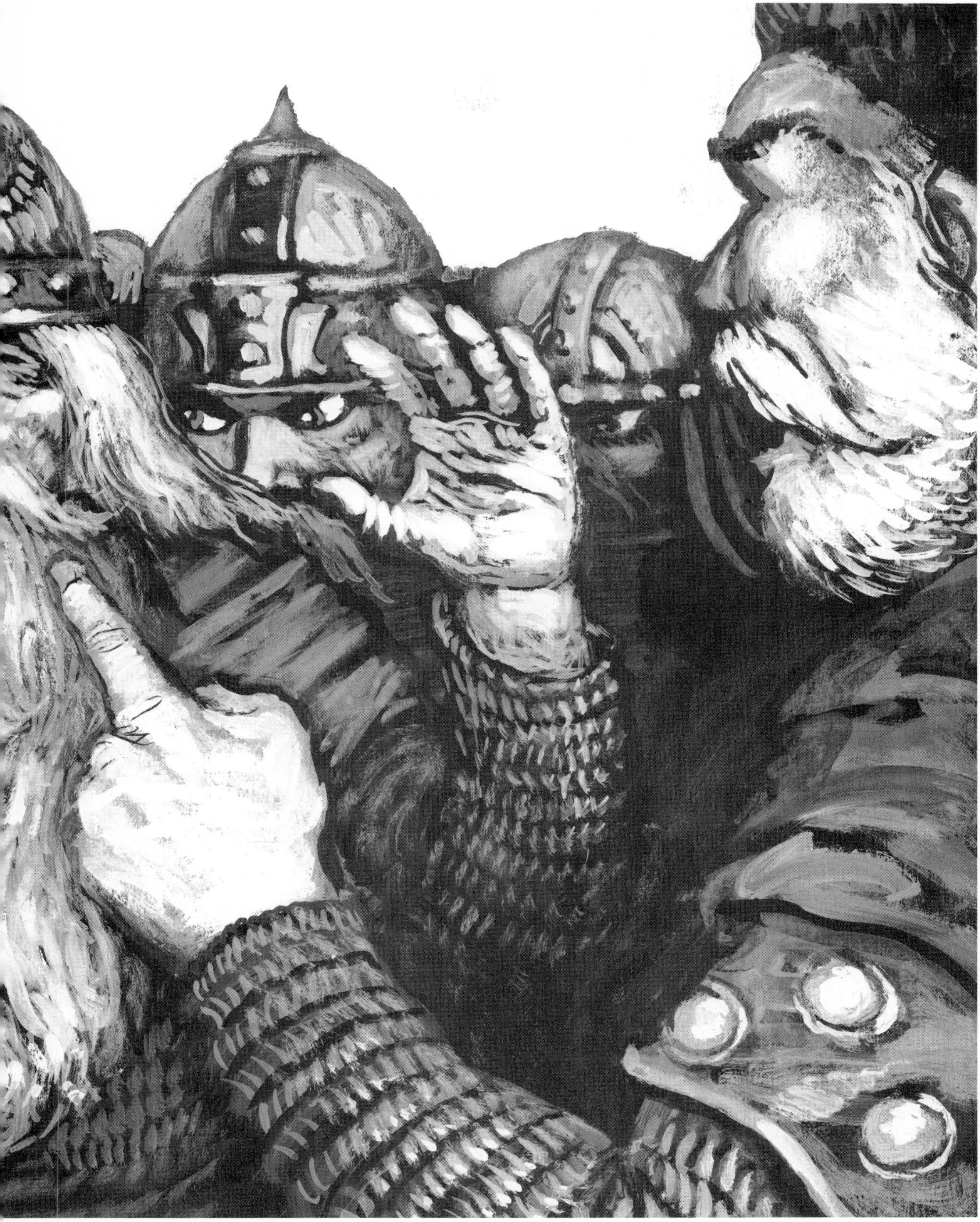

sounds had been them hitting the bottom.

So much for the Weird of the World, he thought to himself. He headed back toward Asgard, picking up Shiro on the way. When they reached the throne-room, they found Odin and many of the others (including Ketil) just coming around. Odin's ravens were lying on the floor, dead. They had killed themselves by pulling their bowlers down over their cigars and inhaling the smoke. Tomokato guessed they would be reviving around sundown.

"But why did they commit suicide?" Odin puzzled.

"Because they thought Asgard was about to fall, I suppose," Tomokato explained. "They knew the giants were coming, and they couldn't wake you."

"The giants!" roared a hundred voices. "Where?"

"Don't worry," Tomokato said. "I took care of them. They're all dead."

Odin and the rest stared at him in stark disbelief.

"Impossible," said the King of the Gods.

"Impossible or not, it happened. Face it, Odin. Ragnarok is cancelled."

Odin chewed his moustache.

"Send out some men if you don't believe me," Tomokato said. "There are lots of bodies out there, including Fenrir and the Serpent and Surtur."

Odin dispatched several warriors. They returned before long, looking amazed.

"It's all true," said one.

"You mean," said another man, "the end of the universe came and went, and we're still here?"

"That's what I've been trying to tell you," Tomokato said.

"But that means we're not going to get to use the last-lines we made up," Ketil said. "Not even the really good ones. Not even our death-songs. All that waiting and planning, for nothing!"

"The hell with that," said Styrbjorn the Strong, who stood nearby. "If there isn't going to be any Ragnarok, then what are we doing here at all?" He glared at Odin. "You didn't have to kill us. You didn't need us for your damn army, but you killed us anyway. You set us up and knocked us off, and all of us in the prime of life, and you never needed us at all. . . . "

The heroes growled, drawing in on Odin, fists clenched.

"I didn't know it was going to work out this way, really guys," Odin protested. "It was all that damn Sibyl's fault. Must've been one of her practical jokes. . . . "

The heroes were unconvinced.

"I'll make it up to you, really," he went on. "I'll hike your salaries. Give you double overtime, medical benefits . . . "

"But what are we going to do for the rest of eternity?" demanded Egill Skallagrimsson, eyes filled with desperation.

"Well, for starters," Odin suggested timidly, "we could go raid Mount Olympus."

Faces brightened at that.

"Pay that old bastard Zeus a visit," grinned Thor.

"Sounds good," Tyr said. There was a general grunt of agreement.

Odin wiped his brow and sighed.

Ketil Jormunreksson turned to the cat. "What about you?" he asked. "Want to come with us?"

"I can't," Tomokato replied.

"Mount Olympus is supposed to be a pretty nifty place," Ketil went on, "just begging to be plundered."

"That sounds tempting," he said to be polite, "but I have duties to fulfill. My vengeance is not yet complete."

Ketil smiled. "Well then, good luck. Perhaps we'll meet again."

"I hope so," the cat said, and shook the Norseman's hand. "Farewell." He cried aloud: "And farewell to the rest of you."

Odin looked round. "Off so soon? Ah well, I suppose it can't be helped."

Tomokato shook his head, waved, and strode off, Shiro in tow.

"Are you going to send me back to my parents again?" the kitten asked as they neared the hall's main door.

"Of course."

"Maybe it's just as well," Shiro answered, sounding surprisingly resigned. "I suppose I could do with a bit of rest."

"One doomsday should be enough for any kitten," Tomokato agreed gravely, as they passed from the hall.

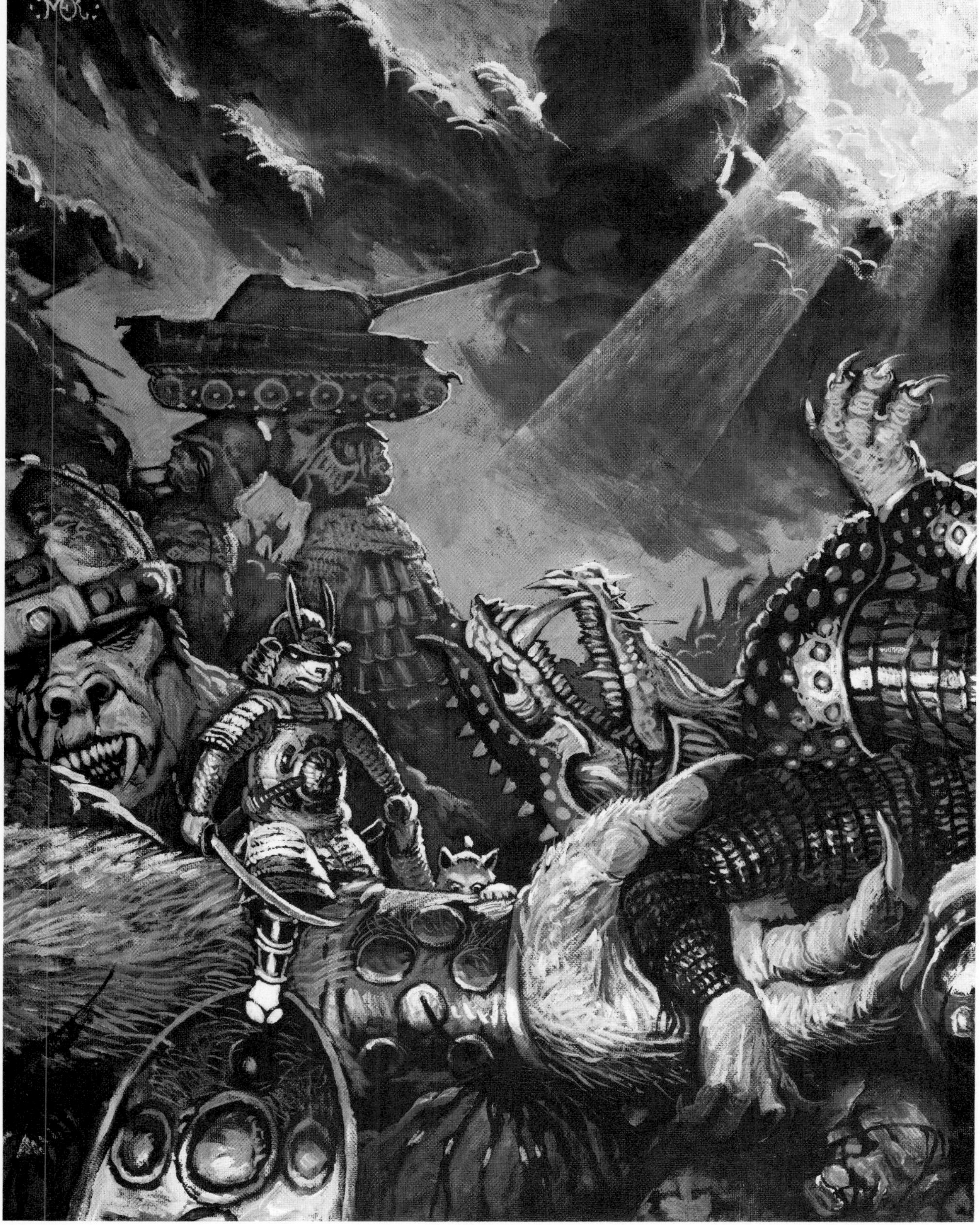

ABOUT THE AUTHOR

Mark E. Rogers was born roughly about 1952 in South Amboy, New Jersey, along with his twin brother Vhong, and spent his childhood in nearby Lawrence Harbor and Point Pleasant Beach. Unappreciated by nearly everyone (he was frequently confused with Vhong, who really *was* a stinker), he sought companionship in a fanatical Roman Catholic secret society, the Opus Joei, founded by the irrepressible and Jesuitical Joe Serrada, who continues to exercise an unhealthy intellectual influence on Mark even now. Mark served faithfully throughout high school as a Garnet Gull, and created a Garnet Gull logo for the other Garnet Gulls; but even this did not bring him acceptance. Seeking higher education, he attended the University of Delaware, where he received a B.A. in English, as well as his wife Kate (she was the prize for graduating Magna Cum Laude); but he became disenchanted with the academic life when he discovered that the secret Phi Beta Kappa signal looked exactly like wiping one's nose — no fooling. After a strange interlude in South Bend, Indiana (is there any other kind of interlude in South Bend?) which lasted just enough for Kate to get her Ph.D. in Philosophy from Notre Dame, he took up residence in Newark, Delaware, where Kate had two darling kids, Sophia and Jeannette, and Mark got several turtles: Anselm, Alberta, and Tertulliana, as well as a pet bat named Mondale. Presently Mark is finishing two books, *The Dead,* an epic horror novel, and *Zorachus,* an heroic fantasy, although most of his efforts have been directed toward funding the Lycanthropoi Christi, a group dedicated to maintaining theological orthodoxy at science-fiction conventions. There might be some more Samurai Cat stuff though, if you're all nice to him and he can work up the steam.